THE VENGEANCE SQUAD

Sidney W. Frost

DEDICATION

This book is dedicated to my wife

Celeste Frost

God's response to my prayers from the belly of a whale.

BOOKS BY SIDNEY W. FROST

The Vengeance Squad
Where Love Once Lived

ACKNOWLEDGEMENTS

Writing is a lonely business, but getting it right involves having many friends who will read early versions of your books and tell you honestly what works and what doesn't. I am fortunate to have a long list of such friends.

Early readers and editors for whom I am indebted are San Gabriel Presbyterian Church friends Ann Stewart, Cordelia Razek, and Peg Case, my wife Celeste Frost, and my professional editor Ashley Boquist.

I would also like to thank my friends at the John 3:16 Marketing Network, the San Gabriel Writers League, and American Christian Fiction Writers as well as my friends and students at Austin Community College for their support and inspiration.

The Vengeance Squad would not be possible without the encouragement received after *Where Love Once Lived* was published. I am grateful to the Combine, my family and my church families for buying books, reviewing the book, attending book signings and cheering me on.

While many helped with the editing chores, any mistakes remaining are due to my last-minute changes.

Sidney W. Frost
Georgetown, Texas
August 2011

Beloved, never avenge yourselves, but leave room for the wrath of God; for it is written, "Vengeance is mine. I will repay," says the Lord.

—Romans 12:19 (NRSV)

Bear with one another and, if anyone has a complaint against another, forgive each other; just as the Lord has forgiven you, so you also must forgive.

—Colossians 3:13 (NRSV)

You have heard that it was said, 'You shall love your neighbor and hate your enemy.' But I say to you, Love your enemies and pray for those who persecute you, so that you may be children of your Father in heaven; for he makes his sun rise on the evil and on the good, and sends rain on the righteous and on the unrighteous.

—Matthew 5: 43-45 (NRSV)

I'll never forget the look on her face. It sustained me for months afterward. Without the memories, I wouldn't have survived.

CHAPTER ONE

Sometimes it worried me because I thought I must be wrong, but there were times I could read her mind. I'd heard stories about couples who had been married for years who experienced a level of silent communication, but Sarah and I had known each other for only two years. Perhaps it was the intensity of love for one another rather than the length of time together that made the difference. Quite honestly, the love we shared was stronger than I believed possible. It was as if God brought us together and blessed the joining of two faithful servants of the Lord. I thanked Him daily for that.

That day, for example, as I sat across from Sarah at the coffee shop's outdoor table, I knew for a fact she was thinking about our wedding. I knew that didn't prove I could read her mind. Any bride would be thinking about her wedding if it were coming so soon. But I recognized a deeper expression of happiness than was usually there. Realizing what she was thinking and knowing for sure I was right made me shiver. I took a deep breath and swallowed for fear I would tear up.

I watched as her eyes twinkled, her cheeks puffed out, and her lips quivered ever so slightly. Her lips. I forgot about reading her mind and realized all I could see were her stunning lips. I had to kiss her right then, so I leaned across the table and placed my lips on hers. She didn't stop smiling as she kissed me back and just barely stopped talking. I couldn't believe how lucky I was as I thought about how we'd soon be Sarah and Christopher McCowan.

Sarah was a nurse at Georgetown Hospital, and I was a professor of computer science at Austin Community College in Cedar Park. The outlet mall in Round Rock, Texas, was a convenient meeting place for us. We sat at one of the outdoor tables at the mall enjoying the mild October weather. I'd grown up in California and she on a farm near Bath, England, so we both had to adjust to the Texas weather at times.

She leaned back in her chair and looked at me, eyes still twinkling, as if she had a serious speech to make. "Do you realize we'll be husband and wife in two weeks and one day?"

Her English accent was delicious and more pronounced when she was excited. I loved it. I often tried to analyze what made her speech different from mine. Mostly, she pronounced each letter in a word, automatically adding ending consonants as if they were separate words, while I slurred my words around, often letting the listener fill in the gaps.

I couldn't take my eyes off her. An auburn lock swung

playfully on her freckled forehead, distracting me as I tried to look into her green eyes. I wanted to kiss her again. Here she was bubbling over about marrying me, while it was I who was blessed to be with her. I squeezed her hand without saying a word. Surely, she could tell how I felt by looking at me. My face had to be glowing.

She stared at me for a few seconds. "What are you thinking? Are you as happy as I am?"

She didn't wait for my answer. "Andrew called today. He's coming to the wedding, you know. Uncle Roger and Aunt Ruth—they'll be here, too. It'll be super seeing them all again. With everyone flying in from England, we'll surely have to get married now." She smiled, glancing at me for a reaction.

Andrew was her brother. He hadn't joined Sarah and their mother and dad when the family moved to Texas. Andrew worked in London, but they were close and talked to each other on the phone at least once a week.

Paul and Ann Eason, Sarah's parents, were part of an American European farm exchange program. They had visited Central Texas only once when they saw the potential for farming just north of Georgetown, Texas. They jumped at the chance to move to Texas, especially after the government had taken much of their Hemington farm for a new motorway interchange. Having the opportunity to be near their daughter probably influenced their decision as well.

She continued to look into my eyes with the same smile that melted my heart every time I saw it. I knew she wanted to hear me say how happy I was, too. And I was. I straightened my coffee cup so the handle was parallel with the edge of the table in front of me. I don't know why; it's just one of the things I do. I started to straighten hers, too, but was afraid she'd question why once more.

"Yes, I'm happy! Can't you tell by the way I look? I'm happy, happy, happy and, quite honestly, a little proud you are happy, too. I'm the happiest man on earth."

I saw her lips moving, but the roar of an engine covered up whatever she said. Seconds later, a whirlwind of debris spread over the area where we sat. Our coffee cups splattered to the concrete as I tilted the table in my haste to get to my feet.

"What?" I yelled. For a fleeting moment, I thought I might have overreacted and ruined some especially good coffee, not to mention the two ceramic cups now in pieces around our feet.

"It's a helicopter," Sarah said, blocking the sun with a hand as she gazed at the sky. "It nearly hit the top of the building. Something's wrong."

I could tell the nurse in her had taken over, and she was concerned about the safety of those in the helicopter. We were near the center of the mall, and the helicopter had flown over us heading south and slightly east. It was out of sight now, but the sound of its engine still roared. We walked toward the noise without discussing why. Others did, too.

Rat-a-tat-tat. Machine gun fire sounded repeatedly in short bursts. I couldn't see the guns from where we were, but I knew the sound from televised wartime reports. Sarah looked at me with concern, but she kept moving toward where the helicopter had gone down. I thought we should be going the other way, but I stayed by her side, knowing she had a professional need to help. As we made the turn around the building, I saw the helicopter on the ground, not as loud now, its rotors turning slowly. More gunshots sounded. A woman screamed. Off to our right, fifty yards or so from the helicopter, a man in what looked like a security guard uniform was lying facedown on the ground with one arm under his body and the other behind him. The woman who had screamed and others were running toward us, away from the security guard sprawled awkwardly on the ground.

Sarah walked through the retreating figures toward the downed man.

I grabbed her arm and dug my feet in to stop her.

She turned to me, eyes pleading for me to free her arm. "Chris, I have to help."

I didn't want to let go of her, but I knew I had to. As soon as I released her arm, she raced toward the wounded man. Another guard joined her, and they knelt next to the wounded man.

I walked cautiously toward her and the two guards as I scanned the area trying to see what was happening. Then I understood. The back doors of an armored vehicle stood ajar. Two or three men in military uniforms passed bags from an armored vehicle to the helicopter. Several others stood guard with machine guns at the ready. They all had long, black beards that, along with the khaki uniforms they wore, reminded me of the way Fidel Castro looked when he first came into power in Cuba.

With military precision, the men moved together toward the waiting helicopter, some carrying the booty from the armored vehicle and the others guarding them. The ones with the guns walked backward, looking left and right as they did.

I felt relieved to see they had what they wanted and were leaving. A robbery. That's all. Too bad the security guard was shot, but this bunch of thugs would be off the ground in a matter of minutes. They got what they came for.

But before the last one climbed aboard the helicopter, I saw him point his gun toward Sarah. I jerked my head toward her and saw why. The unwounded security guard beside her was aiming his pistol at the helicopter.

"No!" I yelled as loud as I could. "Don't shoot! Let them go! Get down, Sarah!" I ran toward her as fast as I could move.

I heard the gunshot and saw Sarah's body jerk in sync. The guard's pistol leaped into the air as his body bounced and fell on top of hers. I kept running toward them. The helicopter's engine was louder as it lifted off the ground.

Please, God, let her be okay. I knew the bullets had hit her, but I hoped the guard had taken the brunt of the blasts, saving her from serious harm. I stood over him surveying the situation when the machine gun fired again, this time from a distance, and I felt a hard slap to my right leg and knew immediately what it was. I moved the guard off Sarah and cradled her in my arms.

There was blood everywhere, but she looked at me and smiled.

"Thank God," I said. "I thought…" I couldn't say what I had thought.

Her lips quivered, and I saw blood come out of her mouth. I pulled her closer, unable to look at her pain. When she spoke I could barely hear her.

"At least you're okay." She smiled.

"You'll be okay, too." I looked around for EMS. People were coming out of hiding places. I looked at one group of spectators and yelled, "We need help over here. Get EMS here now."

Sarah whispered again.

I moved my ear to her mouth. "What?"

"I'm not going to make it."

I leaned back to see her. "Don't say that. Just tell me what to do. Do you need a tourniquet? What can I do? Teach me. I can do it."

She pulled me closer so I could hear her weakened voice. "This is God's will. I'll see you again when it's your time. Until then, be happy. Find someone to love you as much as I do."

"No!" I screamed. I looked around. "Help us, please." I relaxed my grip to look into her face once more. She was always beautiful, but I saw something beyond beauty.

She smiled at me even though I knew she must be in extreme pain. "Thank you for loving me," she said.

I was the one who should be thanking her for loving me. I couldn't think about that right now. There was too much blood. I had to help her. "Tell me how to fix this."

She coughed and cleared her throat. "Your love has fulfilled me."

"No, please," I said, "don't talk like that. You're in shock. That's all. We'll get help soon."

"Chris," Sarah said. "You have to let me go. I love…"

She sank into my arms as her life left her body.

"No! Please, God, no."

***

I was awake—just barely. Drifting…drifting…in…out. At some point I knew I wasn't dreaming, but I didn't move. Instead, I peeked through my eyelashes to see where I was: *dimly lit room…antiseptic smells…hospital…different…not like the last room I woke up in with all the bright lights and people rushing about in gowns and masks. That's where I saw Sarah's parents standing over me in the midst of it all. Was that a dream? Oh no!*

I sat up in bed, now fully awake. "SARAH!"

A nurse ran into the room.

I pleaded with her. "Where's Sarah? Is she okay?"

The nurse cried and left the room without saying a word. I was stunned. Nurses aren't supposed to cry. I began to get out of bed and found myself in midair falling toward the floor when I saw my right leg was in a cast. Funny thing was I didn't care. Two people appeared from somewhere and helped me back into bed.

One of them straightened the wires and tubes I'd pulled down with me when I fell, and she patted me on the shoulder. "Chris, you've got to stay in bed a while longer."

She looked familiar, but I didn't know her name. I stared at her name tag, but couldn't read it. They must have drugged me. Everything was blurry; however, I could see enough to know the name tag was the same as Sarah's.

I grabbed the woman's arm. "This is Sarah's hospital, isn't it?" It would make sense to send us to the nearest hospital, the one in Georgetown, a short distance on Interstate 35 from where the shooting took place.

This woman had tears in her eyes now, same as the other had. I begged her with my eyes, but she was mute.

A man with a stethoscope hanging around his neck moved closer to me, leaning into the bed to look at me eye to eye. "Yes." He said it clearly and without emotion. "This is Sarah's hospital, and that's why it is so hard for us to tell you she didn't make it. We all loved her, and she will be missed. Right now, the whole staff is grieving. Let us take care of you."

I didn't think anyone would be insensitive enough to tell me Sarah had died unless it was the truth, but still, I didn't believe it. Everyone thought she hadn't made it, but she'd probably been taken to another hospital because of her injuries. After all, she'd been shot multiple times. And it was like a battlefield out there. Not everyone who had been injured would be taken to the same hospital. I stared at the man for an eternity trying to look into his eyes. I didn't reply, just nodded—no use confusing everyone with the facts. That's when I felt the needle prick in my arm.

***

The next time I woke up I was in the same room, but it wasn't dimly lit this time. A sunbeam warmed my face. There was a window I hadn't notice before, and the curtains were wide open, allowing the bright light to fill the room. I realized I didn't know what day it was. I sat up to see my right leg was in a cast. *Oh yeah.* The events leading up to my injury came back to me rapidly. My concern for Sarah grew to near panic. I looked around for a call button. *Surely there is one here somewhere.*

"Sarah!" I screamed.

The sound of a toilet flushing in the bathroom gave me hope. *She's here. She was using the toilet. She's coming now.* I turned toward the door, and out walked my mother.

"Mom?"

She ran to the bed and held me in her arms. "Chris, you must have had a bad dream. You know Sarah's gone to heaven, don't you?"

I couldn't remember. *Did I know that?* I wasn't sure.

"Mom?"

"Yes, dear. I'm here."

"Sarah's gone." It wasn't a question. If Mother said it, I had to accept it.

"Yes, dear. I'm so sorry." She held me tighter. I was thirty-one years old and had been on my own for more than ten years, but when she held me this way, I felt I would survive.

"How did you know I was here? I thought you and Dad were in Scotland."

"Sarah's mother had our itinerary. We've been talking about the wedding for months." Her eyes moistened. "I'm so sorry, dear. Such a terrible, terrible loss. I loved that young lady." She hugged me again. The knit sweater she wore felt comforting.

"Where's Dad?" I needed both my parents. Mom always knew just what to do and say in unusual situations, but only Dad understood how I felt deep down.

"He's parking the car. He dropped me off at the lobby because I couldn't wait to see you. Then, since you were asleep, I popped into your bathroom. Sarah's mother said you would recover, but we got here as soon as possible. Are you really okay?" She brushed her blond hair off her forehead in a familiar way.

"I don't know." I showed her my leg. "Every time I wake up they give me a shot to knock me out again. So far, this time I don't feel so groggy."

"Oh, you poor dear. We'll get a doctor in here and find out what's going on. I'm afraid I may be responsible for them sedating you. I said something to Ann about your having to grieve at the same time you're trying to recover from the gunshot wound. She probably said something to the doctor."

Grieving. I have to grieve. I will now grieve. Sarah is...Sarah is...

Mom dabbed eyes I didn't know needed dabbing. "Chris, I'm sorry. Let it out, Son. It's okay."

But I didn't let it out. I took a deep breath and held it all in.

"It's a natural reaction to death."

"But, Mom, you don't understand. I let her die."

She moved away to look into my face. "No you didn't. Ann and the news accounts said you did everything you could to save her. You ran into the gunfire to protect her. You could have been killed." She hugged me again as she patted my back.

Some stray tears tried to get out, but I stopped them. "I

shouldn't have let her go where there was danger. When she pleaded with me to let her go because she was a nurse and had to help, I let her. I could've stopped her. I'm strong enough; I could have held her in my arms so that she couldn't go to that wounded man. I caused her death because I didn't stop her." I could hardly breathe.

She rocked me as if I were a child. It passed through my mind how silly it might look if someone walked in, but I didn't care. It was comforting, and I didn't want her to stop.

"You did the right thing. You didn't know what would happen. You did what she wanted."

"I'd rather have her alive and hating me than this."

"I know, dear," Mom said as she let go of me and sat on the edge of my bed, "but we don't get to make those decisions—God does."

I sat up with my arms crossed. "God sure messed up this time."

"Now, dear, don't talk like that."

"Why would God let Sarah die so young? She is…was…the sweetest person I've ever known."

"We will never understand why these things happen. We have to trust God."

"I don't." I always had trusted God, but suddenly, it was clear. *God shouldn't have let this happen. Therefore…* Still, I couldn't say the words I was thinking.

"That's normal. It is part of the grieving process. You'll get past it with time." She patted me as if I were a child who didn't understand the mysteries of life.

I knew better, but the words came out anyway. "I'm going to get revenge, you know." I said it looking squarely into her eyes. I wanted her to know I meant what I said.

She gulped before she responded. I didn't know if she was trying to figure out if I was serious or trying to think of what to say. Either way, there was a long pause in the conversation as I continued to keep my eyes locked on hers, daring her to speak.

After what seemed like minutes, but was more likely seconds, she laughed. That wasn't the response I expected.

"Of course you are, dear. You'll get your revenge by not letting this change the way you live your life. I'm sure Sarah would want you to be happy." She walked over to the door and looked out. "Your father was supposed to be here by now. How long does it take to park a car?"

"Mom, I'm serious. They're going to pay for what they did." I tried to get out of bed, but the pain in my leg flared and kept me down. "I'm going to track them down and make them wish they'd never messed with Sarah." My voice was louder and steadier than it had been since I woke up. It felt good.

Dad walked in wearing the same slacks and polo shirt I'd seen him in back home in California. He looked me over as if to see if I was okay, then gave me a quick hug. I knew he was glad to see me, but I saw the pain in his eyes.

"I'm sorry, Son."

Mom grabbed Dad's arm. "Jason, dear, Chris must have been hit in the head. He's talking crazy." She was talking to Dad as if I weren't there. That reminded me of California, too.

"What do you mean?" Dad looked me over again while gripping my arm before he turned to Mom.

"He wants to go after the killers." She was wringing her hands.

"So? I'll help him." He looked at me with a slight smile that could mean he agreed with me or didn't believe me.

Mom put her hands on her hips. "Help him? Oh, you're both crazy." She turned to me, pleading, "Let the police take care of it. That's their job."

I almost laughed out loud because of the way she said it slowly and loudly as if I had a hearing problem, but I didn't. "I bet the cops won't tell me anything about the investigation because I'm not family. I'm just the fiancé." If this had happened two weeks later, I'd have legal standing.

Dad sat on the bed beside me. "There's not much the police can do anyway. This is a big story now, but it'll be forgotten in a week or so."

Mom turned her back to us and walked toward the door before she twirled around and pointed a finger at Dad. "Maybe so, but Chris doesn't know how to catch a killer."

"What about that, Son? You're a computer science professor same as me. What do we know about law enforcement?" He asked the question as if he hoped I had an answer.

I hadn't worked out the *how* part yet; the *what* part had just come to me while I was talking to Mom. I knew what I had to do. It was impossible for me to live my life until I found the goons who killed Sarah. Even then, life would be difficult.

I looked at Dad and tried to tell him what I thought he wanted to hear. "I don't know how to do it, but I'm a researcher. You know what it takes to get a PhD. If I can do that, I can learn what I need to know. I'll use the computer to find them. It may take years, but I have to do this."

Dad winked at me before turning to Mom. "See, dear, there's nothing to worry about. He sounds rational to me. Chris isn't doing anything dangerous. He's just planning. Nothing to worry about."

"Are you sure?" She looked at me and pleaded.

"Yes, ma'am," I said to her. Dad understood I was serious about my desire to find and wipe out the killers. I think he just wanted to ease Mom's fears. That's why I went along with him.

She smiled. "You know, dear, Jesus tells us to love our enemies."

"Yes, ma'am, I know." I was going to find and kill my enemies. Only thing was I'd have to be careful whom I told.

"That's a sweet boy." She turned toward the door. "I'm going to track down the doctor and find out how you're doing."

"Good idea, dear. I'll visit with Chris some. There's something he needs to know."

She stared at Dad in a way I hadn't seen. "Now, don't you go putting ideas into his head. You think you know more about law enforcement than you do. Chris doesn't need any encouragement from you."

Dad stayed calm even though I could tell Mom was threatening him. "It'll be okay." He turned his back to her and winked again, the way he always did.

"Jason, please don't tell him what I think you're going to." She paused before making a sound of frustration. "If you do, I don't want to know about it." She walked out of the room.

Dad sat on the bed next to me, grinning. "That's what I do, too."

"What?" Maybe it was the medication, but I was having trouble following the conversation. I have a photographic memory, or what most folks think of as one. I have an excellent memory for anything. I can look at a page in a book, a list of numbers, whatever, and know exactly what I saw days later. I liked being able to do that and hoped the medicine hadn't changed that.

I also have this thing about neatness. Not the kind of neatness most people think about. I mean symmetry and parallelism. I feel better in an environment where everything makes sense. Why have some objects turned one way and others turned another? I wouldn't mind if the medication changed some of that, but it hadn't. I had a terrific urge to get out of bed and line up all the medical devices in the room. Even the tissue box on my crooked table was askew.

"Tell her what she wants to hear." He laughed. "You've got that 'Yes, ma'am' down pat."

I smiled without responding while reaching toward the tissue box.

Dad lined up the edge of the tissue box with the edge of the table. "You're going after those killers, aren't you, Son?"

"Maybe." After Mom's reaction, I didn't know if I could talk about this with him.

"I thought so. Okay, there's something I need to tell you."

"Is this thing you're going to tell me why Mom's so angry?" Dad and I had been close for as long as I could remember. I couldn't think of anything I didn't know about him.

"Yes, so don't mention this to her. She doesn't like me to talk about it. Okay?" Dad's voice was almost a whisper, and he looked around the room as if checking to see that we were alone.

"I won't say anything." I sat up on one elbow to hear him better.

"A couple of years ago, I took a second job doing research work for the federal government. It's secret work." He looked around the room again.

"Mom knows, right? Is this what she didn't want you to tell me?"

"Sure. Otherwise, how would I explain the income? She doesn't know exactly what I do, and she doesn't want to know."

I looked at him in a new way. "What do you do?"

He ruffled my hair in a way that took me back to grade school. "Nothing you couldn't do. I help the government track down criminals—white-collar crime mostly. It's desk work."

I smoothed my hair back into place. "Really? What else?"

"I'm a hacker, too."

"You? A hacker?" He had all the same training I did, but to think he'd break into a computer went against everything I'd ever believed about him. It was a little scary but, at the same time, made me proud. To find Sarah's killers I would do more than just break into someone's computer.

"You know, a white-hat hacker." Dad rubbed his hands together the way I do just before I reach for a keyboard. "Criminals have computers, too. What I do is look at their computers from time to time. If I find anything interesting, I pass the information on. I don't disturb their computer. They never know I was there."

My arm ached from sitting up so long. I lay back on the pillow to rest. "Why didn't you tell me before now?"

"Why? It's no big deal. It's not the type of thing to talk about in an email or a telephone call."

"I was home last Christmas." *With Sarah...our last Christmas together...the last time my parents saw her*, I thought, trying to focus on what Dad was saying.

"I know, Son, but it wasn't the time to talk about my work. Everyone was having fun, and we were getting to know Sarah." His smile suddenly disappeared. "If you re-member, you and Sarah were busy doing things together. You wanted to show her where you grew up, introduce her to your friends, and all that."

I must have looked distant to him.

"I'm sorry," he said, "I shouldn't have reminded you of

that."

"That's okay. I'm glad you met her before…you know." Every time Sarah came into my thoughts she took over and made it difficult to think about anything else.

Dad nodded, his eyes moist.

"The secret work doesn't interfere with teaching at Long Beach?" I asked.

"No one there knows about my research work, and I never let one job interfere with the other."

"And your trip to Scotland? Was that for the university or the feds?"

Dad laughed. "Neither. That was for fun."

"Thanks for telling me about your so-called research. But why now?"

"So I can help you catch those killers." He looked at me the same way he did one Christmas morning long ago when I saw the bicycle with all the latest gadgets on it. I wanted a dirt bike, not the fancy one, but he was so excited about the more expensive one he'd picked out that I never told him. This time he had a gift I could use.

"What? Are you serious?" I sat up as straight as my bum leg would allow.

His pleasure was evident in his eyes as he stood next to the bed. "Of course I'm serious."

"Great." I had no idea how to get started, but with Dad's help, it might be possible.

"I can't promise you we'll find them. It's not my area of expertise, but I know people. I'll get the information you need if it's available. That's all I can promise."

"That's more than I had ten minutes ago." My body relaxed some. Sarah was gone. All I could do now was settle the score.

"Are you still teaching in that little junior college, Son?"

"Austin Community College—we don't say 'junior' college anymore. Yes, and I'm proud of it. We're not so small, either." We had this conversation every time I saw him.

"When are you going to get a real teaching position?"

"I've got a great job."

"With your credentials and a few high-ranking recommendations, you could get a position anywhere in the country." He looked serious. "Maybe this is the time to move…you know, get away from the memories here."

I loved my memories. I realized at that moment that memories were all I had—all I would ever have.

"I do okay here. I'm making a difference. They let me plan the curriculum, select textbooks, and counsel students. I'm writing another textbook based on my classroom experiences."

Dad hugged me before he walked toward the door. "You could do better. Well, I better go find out what happened to your mother."

What a surprise to learn Dad could help me find the killers. Now all I had to do was to learn how to shoot a gun.

Before Mother and Dad went home to California, Mother must have had a stern word or two with my doctor because she stopped by at least twice a day to give me progress reports. I learned the bullet had messed up some muscle and cracked a bone. The doctor told me I'd need to use crutches for a while and that I may limp after that. I didn't care. I would trade both legs for Sarah's life. I would die for her. I should've died for her. There was also a nasty-looking scar on the side of my right leg slightly above the knee. Even after leaving the hospital, she'd said, I'd have to continue the physical therapy they'd started once the cast came off.

I was sitting in one of the visitor chairs looking at, but not reading, a textbook. I was going home, that is if the doctor was pleased with her latest look at me. That's why I was nervous as she came into the room.

"I guess you're getting sick of us poking and prodding you," she said.

"I'm ready to go home," I said in reply.

She looked at the chart book she'd carried in with her and didn't say a word for the longest time. I hoped she wouldn't find a need to keep me longer. I longed for my apartment, even if it would be a lonely place. All I could think of was my time with Sarah and how we had planned our wedding. Now it would never be. I wasn't a widower; I was someone who had been engaged to the most wonderful woman in the world. Her parents had talked to me about the funeral, but I could tell they had already made all the decisions without me. It was to be on the same day we had planned to get married. And, in a way, it made sense to do so, as Sarah's family members from England had made arrangements to be here at that time, but oh how much it hurt to think of burying her instead of marrying her. Same church. Same guests. *How cruel could God be?*

"Okay," the doctor said as she signed a form and tucked the chart under her arm, "I'll take care of the paperwork, and you can leave as soon as it is done."

I stood. "Thank you." I was excited inside, but I know it didn't show. I'd been that way lately, that is not wanting to show any feelings to another person.

She took my hand as if to shake it, but instead, she pulled me into a hug. An unknown mixture of smells arose from her body as I got closer—medical stuff, I guessed. Dr. Joyce Johnson was probably my mother's age, and she reminded me more of a mother than a doctor. While she certainly couldn't be considered obese, she didn't quite have the build you would expect for someone trained to take care of the human body.

"Listen," she said as she backed away while still holding onto my hand.

I waited while she brushed away a tear.

"You know, all of us here at the hospital know how you feel. We loved Sarah, too. We're all grieving with you." She patted my hand and then turned to leave before suddenly twisting around to face me again. "I guess what I'm trying to say is that if you need someone to talk to…someone who understands…then we're here. Come in or call anytime."

"Thank you. I will." I knew, even then, I would never see her again. I didn't want a constant reminder of Sarah's death. *And how could anyone know how I feel?* No one would ever understand how deeply I loved her.

Dr. Johnson pulled out a card and wrote on it before thrusting it toward me. "Here, this is my home phone number. Call me anytime." With that, she was gone.

As I stood there staring at the door, in walked Father Jesse Williams. He'd been to see me almost daily during the past week, and I had never told him how I felt about his God. Here he was again, probably wanting to pray with me, and I didn't know if God existed. If there was a god who'd let Sarah die the way she did, I wasn't sure I wanted to worship that god.

"Hello, Chris," he said. "I hear you're going home today. How do you feel about that?"

What a stupid question. "Fine," I said.

He walked on in as I tried to think of a way to not talk to him that day. I couldn't keep acting as if nothing had changed. Everything was different now, but people kept doing the same old things they did before Sarah was shot and killed.

"Yes," I said, "I'm going home today. In fact, I was just getting ready to pack for the trip home. My friend Tony will be here soon to give me a lift."

Father Jesse had his well-worn Bible in his hand and was about to open it.

"So I don't think I better take time to talk today. You understand?" I asked.

"Yes, of course," he said. "How about a short prayer to get you safely home then?"

"I already did that," I said. "I went to the chapel earlier today with the hospital chaplain, and we prayed there." I had never lied to a priest before, and it felt weird. I couldn't look him in the face, instead busying myself with pulling clothes out of a drawer.

"Okay then," he said, "I guess I'll see you at the memorial service." He hugged me before leaving.

I felt so guilty for lying to Father Jesse I decided right then I should at least find the hospital chapel and see what it looked like.

I found the Brightwell Chapel on my own by reading signs. For some reason, I didn't want anyone to know I didn't know where it was. It was still difficult getting around on crutches, so as soon as I entered the dimly lit room, I sat in the first chair I came to. It was a peaceful place, and I'm sure it brought comfort for those seeking such. That wasn't why I was there.

I straightened the books sitting near me and asked myself why I came to the chapel, not the fake reason. I had loved God all my life and attended church almost every Sunday for as long as I could remember. I met Sarah at the church, and we talked about how God had brought us together. "How else," she asked once, "could such a perfect union be orchestrated?" I loved her for saying that, and now I wished she hadn't.

Maybe she was right. Even as she lay dying in my arms at the shopping mall, she knew something I didn't. There wasn't sadness in her eyes. She knew she was going to see her Lord.

Was there something I was missing? My life is in shambles because of a bunch of low-life thieves with no regard for human life. Am I supposed to let them get away with that? Turn the other cheek? "Vengeance is mine," saith the Lord. *What does that mean?*

I looked at the cross on the wall and stared at it for a few minutes, hoping I might hear something in response to my question.

Nothing.

I knew what it meant. It meant I wasn't supposed to take the law into my own hands to extract justice. It didn't mean God would settle the score for Sarah's death; he'd just try to save their souls.

No way was I going to let them get away without punishment.

I used to go to a place like this chapel and pray. It was quiet, with a soothing ambience. But I couldn't bring myself to believe that prayer would work. I looked around the room and saw an Episcopal prayer book. Perhaps that would help. I had parts of the book memorized from years of worship in an Episcopal church and my strange memory capabilities.

I leafed through it looking for something to help me accept what had happened. The only thing that came to me was the prayer said after communion:

Almighty and everlasting God, we most heartily thank thee for that thou dost feed us, in these holy mysteries, with the spiritual food of the most precious Body and Blood of thy Son our Savior Jesus Christ; and dost assure us thereby of thy favor and goodness towards us; and that we are very members incorporate in the mystical body of thy Son, the blessed company of all faithful people; and are also heirs through hope, of thy everlasting kingdom.

And we humbly beseech thee, O heavenly Father, so to assist us with thy grace, that we may continue in that holy fellowship, and do all such good works as thou hast prepared for us to walk in; through Jesus Christ our Lord, to whom, with thee and the Holy Ghost, be all honor and glory, world without end. Amen.

How many times over the years had I said this prayer? I stared at the words, waiting for them to make sense. Now it sounded like black magic or brainwashing material. It didn't mean anything. I was alone in the world now because there wasn't a god after all.

I stood and held the prayer book up toward the cross. "SARAAAAAAH! I PROMISE I WILL AVENGE YOUR DEATH."

A candy striper looked into the chapel. "Are you okay, sir?"

I threw the prayer book against the wall as hard as I could, knocking the cross to the floor and eliminating the serenity and silence of the chapel in a matter of seconds. When I turned around, the candy striper was nowhere to be seen. I went back to my room and checked out of the hospital.

CHAPTER TWO

Mother and Dad returned to Georgetown for the burial service. If they hadn't been staying at my apartment and hadn't expected me to go to the service, I probably would have stayed in bed all day. I didn't discuss any of this with them. I just knew there'd be a fight if I didn't buckle up and do what everyone expected of me. I sure wasn't interested in talking about how I felt with Mom and Dad—or anyone, for that matter.

I did talk to myself about it and came up with the answer. I didn't want to go to the service because it was being held at the same time and place as our wedding day—well, the same time our wedding was *supposed* to be. I couldn't bear to be in the church without Sarah at my side. Sarah's parents and relatives were farmers; practical, down-to-earth people; and good stewards. I'm sure it made sense to them to have the service on this day because the out-of-town guests had made travel arrangements to be here for the wedding. So I understood why they selected that particular day for the burial service, but that didn't make it any less painful.

As I discussed this with myself, I also came to realize a part of my not wanting to go to the service was because of it being in the church. I didn't want to have anything to do with the church again. This was also something I couldn't discuss with anyone because they would want to change my mind. I couldn't believe in a god who would let Sarah die the way she did.

All through the service, I looked around the sanctuary and felt like an outsider. This wasn't part of my life any longer. I also felt like I was living a lie since I didn't want to tell anyone how I felt. I'd have to do that eventually. Father Jesse had been calling nearly every day, and I was running out of excuses for not talking to him.

After the service, the family and close friends met at the Eason farm. My parents couldn't stay for the gathering since they had a flight back to Scotland to finish the vacation that had been suspended when I went into the hospital; however, they wouldn't let me go back to my apartment. Since I was on crutches and not driving yet, Mom asked Father Jesse to drive me to the reception and make sure I got home afterward.

The reception was strange. I never know how to act at these things, even when it is because of the death of someone other than my fiancée. I thought everyone would be sitting around crying. Instead, it was more like a party. I heard laughter from time to time. People I didn't know walked around with small plates of finger food trying to find a place to set down their drinks.

I had been introduced to most of the family, but I still felt like a stranger there. Besides Father Jesse, I didn't know anyone except for Mr. and Mrs. Eason. I was still a bit unsteady on the crutches, but I worked my way over to Sarah's parents. They had visited me in the hospital, but we hadn't talked about the shooting. This was the time to say something meaningful to them, but my mind was blank.

As I approached Paul and Ann, the conversation in the room diminished. I could feel the stares around me. I steadied myself on the crutches and opened my mouth. No words came. I swallowed and tried again. Still, there was only silence. I bowed my head, unable to look them in the eyes. My whole body drooped.

Ann stepped toward me and hugged me as only a mother can. "It's okay, Chris." She had a way of sucking in the end of her sentences that made me wonder if she was getting enough air.

"I know you want to comfort us in our loss, but it's not necessary. If one believes in God as we do, one must accept death. We don't like it, and we don't understand it, but we accept it as joyously as we can." She took a deep breath.

Her voice was so soft I was sure no one else in the room heard her, other than Paul who was nodding in agreement while looking at me over the top of his half glasses. His face showed strength, not fear or anger. I couldn't believe what I was hearing. *Why don't they do something? How could they sit around and accept the evil perpetuated by those monsters who killed their daughter?*

Ann helped me to a chair, and Paul brought me a glass of punch. The volume of the conversations in the room returned to normal. Several family members came to where I sat and introduced themselves. I knew most of the English guests were from Sarah's hometown of Bath.

Sarah's brother, Andrew, who was about my age and had Sarah's red hair, was the first to attack. "How shall I say this?" he began, hovering so close I felt blocked in. "Back home, we protect our womenfolk."

Before I could respond, Sarah's Uncle Roger moved in next to Andrew. "Right you are, my boy. I should like to know how this happened." He looked at me with a frown. "Weren't you there with Sarah when she was so brutally shot to death?"

This should have been our wedding day, my first day with my lifelong partner. I loved her more than anyone there could ever know. I didn't need to explain anything to them. I wanted to get up and walk away, but with a glass of punch in one hand and both crutches in the other, I stayed put.

But not for long. Sarah's mother appeared and took the glass from me. Paul was at her side, helping me stand.

"Andrew, Roger, knock it off," Paul said. "Neither of you knows what you're talking about. Don't you see the crutches? Don't you know Chris was shot with his body covering Sarah's? Read the news. His actions were heroic."

"Yeah? Well, she's still dead, isn't she?" Andrew turned to walk away.

Paul grabbed his arm, forcing him to stop. "Listen to me, Son. I know you're angry, but don't blame the person who loved your sister. I saw him with me daughter many a time over the years, and he was always the perfect gentleman. He's no coward. I can vouch for that."

Ann wrapped her arm around her son's arm. "Think how Chris must feel. Today was to be their wedding day." She touched my shoulder with her other hand and took a deep breath before continuing. "I'm sorry, Chris. I just realized myself how you must feel. We should've had the service on a different day."

Ann sounded so much like Sarah it hurt to hear her speak. The accent. The way she popped the ending consonants.

"It's okay, ma'am," I said. At least she understood— Paul, too. They seemed to know how I felt. But I didn't understand them. *How could they accept Sarah's death so easily?*

Ann turned from me to Andrew without saying a word.

Andrew looked down. "Sorry, Mum."

"We need to help Chris, not blame him," Paul said. "He's going to be rid of these crutches soon, but he'll always be in pain because of Sarah's death, just as we all will be."

Andrew stared at me for a long time, and the anger I

had seen on his face diminished some before he turned and walked away.

Paul helped me to another chair, one with a side table, and Ann brought me a fresh punch and a plate of sandwiches.

"Don't let anyone upset you, Son," she said. "Sarah talked about you all the time. She loved you dearly and so do we. You are our link to her memory."

I looked at her in a new way. Her eyes were moist even after her speech about God's will. Maybe she was hurting as much as I was. A simple thank-you was all I could manage. I hoped she could read the depth of appreciation in my eyes.

A woman Ann's age sat next to me, and Ann left us alone.

"Hi, I'm Ruth—Roger's wife. I'm sorry for what he said to you. He had no right to blame you for anything. I hope you'll give us another chance."

"It's okay." She was being so nice I didn't want to tell her Sarah's death was my fault. Perhaps an Englishman would have been tougher about keeping his fiancée away from danger.

"I read the news stories," Ruth said. "You did your best."

"Yeah, but that wasn't the whole story."

Ruth's hair was gray and she tugged at the waistband of a black dress that was probably a size or two too small for her. When she finished with the dress, she clasped her hands and rubbed a thumb. "What do you mean?"

"Honestly, I believe Sarah had received the fatal shot before I got to her." I didn't know why, but I could talk to her in a way I hadn't been able to talk to Ann and Paul. "She talked to me before she died, and I believe she knew she wouldn't make it—probably her medical training. I don't know."

Ruth moved closer. "If you don't mind my asking, what did she say?"

That surprised me. No one had asked me that. I didn't want to share the exact words. "I don't recall the exact words, but I guess you could say she told me good-bye. She told me to enjoy my life, and we'd…"

My voice shut down, and both Ruth and I had tears in our eyes as she finished the sentence for me.

"Meet in Heaven? Yes, that sounds like Sarah, trusting in God right up until the end. We should all have such faith." She wiped away her tears.

I saw pride on her face.

Everyone was nice after that, so much so I wondered if Paul and Ann had warned them to lay off. About the time I thought I couldn't stand being there another minute, Father Jesse showed up and said he was ready to go. I got out of the chair as fast as one could with only one functioning leg. Father Jesse and I walked side by side to where Paul and Ann stood to say good-bye, then nodded to the others as we walked toward the door.

When we got to the front door, Andrew stopped me. "Can I talk to you a minute?"

"I'll get the car and move it up closer," Father Jesse said, looking at me. "Take as long as you need."

Andrew watched Father Jesse walk away before saying a word. "I'm sorry for what I said earlier. Dad told me more about what happened. It's a bloody shame, it 'tis. I know you loved her, and I want you to know Sis was special to me, too. Someday, we'll talk about it. Okay?" He held out a hand.

"I'd like that." I balanced on my crutches to free my right hand and took his in mine. I suspected we had a special bond neither one of us yet understood, but with him going back to the UK, I wasn't sure we'd find out anytime soon.

"Listen, there's something else." Andrew looked around as if to see if anyone was close enough to hear him. "I'm just a farmer's son, but I've got mates—close mates—in London, if you know what I mean. Two of them are in the government. When they heard about Sarah, they got in touch with me. I haven't told Mum and Dad, but my mates think the killers have terrorist connections."

"Terrorists?"

He looked around the room. "Shh. Don't say anything about this yet. I'll check it out when I get home and let you know what I hear. It might make it easier to understand if we find out it was more than a robbery."

"Maybe. Yeah, please let me know what you learn. I'd like to find the people responsible and…" I couldn't finish that sentence. I said good-bye and hobbled to Father Jesse's car wondering what I'd gotten myself into.

***

As Father Jesse drove away from the farmhouse onto the dirt road that led to the blacktop county road, I watched him. I guessed he was in his sixties based on the wrinkles around his eyes and his gray sideburns and salt-and-pepper hair. But he wasn't fragile looking—just the opposite. I remembered the day Sarah and I went to his office for marriage counseling. He was wearing a golf shirt and his biceps were so well developed I thought he must have been lifting weights on a regular basis. I never did know for sure if I was right, but I did learn he was an avid golfer, which explained why his face and arms were tanned.

Now he wore a gray wool jacket with leather elbows, which seemed too heavy for November in Central Texas.

He drove silently until we reached the end of the dirt road and turned onto the main highway. Once we were on the paved road, he said what I'd been hoping he wouldn't say.

"Your mother is worried about you, Chris."

Since Mom had arranged for him to give me a lift to the reception, I knew she'd talked to him. Still, I hoped she hadn't told him what I'd said about revenge. His expression didn't offer the slightest hint of what he knew.

"I know she is," I managed to say.

"She thinks you might go after Sarah's killers." He looked toward me long enough to lock eyes before turning back to the road. Well, there it was—my blabbermouth mother at work again. I had a good idea what a priest would say about revenge, but his voice didn't sound accusatory.

"Would that be so crazy?" I watched him as I said it, knowing exactly how he would answer. He was a man of the cloth, after all. Sarah introduced me to him two years before when I joined the church. Before that, I had been attending a larger Episcopal parish in Austin. I grew to love Sarah's Anglican Church and was comfortable there. Also, I learned to respect Father Jesse. Now, here he was, obligated to tell me how wrong I was. I knew the Bible verse he'd use: "Beloved, never avenge yourselves, but leave room for the wrath of God; for it is written, 'Vengeance is mine. I will repay, says the Lord.'" Sometimes my memory of such things worried me, but there it was. I could actually see the words on the page of my Bible. So let him say it. I knew what I wanted to do was wrong, according to the church. I didn't care. Sarah was dead, and that changed everything— even the importance of God's rules.

He didn't answer right away, but I kept my mouth shut.

"Look, Son, I can't lie to you and tell you I know how you're feeling. I hope I never know. What I can say is if anyone came after my wife or my children, I would protect them to the death."

That surprised me.

"You're fairly new to the congregation, so you may not know this is a second career for me. Those who have been around a while know I'm a retired military officer, but no one in the church, other than my wife, and now you, knows I had to kill or be killed in Vietnam."

"Then you understand," I said.

"Hear me out on this. If my family was in danger today, my military training would override my theological training, and I would be all over the attackers like a mad dog. I'd kill them with my bare hands if I had to. I wouldn't turn the other cheek if my family was endangered."

This killer sitting next to me was the same gentle man who led our worship services, the same man who had counseled Sarah and me about the give and take of marriage. He seemed different now. His words were chopped, sounding more like those street toughs seen on television.

"I didn't know. So, you don't think I'm loony for what I'm thinking?"

His softer, more familiar counseling voice gradually came back as he spoke. "I don't think you're crazy at all. The feelings you're experiencing are normal. You're angry, and you want to strike out at those responsible for Sarah's death. I understand that."

This guy was smarter than I thought. "So I'm right."

"What you feel is neither right nor wrong. Feelings just *are*."

I looked at him, but he had his eyes on the road again. "I don't understand. Are you saying I should go after the killers or not?"

"Certainly not." He parked the car, opened the windows, and turned off the engine. I was surprised to see we were in front of my Georgetown apartment. He swiveled slightly to the right to face me. "I'm saying it is okay to recognize your feelings. It is quite another to act on them."

"You said you'd kill anyone who attacked your wife or kids."

He shook his head. "That's not the same. If you'd gone after the killers at the time they shot Sarah, okay. To track them down now is taking the law into your own hands. It also violates God's laws: 'Vengeance is mine,' saith the Lord, 'Forgive your enemies,' and the big one, 'Thou shall not kill.' If you find those killers and wipe them out, you're no better than they are."

"What about soldiers in wartime? They go after the enemy. You did yourself."

"Only when representing our country. Remember what happened to the U.S. soldiers in Iraq who acted outside the rules of war? They were severely punished for it, same as in Vietnam."

I should've known what he'd say. "I'm sorry, but I can't believe God would allow this to happen. Sarah was the best Christian I've ever known. She did everything right." I took a deep breath to keep going. "She only lived twenty-four years. Why did she have to die?"

He patted my shoulder. "We can't understand everything that happens in the world, but I can assure you God knows why she died."

What a bunch of bull. I dabbed my eyes and shook off the pity I was feeling and decided to tell him the rest. "I could have saved her."

Father Jesse didn't say anything, but his look invited me to continue.

"I should have. She's gone because of me."

"I don't know what else you could have done, Son. You took a bullet trying to protect her." He spoke softly, still looking into my eyes.

I had to look away. The truth was painful. "My getting shot—that was too late. She shouldn't have been in the line of fire in the first place. If I'd been thinking clearly, I would have picked her up and carried her behind a building to safety."

"She was a nurse. She felt she had to help, even if the situation was dangerous."

"I shouldn't have let her. I stopped her, but I got caught up in political correctness and let her go. That's when she was killed."

Father Jesse was disagreeing with his headshake again. "She went in there in the same way a medic does in the time of war. She faced danger to help that guard."

"Except she was killed before she could help." Tears filled my eyes. "Such a waste."

Father Jesse looked at me questioningly. "Don't you know she saved the guard's life?"

That shook me. "No, I didn't know." I hadn't read a news report about the incident. I still had the newspapers, but it was too painful to look at them.

"She did. There were reports from many witnesses. The second guard died because he fired on the helicopter as it was taking off. That's what caused Sarah's death, too. But before she was hit, she used part of her dress as a tourniquet that stopped the first guard from bleeding to death. He's alive and well because of her. His wife and children are in Sarah's debt."

I blew my nose. "I'm glad he lived." If I had hung around, Father Jesse probably would have said God's will was to save the guard because of his family, but I didn't want to hear that. There was no justification for Sarah's death. I climbed out of the car before he had a chance to say more. "Thanks for the ride home."

I walked slowly to my apartment. Not because of the crutches, but because of my thoughts. With every step, I silently denied the existence of God.

***

The Tuesday after Sarah's memorial service, I taught my first Fundamentals of Programming class at Austin Community College's Cypress Creek campus. It was my first day back to work since the incident.

Incident.

That's what people around me called it. No one could say, "Sarah's death," for some reason. Actually, everyone had been supportive in many ways. My colleagues had covered for me while I was in the hospital, and the dean had offered to give me the rest of the semester off. I declined, and I'm glad I did. Conducting the class was the first time I'd gone more than a few seconds without thinking about Sarah and mourning her loss. Remembering that now that the class was over and the students were leaving made me feel guilty. I wanted to never forget her, not even during a class.

Besides wanting to get back to what I enjoyed, I also needed the classroom experience to help with a textbook I was writing. I hadn't written a word since the incident and had probably missed a deadline by now. *I'd better check that today*, I thought, making a mental note. The textbook income was to help pay off college loans that were also coming due.

After class, I straightened the chairs, once again shaking my head over how students could get up and walk out without putting their chairs back under the desks. Of course, if I didn't have this thing about neatness, I never would have noticed the cockeyed chairs. Tex, my wheelchair-bound student, was the only one left in the room. He was putting his textbook into the backpack that hung on the back of his chair. As soon as he left, I'd move a regular chair to his desk. He was the only one I didn't object to straightening up after.

My mind wandered while I continued to clean the classroom and erase the whiteboard. And, as usual, I started thinking about how I'd sworn to avenge Sarah. I was beginning to think it wasn't going to happen. I didn't know if it was because of what Andrew had said about the killers being terrorists or whether those thoughts of vengeance had been simply a part of the grieving process. Actually, as I thought about it now, I suspect it was more the fact that I didn't know how to find the killers if I'd wanted to. I'd blabbed to Dad about my research abilities and how I could use the computer to track them down. *But what then?*

I gathered my books and prepared to leave. Tex didn't go toward the exit. He wheeled up to my desk, holding his cowboy hat in his lap, a hat he'd told me he'd started wearing when some buddies in the marines gave him the nickname "Tex."

"What can I do for you, Mr. Thompson?" Tex was older than the average student in my classes, probably in his forties. Although he was in a wheelchair and appeared to be paralyzed from the waist down, he didn't act as if he were disabled. He always had an opinion, and through it all, he remained positive about life. I respected him for that.

He'd started this class last semester, so I knew him better than the other students. He'd dropped out near the end, saying something about a family emergency. Still, I knew little about him other than what I saw and heard in class.

I'd overheard other students say Tex had spent time in prison, but I didn't know if it was true or not. He was always a perfect gentleman around me. He knew the material and participated in class discussions, often helping the other students. To be honest, he could teach the class if he had the credentials.

"Listen," he said, "I heard what happened. I'm sorry, sir. I wish I could help."

It always made me nervous when an older student called me sir, but I didn't correct him. I wanted to get out of there as quickly as possible because I knew what was coming next. I'd seen him at the Bible discussion groups in the student union, and on one occasion last year, he told me how his church had helped him get through the rough times in his life. He was getting ready to preach to me about Sarah's death being God's will, not something I wanted to hear right now—or anytime, for that matter.

I stuffed my textbooks into my carrying case and turned off the projector. I should have walked away, but I couldn't leave it alone.

I looked Tex in the face, leaning over until we were eye to eye. "You want to help? How about praying for a way to find the creeps who killed my fiancée so I can wipe them off the face of the earth." I shouldn't have said that for a number of reasons, but I was angry and the words were out before I knew what was happening.

Tex looked surprised and was uncharacteristically at a loss for words. When he finally spoke, he did so with a serious tone. "Don't talk like that, Dr. McCowan. They're not worth it. If you break the law trying to get revenge, you could end up in prison yourself. A person can get hurt bad in prison."

I motioned toward the wheelchair. "Is that what happened to you?"

He grinned and slapped his armrests. "This? No, I got this after I was out of prison."

So the rumors were true. "Mind if I ask what happened?" I

didn't usually get into the personal lives of students, but I felt at ease talking to him.

Tex cocked his head. "You mean prison or the wheel-chair?"

"Both," I said. "Why were you in prison?"

He leaned back in his chair and looked comfortable with my question. "The usual—drugs and alcohol. Incarceration didn't help with either one. I was in for two years, but lived on the streets for several years after that. I'm not sure which is worse—prison or homelessness. The food was a little better in prison, just wasn't enough of it."

I couldn't imagine what he'd had to do to survive. I'd never known anyone who'd lived on the streets. "That's awful. How'd you get past it? You seem so different from the person you're describing."

"Patriotism and God." Tex held his chin high as he said it, then nodded slightly as if agreeing with himself.

"How's that?"

"I was a straight-A student in high school, and I took all the college-prep classes. Never a problem. But when the time came to pick a college, I wasn't ready. I joined the marines instead. I ended up staying in the Corps for ten years. The only reason I got out when I did was to get a college degree and go back as an officer."

"What happened?"

"Once I was in college, I started partying too much, and things went downhill from there. Finally, I dropped out and worked as a busboy to pay my bills." He rubbed his legs as he talked, and I could see how thin his thighs were. "One thing led to another, and I ended up in prison."

"And you found God in prison?"

He laughed. "No. God was there for others, but I managed to escape his notice. I got my wake-up call when the World Trade Center buildings went down on nine/eleven.

That day I started thinking there were some things more important than where my next drink came from. I knew I had to get back in the Corps and go after those terrorists. I would've, too, if it hadn't been for the accident."

"The wheelchair?"

"Yeah," Tex said, laughing, and slapped his thighs. "This was God's little joke on me. I sobered up with the help of AA and my church. After that, I was accepted by the marines for reenlistment. A few days before I was to report for duty, a drunk driver hit me. Ironic, huh?" He laughed again.

"I'm not sure I could laugh about it the way you do."

He shrugged. "What else we going to do? If we believe in God, we have to accept the life he gives us."

Here it comes. That's what Sarah's parents had said. "I've been hearing that a lot lately. Sounds like bull to me."

"Sorry, sir. I didn't think." Tex turned serious. "I understand. God and I didn't get along at all until I was ready."

"It's okay. I'm glad you were able to turn your life around the way you did. I'm sure it was difficult."

His face went somber before he answered. "I couldn't have done it without help. I might have gone back to drinking if it hadn't been for the hospital chaplain. She not only saved my life, she married me. I'm in school now studying to be a drug and alcohol counselor so that I can use my experience to help others."

"You'll be good at it," I said. "I bet your parents are proud of how you've changed."

"Don't know. They gave up on me long ago." His voice was softer as he spoke.

"Have you told them how you're doing?"

Tex turned his wheelchair around as if he were trying to get away from the question. "I haven't talked to them in years."

"I'm sorry. It's none of my business." Tex had been through terrible ordeals, but so had I. Without Sarah, there would be no more joy in my life. All I had to look forward to was taking revenge for her death, and now that didn't seem possible. Even with Dad's help and whatever Andrew's friends could do from London, I didn't know where to start. Even if I could find the killers, what then? Besides, I didn't know the first thing about weapons.

We were the only ones in the room, but Tex moved in closer and spoke softly. "I didn't know your fiancée, of course, but I bet she wouldn't want you to endanger yourself. She'd want you to live your life to the fullest."

I had to turn my head away before he could read the truth in my eyes, because that was almost exactly what she said to me as she died in my arms. I reached for my crutches. *Time to get out of here. Why should I expect anyone to understand how I feel?*

Tex handed me a piece of paper he'd been scribbling on as we talked.

I looked at it as he held one finger vertically against his lips.

It said, "Room is bugged."

I looked around, and he motioned toward a black half globe on the ceiling. In it, I knew was a video monitor used to prevent someone from walking out with a computer. I doubted if it picked up sound. In fact, I wondered if it was working.

I hoisted my bag over my left shoulder and climbed onto my crutches. "Why don't we go outside?"

As soon as we were outside and away from the building, Tex picked up the conversation where he'd left off. "As I was saying, I don't think your fiancée would want you to endanger yourself. Even so, I think you're going to do this thing anyway." He paused, but when I didn't respond, he continued. "And I want to help. Let this be my nine/eleven. After that drunk hit and paralyzed me, the marines wouldn't take me. I know how to do the job. It's this wheelchair they didn't want. If you insist on doing what I know you're going to do, let me help." He had an eerie smile on his face.

My hands were sweating in anticipation. "What'd you have in mind?" *Was it possible I hadn't hit a dead end after all?*

Tex wheeled back a few feet and straightened his back. His voice was a strong stage whisper. "You'd be surprised. I can teach you what I learned in the Corps, on the streets, and in prison. I can tell you about criminals, drugs, guns, hand-to-hand combat, disguises, security systems, the whole bundle. I can get fake IDs, and I have contacts with a variety of useful people. Need I say more?" Tex paused to take a breath, but didn't wait for a response. "As soon as your leg heals, we'll start by getting you into better physical condition. You're a great teacher, sir, but you've been sitting in front of a computer screen too long. You're too flabby to fight."

I was taken aback by his offer and surprised by how quickly he'd summarized what might be needed. He made it seem as if this could happen. I could provide the research skills with the help of Dad, and Tex could provide the rest. We'd make a strange team, with me on crutches and him in a wheelchair, but we had the combination of skills needed for this project.

"Well, sir, do I get my nine/eleven or not?" Tex smiled as if he knew the answer.

I looked at him and smiled back. "Let's roll!"

CHAPTER THREE

It was dark by the time I got home from school that night, and I was excited, in a strange way, about the discussion with Tex. I couldn't think about that now. All I wanted to do was crawl into bed and sleep. It didn't help having to climb three flights of stairs on crutches to get to my apartment. I was breathing heavily when I got there, which reminded me what Tex had said about my being out of shape. I unlocked the door, hoping to make it to the couch to rest. Instead, I froze as soon as I opened the front door and looked in.

Someone was in my apartment. I couldn't say how I knew, but someone was either there or had been. I have an uncanny sense of my surroundings most of the time. If I see a drawer not completely pushed in or a cabinet door opened slightly, I feel out of balance until I push the drawer in flush where it should be or shut the cabinet door. Perhaps everyone who works with the unwavering requirements of computers had the same sense of space. I don't know what it is.

But I did know something in my living room was different from the way I left it this morning. I quietly removed my left crutch from under my arm and held it up like a baseball bat. I was just mad enough at criminals in general to take a swipe at one, even if it caused me to fall on my butt.

There was enough light from the covered landing outside my windows to allow me to see the room clearly, so I didn't flip the light switch on for fear the light might scare the intruder away, assuming he or she was still there. I hobbled in with one good leg and one crutch, still holding the other crutch at the ready. There, I found it. The bedroom door was closed. I never close the bedroom door unless my parents are visiting.

I knew it isn't smart to confront a burglar; it is best to leave and call for help. But all I had so far was intuition—not enough to call 911.

I moved as carefully as possible toward the bedroom door. That's when I heard the noise that caused me to stop in my tracks. There was definitely someone rummaging in my bedroom. Now it was okay to leave and call 911. As much as I wanted to whack a bad guy, I decided against it and turned to shuffle toward the front door, using both crutches for what they were intended. I pulled out my cell phone to be ready to make the call as soon as I was out the door, forgetting I needed both hands for the crutches. I managed to drop the phone on the ceramic tile floor, and as I watched it split into two pieces, I knew the crashing sound would alarm the burglar and leave me without a way to call for help.

Sure enough, the bedroom door opened so fast it hit the wall with a bang. A man ran from the room, slowing down just long enough to knock me out of the way with a football block. He probably didn't see the crutches, or he wouldn't have hit me so hard. It happened so fast, and he held his head so low as he rammed me that I couldn't see his face. All I knew when he was gone was that he was a male of about my height, six two—so much for whacking a bad guy.

It was an effort to get up and back on the crutches, but I managed. I closed and locked the front door before checking the bedroom. My chest of drawers had been moved away from the wall, and the contents were dumped on the floor.

After searching the rest of the apartment and finding everything where it should be, I made my way to the guest room I call my office and sat at the desk and called Tex on my landline. While waiting for him to answer, I noticed my mouse was out of position. Someone had messed with my computer. No, I'm not that kind of neatnik. I don't leave my computer mouse in an exact location. The only reason I noticed it was the fact that the mouse was on the right side of the computer. Since I'm left-handed, I keep it on the mouse pad on the left. The burglar was either stupid or didn't care if I knew he had been on my computer. I'd also reprogrammed the mouse buttons. I bet that drove him crazy.

"Hello." Tex's voice sounded strained. It was the first time we'd talked over the phone, so I couldn't tell for sure, but he may have been asleep.

I checked my watch. It was only 9:30 p.m. I stayed up until midnight most nights, but I'd been sleeping more since the incident. "Sorry to call you at home so late, but someone broke into my apartment. Thought you'd want to know. Nothing seems to be missing. Any reason why I shouldn't call the police?"

"Call 'em. After they leave, meet me at the place where we had lunch today. Understand, sir?"

"You mean—"

"Shh! Don't say anything on this phone. Call me on your cell if you want to talk more. Otherwise, you know where to meet."

I wasn't sure why Tex was being so cryptic. It was as if he thought the break-in was related to our vengeance plans. That couldn't be. We hadn't done anything yet. No one could've known about us.

"My cell is busted into pieces thanks to my visitor."

"Then meet me. Good-bye."

I heard the familiar tone letting me know he'd hung up. His reaction seemed overly dramatic, but I was beginning think that was the way he was. I hung up and dialed the police. I told them it wasn't an emergency and I didn't think anything was missing, but I thought it should be investigated. I looked around while waiting for the police to arrive.

A quick check of the computer showed it to be intact.

The police didn't learn much during their investigation; however, they did discover a little fact I hadn't noticed. Whoever had been in my apartment apparently had a key since there wasn't a sign of forced entry. Before they left, they told me I should get the locks changed.

After they were gone, I grabbed my crutches and car keys and headed for the Round Rock Denny's.

I found Tex sitting at a table in the back of the restaurant. He looked around suspiciously as I sat across from him.

"No one followed you here, did they?" he asked, still looking around the room.

"Who would follow me?"

He shrugged. "I'm just being cautious. So, what'd the cops say?" Without taking his eyes off me, he took a sip of his coffee and put the cup down on his saucer with a clink.

With my so-called photographic memory, I pretty much knew the menu since the last time they changed it, but I glanced at it anyway. "Not much. They took notes and said they'd file a report. They said the person who'd been there must have had a key and suggested I get the locks changed."

The server brought my coffee before Tex had a chance to answer. She pulled out a pad, and gave us a bored smile. "What's it gonna be?"

"I'm just having coffee," Tex said.

I handed her the menu. "I'll have coffee and *migas*—no jalapeños."

Tex was silent until the server was gone, then he rolled back from the table a foot or so and moved in closer to where I sat. "I'm probably being paranoid, sir, but I'd rather be safe than sorry. It just doesn't seem like a coincidence to me that your apartment was broken into."

"I'd be suspicious, too, if anyone knew what we've talked about." Tex meant well, but this was a little out in left field. I straightened the fork on my napkin, making sure the edge of the napkin was parallel with the fork, and worried once again if I was crazy because of these silly habits of mine.

Tex leaned in and spoke softly. "Who all did you tell about your little plan?"

"Vengeance" was what he meant. I thought it over carefully before I answered. I counted with my fingers as I responded. "My parents. I wish now I hadn't told Mother. She told Father Jesse. I don't think he believes it, though. He was in Vietnam before he became a priest and had to kill the enemy. When he looks at me, I'm sure all he sees is a computer nerd. As you've noted, I'm not exactly built for fighting."

Tex grunted. "Humph. Don't worry, Doc. We'll fix that. Is that it? Is that everyone?"

I remembered one more and held up a fourth finger. "Andrew—Sarah's brother."

"Why'd you tell him?" Tex frowned. "Doesn't he live in England?"

Tex didn't understand what it was like to lose your fiancée the way I did. I wanted to convince him the break-in at my apartment wasn't related to our investigation so I could go home and get to sleep. *Why should I have to talk about all this now?*

But I did.

"Andrew put me down for not protecting his sister. He implied an Englishman would have kept her safe. Maybe I told him what I was going to do so he'd understand, or perhaps, respect me more. I think it worked. That's when he told me about his friends in London. Who knows, maybe his friends will end up helping us."

Tex leaned back in his wheelchair. "So, your mother told your pastor, and Andrew told his friends in London. I wonder who they told."

I wanted to go home. "All this talk about who told whom is getting us nowhere. I just came here to tell you I don't think the break-in at my place is related to our investigation."

Tex waved his hand in the air as if dismissing my argument. "I know, but humor me. Who else did you tell?"

Dad told me not to tell anyone about his involvement with the FBI, but I knew I should let Tex know I had a contact in the FBI. "I also told a friend who's connected with the FBI."

"FBI?" Tex said it so loud he quickly looked around to see if anyone was paying attention. "Good," he said at a greatly reduced volume, "an FBI source could come in handy."

The server showed up with a plate of *migas* loaded with cheese, a side of hash browns, flour tortillas, and a bowl of chunky salsa.

When she was gone, I turned to Tex. "We're wasting our time analyzing all this. I think the break-in was a druggy looking for something to pawn."

Tex shook his head slowly. "I don't know. That doesn't make sense. Nothing was taken from your apartment, right?"

"Not that I can tell, but maybe I scared him off before he had a chance to steal anything. I looked over the place carefully while I waited for the police to show. I even checked the computer. It had been searched, but nothing was changed."

"You have a nice computer, right?" Tex asked.

"Of course. I need it for my job."

"A burglar would have taken that first and gotten out as fast as possible."

"So, what was he doing there?"

"Your whole apartment could be bugged. Even your computer could be set up to send out encrypted messages to someone, letting them know everything you do."

I laughed. "I don't know about the listening devices, but nothing happens on my computer I don't know about. Computers are my thing, remember?"

"I've got a friend who'll check your place for bugs. Expect him tomorrow. If he says Jimbo anywhere in a sentence, he's my man."

Nothing Tex said that night convinced me the break-in was connected to Sarah's death, so I began to think teaming up with him might have been a mistake. At the same time, the more I thought about it all, the more difficult it was for my logical mind to call what happened a coincidence. I'd let Jimbo check for bugs, but I knew the truth. It was a simple burglary, and I'd come home too early for the crook to finish the job. Of course, that didn't explain why he messed with my chest of drawers or why he used my computer and didn't run with it. It was going to take me a while to have the detective mindset Tex had—if I ever did.

***

Just as I expected, Jimbo, or whatever his name was, didn't

find any bugs in the apartment, leaving me more convinced than before the break-in didn't have anything to do with Sarah's death. Just in case, however, I installed a little surprise for the next person who visited my place while I was away.

As soon as Jimbo was finished, I went to the Apple store in Austin and bought a new iPhone to replace my cheap mobile that had cracked apart when I dropped it trying to get away from the burglar. I was still playing around with my new toy when Tex came over that Saturday for the first official meeting of the "Vengeance Squad." That's what he had started calling us.

When he got there, I realized we had a problem. I hadn't thought about how he'd get up the stairs to where I lived on the third floor. At school, he got around so easily I tended to forget he was disabled. After we stared at the situation for a while, that is he at the bottom of three flights of stairs in a wheelchair and I at the top with my crutches, two of my brawniest neighbors eventually agreed to carry him and his wheelchair up the stairs. Tex sat there like deadweight wearing his ten-gallon cowboy hat and acted as if he enjoyed all the attention.

After my neighbors left, Tex surprised me with a suggestion to expand our team. "I want to invite a friend to join our team. She's a librarian and can help us do research and—"

"Are you crazy?" I leaned my crutches up against the wall in the living room and limped to the dining table, where I jerked one of the chairs out of the way to make room for his wheelchair. "I thought you said we shouldn't tell anyone about this."

The dining table was in a corner of the living room near a counter that separated the living area from the kitchen. It was a two-bedroom unit, with one of the bedrooms being used for my office, but all the rooms were small.

He tossed his cowboy hat on the couch and rolled in behind me, taking his place at the table. "I'm not talking about any ol' librarian. This one's special. Besides, she has friends in law enforcement and government. She also has financial connections."

I put the unneeded chair in the corner of the room. "We don't even know if we can do this yet. Let's not bring in more people until we know if we need to."

He looked at me more seriously. "You haven't changed your mind, have you? We're still going after those guys, aren't we?"

"We'll see." I wanted to, but I had no idea if it was possible.

Tex made a grunting sound. "'We'll see'—that's what my dad always said. He mostly meant 'no' when he said it."

"It means I don't know. We're here to talk about it. Don't make a big deal out of my words."

Tex had a quizzical look on his face. "I see you're getting around better without the crutches, but what happened to your face, sir?"

I rubbed the stubble on my chin. "What do you mean? This is my beard." For no particular reason, I hadn't shaved since Sarah's death and decided that morning to let it grow until we captured the killers.

He laughed aloud. "Beard? You call that a beard? I thought it was some fuzz from a towel or something. I scrape more 'n that off every morning." He laughed louder.

I rubbed my face again. It felt like a beard to me.

Tex wheeled up to the table and turned serious. "So, what's your FBI friend say?"

Tex didn't know Dad was my FBI contact, and there was no reason to tell him. After all, Dad had asked me not to tell anyone. "I learned they're aware of the case. That's all. My contact isn't sure if that means they don't know anything or they can't talk about what they know."

Tex tapped his fingers on the table. "I hope you can get more out of them later. How about your London source?"

I didn't think we'd learn anything from Andrew's friends. "No, nothing yet. I suspect what we have here are some sophisticated crooks with no morals, not international killers. They could be local bank robbers dressed in costumes to throw everyone off."

Tex shook his head slowly. "I don't know. We need to check everything. Your apartment manager said a guy with a strong English accent asked about you the day before your apartment was broken in to—might be someone Andrew knows."

"When did you hear that? I talked to him last week when I asked about changing the lock, and he didn't mention anyone with an English accent."

"I talked to him about ten minutes before your friends carried me up here. Maybe it was my wheelchair. You'd be surprised how people open up to me because of this." He tapped on the handles and smiled. "Or just asking him about it triggered his memory. I doubt if it was the twenty bucks I slipped him. Who knows? People don't usually volunteer information. You have to ask them point blank."

I had a lot to learn about criminal investigation.

Tex reached around to the back of his wheelchair where a well-worn khaki backpack hung from the handles and came up with a note pad. He grabbed a pencil from his shirt pocket and licked the point before putting it on paper. "Now, let's see what we know about this case."

We knew very little, certainly not enough to maintain a log, in my opinion. But if it would make him happy, let him at it. At least he'd stopped talking about adding his librarian friend to our team.

"Let me see." I bowed my head and rubbed my temples as I went over the incident one more time. Most of that last day with Sarah flashed through my head several times each day and woke me during the night, so it was easy to recall.

Tex made notes as I talked. In the end, we hadn't identified much to help with our search. The only thing that stood out was the helicopter. That, and the fact that there were six to eight men with brown skin and black beards dressed in khaki fatigues.

Tex held his note pad up in the air as if it were a trophy. "Good start, sir. Next, we'll review all the news reports again to glean more details. We'll talk to the other witnesses, too. Do you know what kind of helicopter they used?"

I shook my head and shrugged. "Big enough to hold all those guys. That's all I know. Plus, it looked military." I still hadn't read the newspaper reports about the shooting.

"Olive drab, black, what?" he asked.

I thought about the helicopter as it fired toward Sarah. "It was a greenish color, I think." My so-called photographic memory apparently didn't work when people were shooting at me.

Tex suddenly pushed back from the table. "You got a laptop?"

"Sure. Why?"

He shook his notepad at me. "For this. We need to organize our notes. Also, with the laptop, we can get on the Internet and look up more information about the attack to fill in some blanks. Let's use Microsoft Access and build a database to collect the tidbits of information we know. Maybe we'll see some patterns after we get enough data— you know, that stuff you teach in your class."

He was right. *Why hadn't I thought of that?*

I went to the spare bedroom I called my office, brought out my laptop, and put it on the table in front of him.

"Good idea. You have an excellent teacher." We both laughed. "While you're building the database, I'll use my desktop system to see what I can find about that helicopter."

"Great idea. Most robbers don't have helicopters, and it's gotta be hard to steal one. I don't remember seeing any details in the initial news reports, but maybe you can find a follow-up story. If it was a military hijacking, they probably wouldn't talk to reporters about it. If we can't find anything on it, I'm sure Liz can help us."

"Who's Liz?"

Tex had his nose in the computer and didn't look up. "The librarian I was telling you about."

There he goes again. "I'll find it. Don't tell anyone what we're doing, okay?"

I went to my office and sat in front of the computer, leaving Tex to work on the laptop in the dining area. I found the story in about five minutes, printed it, and took it to him.

He looked it over. "Yeah!" Tex was an animated guy from the waist up. "That's it! They stole the helicopter from Camp Mabry right in the middle of Austin. Surely there'll be some clues there." He moved both hands to the keyboard of the laptop in front of him and started typing. "There. I've added the details to our database. Good job, Doc."

We still didn't know a thing really, but it was a start. Maybe Tex was right. If we could find a bit of information here and another there, it could add up to something meaningful in time.

"How can we find out what happened at Camp Mabry?" I asked.

Tex smiled as he rolled away from the table. "I'll get Liz to check on it. She should know something in time for our next get together. Is Monday night okay? We could meet at the Austin History Center. That's where I work."

I didn't want to meet at my place and have to ask neighbors I didn't know to lift Tex and his chair up three flights again. "That's fine. You won't get in trouble with your boss, will you?"

"Nah, she's cool."

Tex shut down the laptop and was putting it in the case when an idea came to me. "You don't have a laptop, do you?" I asked.

"Laptop?" Tex asked. "I don't have a computer of any kind—can't afford it."

I hadn't considered that. "How do you do your homework?"

"I do it at school or at work." He turned the wheelchair toward the door.

"Here, take mine. I only use it for trips. I've got my big system in the office. That way you can maintain the database you started. Okay?"

He grinned from ear to ear. "Okay? Of course, sir." He did a 180 and grabbed the laptop off the table and slipped it into the backpack hanging behind him. "Now, where are those human bearers of yours?" He rolled toward the door.

I called my neighbors, the ones who had lifted Tex up initially, and they said they'd be right over. They didn't sound happy about it, but who could turn down Tex?

When Tex got to the door, he twisted around and looked at me seriously. "Sir, I know you're concerned about the way the investigation is going. Just think about your fiancée and you'll be reminded why we're doing this. Pardon me for asking, Doc, but how long did you and Miss Sarah know each other?"

I opened the front door to watch for my neighbors. "When we're not in class, you can call me Chris. Sarah and

I were together for two wonderful years."

Tex looked surprised. "Is that all? I was drunk longer than that once."

I hoped what he said was a commentary on his life and not a suggestion I hadn't known Sarah long enough to feel the way I did. I'd noticed during class that Tex would sometimes say some outrageous things, but he wasn't mean-spirited. Still, I felt compelled to defend myself.

"It doesn't matter how long we were together. What matters is how much we loved each other."

"Sorry, sir. I did it again. Excuse me while I pull my foot out of my mouth." He sounded as if he meant it. "Man, I'm stupid sometimes. I hope you know I didn't mean it the way it sounded."

"That's okay," I said. Even so, I wondered if this arrangement was going to work. He wasn't the type of person I was used to hanging out with, but I could put up with his antics as long as it helped me find the killers. Besides, my so-called friends hadn't been around much since Sarah's death. I was surprised to learn how most people don't know what to say when someone dies. Many of them just don't come around; that way they don't have to say anything.

Tex was all smiles by the time the guys got there to carry him downstairs. "Let's meet about six on Monday night," he said from his perch on the way down the stairs. "That's when I get off work. It'll be a lot easier than lifting this hunk of steel up and down here."

As soon as my neighbors deposited him near his car and were far enough away, he dropped the bomb.

"I have a confession." He was as serious as I'd ever seen him

"What?" I never knew what Tex might do or say.

He locked his eyes on mine. "The librarian is already

doing some research for us. I hope you don't mind."

I did mind and could feel my face begin to flush. I'd told him not to involve anyone else in this. "You mean you told your boss, and you told your librarian friend, too?"

Tex laughed. "Well, sir, maybe I didn't goof up as bad as I thought."

"What do you mean?"

"As it turns out, they're one and the same. My boss is the librarian." He drove away still laughing, leaving me wondering what I'd gotten myself into.

CHAPTER FOUR

I used to get up early every Sunday to go to church with Sarah. Even before I knew her, I missed very few Sunday worship services. When I did miss one for some reason, I'd feel out of kilter for the rest of the week.

On this particular Sunday, I didn't just miss church; I missed the entire day. I was up and about, but just barely. I hadn't even gotten dressed, and I didn't know when I'd last eaten a decent meal. I was going to have to take better care of myself if I wanted to go after those killers, but I couldn't seem to get started. With my so-called photographic memory, I could see the section in the grief pamphlet Father Jesse had given me that warned this could happen. Sundays were the hardest. I didn't care. Besides, I got out of the house most days. I had my job.

Right now, I was more concerned about why I was in the kitchen. *Had I come here to eat?* Probably. I poured cereal into a bowl and added milk, but just as I took the first bite, the doorbell rang. I walked to the door, carrying the bowl with me and wondering who it might be. My onetime friend Tony had been over a few days before, but when I told him to go away, he did—so much for friendship. Maybe he was back to try again.

I opened the door.

"Hello, Chris. We've missed you." It was Father Jesse carrying a black case with him. "I've brought communion."

"Come in." That was the last thing I wanted, but I couldn't slam the door in his face.

He walked to the sofa and sat with that ominous black case in his lap. "I have to say, you look pretty bad, Son. Nice beard, though."

"Thanks." I knew he was just being nice. Tex was right; I should shave. *But why?* No one cared. I placed my bowl on the dining room table and sat on the chair across from him, rubbing the blond stubble and then brushing back my hair. I couldn't remember when I'd last combed it. I stared at the case he held, and knowing it contained the communal elements made me more uncomfortable.

"I've been hoping you'd come back to church," he said.

"Oh, well, you know…" *How do you tell your priest you no longer believe in God?*

"You need your church community more than ever before." He studied me before continuing. "I've left you alone because I know how difficult it must be to go back to the church where you were to be married."

He doesn't know how I feel. No one knows. "Yeah, that's it."

"But I hear you aren't letting anyone from the church talk to you or assist in any way. We can help you get through this. Several members have tried to bring you food, and you won't let them. Also, I can assign you a Stephen Minister, a man experienced in listening and helping you with your grief."

I felt the same tightness in my head I had learned recently preceded tears—tears I had to stop before he saw them. I walked to the kitchen, poured a glass of water, and took a big gulp.

"Would you like a drink of water, Father?"

He walked to the counter that separated the kitchen from the living room. "Yes, thanks."

I poured him a glass, and he took a drink before he continued.

"Don't try to do this alone. Use the church as your safe

place even though there are memories of Sarah there. Enjoy the memories, and let the church help with the grief."

I focused on the window above the kitchen sink to keep from looking him in the eyes. The sun was below the horizon, and the sky was a glimmering red-orange, unlike any other color. *Sunset? What had happened to the day?*

"It's not the memories of Sarah that bother me, it's not the church building that's a problem, and it's not the congregation." I swallowed hard and turned my gaze to him. "It's that God let her die." I didn't like saying it, but now he'd understand how I felt.

He led me over to the sofa, and I found I was sitting next to him. He'd want me to take communion from his portentous black case, but there was no way I'd do that. Just seeing him and talking to him was too much for me to handle.

"I'm sorry. I can't take this right now."

He took my hand in his. "Could we pray about it?"

I jerked my hand away and jumped up from the sofa, stronger now. "Pray? Aren't you listening to me? How can I pray?"

He stood also. "Son, we can't understand it all, but we have to have faith."

I turned my back to him. "Yeah, I've heard it all before. Come see me when you can tell me why this happened." I opened the front door and waited for him to leave.

He picked up his case and slowly walked out onto the landing before he turned to face me. "I'll continue to pray for you, Chris. We all will. God loves you even when you can't feel his presence." He stood there for a minute staring at me as if waiting for a response. "Look, Chris, I would understand if you decide to go to another church, one without the memories of Sarah, but please don't give up on our Lord."

I slammed the door shut without saying anything. I felt bad about that and started to open the door to apologize, but then my cell phone rang.

Father Jesse wasn't so bad. At least he had the decency not to open the communion case. I stared at the phone. I didn't want to talk to anyone, but thought it might be Tex. When I saw the caller ID, my heart skipped a beat. It was Sarah's phone number, not her parents' home phone where she'd lived, but her private cell phone number—a number I'd seen displayed hundreds of times. When I brought home my new iPhone, I'd synced it from the backup on the desktop, not thinking her name and number were still there. *What is happening?*

The sound of the ring grew louder in my mind, and for a split second, I thought it had all been a bad dream, and Sarah was calling to say she was fine. For that moment, my life was whole again. God had somehow fixed everything. As I pressed the talk button, everything I'd said to Father Jesse haunted me.

"Chris?" The caller had an English accent, but it wasn't Sarah. It was her mother.

"Mrs. Eason? Why are you calling on this phone?" I know my voice cracked, but I couldn't help it.

"What do you mean, dear?" she asked, swallowing the last couple of words as usual.

My heartbeat was still not right. "This is Sarah's phone."

"Oh, I'm sorry. I've upset you. We'll fix that, dear. I'll get rid of this number right off."

I wish someone could fix what happened. "I'm sorry, too. I didn't mean to snap at you." I took a deep breath and sat on the sofa, not wanting to talk to her and not wanting to hang up.

"Paul and I would like to talk to you, dear. Can you

meet us tomorrow at the Monument Café for lunch?"

I didn't want to see them, or anyone. *But how could I say no to Sarah's parents?*

***

The next day, I met Sarah's parents for lunch because it was what she would have wanted me to do. Besides, they were grieving, too. Perhaps I could help them. I just wish they hadn't picked Sarah's favorite restaurant, but I met them at the Monument as I said I would.

When I got there, I saw Paul and Ann in a booth near the door.

Paul waved. "Over here, Chris."

I pecked Ann on both cheeks because that was what she expected each time we met. The softness of her skin reminded me of Sarah. Paul took my hand and shook it vigorously as if we hadn't seen each other for years. His face was dark brown from working the fields. The top of his forehead was as white as mine, testimony to the protection provided by the hat he wore while outdoors. As we shook hands, I felt the thick, leathery skin of a man who labored in the fields. They seemed so happy as they greeted me that I felt uncomfortable. *We should cry together, not laugh.*

I saw Sarah standing at the blackboard. She couldn't read the daily specials board from where we usually sat when we dined there, so she moved in close to study the choices. That's how she got to know everyone who worked there. I saw her standing there so clearly I thought for a minute she was still alive.

"Don't you think, dear?" Ann looked at me.

"Pardon? I'm sorry, I didn't hear you."

"Chris, I'm sitting next to you." She took a deep breath. "What do you mean you didn't hear me? Are you okay, dear?"

"I'm fine. I was thinking about the last time I was here with Sarah."

Paul leaned back in his chair and smiled. "There you go, then. That explains it."

Ann raised her eyebrows. "That doesn't explain anything. You can't continue living in the past, Chris. You need to get on with your life." She took a deep breath. She seemed out of place in her fancy pink dress sitting next to Paul in his jeans and cowboy shirt. Sarah had told me how quickly her father had adjusted to Texas farming. He and Ann had quickly decided to participate in the farm exchange program when they learned they could be close to where Sarah worked.

"My mother called you, right?" I didn't need to ask.

Ann straightened her fork, took a sip of water, and put her napkin on her lap. She didn't respond, other than for a miniscule nod toward Paul.

"Sorry, dear?" Paul leaned in toward his wife for a second before facing me. "Ah, Chris's mother. Yes. She's worried about you, Son. If you were me son, I'd be as well."

Before I could respond, the server showed up to take our orders. After that, I managed to keep the conversation on less controversial subjects by asking them questions about their lives. When the food arrived, Ann insisted on saying grace, then asked Paul to do it. I didn't participate, but I was careful not to let them know. I may have bowed my head slightly. There was no reason to give them more to fuss at me about.

After the prayer, Paul held his knife and fork in midair, looking puzzled. "What was I going to say?" He often started his conversations that way, and of course, no one knew.

"Ah, yes," he said. "We're all concerned about you,

Chris."

Of course, that's why they'd invited me there. Mother had been calling nearly every day, and then there was Father Jesse. Now the Eason's. No one understood how I felt, but I would have thought Ann and Paul would know best. After all, it was their daughter who had been killed.

I lost my appetite thinking about it. Actually, I hadn't been hungry since Sarah's death. At home and at school, I had started using a timer to remind myself to eat.

Sarah's presence was strong in the restaurant. One would think having the person you loved near you in any way would be good, but feeling her presence and not being able to reach out and touch her hurt so much I wanted to run away.

Ann patted my shoulder. "Aren't you going to eat your salad?"

I shook my head, unable to speak for a few seconds. Finally, I waved to the server. "May I have a to-go box, please?"

"Now, Chris," Ann started with a deep breath this time, "let me tell you what we've decided."

That had an ominous sound, and I didn't want to hear the rest of what she had to say. But I didn't have a choice. These were Sarah's parents after all. I respected them.

Paul leaned away from the table and smiled as if in anticipation.

Ann continued. "I've talked to some of Sarah's friends at church and the hospital, and we've planned a party. It'll be a celebration of Sarah's life, and since you were such an important part of that life, you will be celebrated as well." That was a long speech for Ann. Two huge breaths were needed to finish it.

The word *celebrate* rubbed me the wrong way. "Celebrate? No way. I'm barely managing to get through this meal. Don't ask me to go to a party."

"What's wrong with the meal?" Paul looked at my untouched plate and back to his empty one as if he'd just noticed I wasn't eating.

My heart was racing. "Not the meal. The place. I was here with Sarah three weeks ago." I pointed to the booth on our right. "We sat right there in that booth. I can see her now." I could feel my nose getting tight. The tears would be there soon enough.

Ann rubbed my shoulder. "Of course you can dear, but she's with the Lord. She'd want you to be happy."

I jerked away from her. "Happy? Why can't you understand? That's impossible! I'll never be happy." It came out more like calling her a liar than I meant it to.

"Mind your manners, sir." Paul placed his fork on the table and moved back from the table. He spoke softly, but he was visibly agitated.

Ann took Paul's hand. "It's okay. Chris needs time. He's right. It's only been three weeks. Let's talk about this later."

Three weeks or three decades—it didn't matter. I would never celebrate her death. I'd planned to be with her forever. Without Sarah, I had no life. Revenge was all I had.

My phone rang, and when I checked the caller ID, I knew an uninvited guest had entered my apartment. "I'm sorry. I have to go." I stood, with my billfold out.

"Never mind," Paul said. "We've got it, Son."

I ran out of the restaurant without my to-go box.

I called Tex while driving home. "Someone took the bait," I said, trying not to sound too excited.

"Huh?" He sounded as if he had just woken up.

"The rattrap I set at my place went off." Technology was wonderful. For a few bucks, I'd installed surveillance equipment that not only made a video recording of the intruder, but it also called my cell phone to let me know. It could have been the manager, but he usually let me know before he entered the apartment for maintenance reasons.

"Hot dog!" Tex's voice was back to normal. "Does that mean you'll have a video of the perpetrator?"

"If everything worked properly." I knew it'd work. I'd tested it several times.

"Where are you?" Tex asked.

"I'm on my way home to find out who's there."

"But, sir, you can't walk in on a burglar. That's dangerous. Besides, you don't need to. You'll have the video."

"What then? I can't stand around waiting while some lowlife ransacks my apartment." Tex was too careful sometimes. I wanted to catch this guy and maybe bang him up a little.

"Wait in your parking lot. If you see a stranger come out, fine. You'll have an eyewitness account of what he looks like. But stay in your car and wait. I'll send help."

He hung up before I could respond.

Five minutes later, I sat in my car near the stairway to my apartment. I scanned the area, but didn't see anyone suspicious. A dark-haired woman I didn't know came down the stairs, but she could have been visiting any of my neighbors. I watched her anyway. She didn't get in a car, but walked through the parking lot and disappeared around a building. She was so attractive a pang of guilt hit me for noticing so soon after Sarah's death. Then I kicked myself again when I realized the burglar could have left my apartment while I watched the dark-haired woman. I needed to focus.

I looked toward the stairs, hoping I hadn't missed seeing him, and was startled by a knock on the driver's-side window. It was Jimbo. Tex must have sent him to help. I climbed out of the car.

"Hi, Jimbo. Thanks for coming so quickly."

"Yeah. What's up?" Jimbo wore blue jeans with a white T-shirt that was too small to cover his midsection, which I could see through the opened black jacket. He had tattoos on both hands that probably went up his arms, and he was built like a football lineman who hadn't worked out in years.

"I'm not sure," I said. "I had a trap set in case someone broke in again, and the alarm was triggered about fifteen minutes ago. I've been watching for someone to come out, but there was only one person who came down the stairs so far, and I don't think she was the type to break in."

Jimbo looked up the stairway. "Technically, no one broke in last time. I'm not sure how they got in, but nothing was broken. And, keep in mind, you can't identify creeps by how they look." He went up the stairs five or six steps at a time.

I followed, but lagged behind because of my wounded leg. At least I no longer had the crutches to slow me even more. Jimbo was at the door with his right hand on the knob when I got there. The index finger of his left hand was on his lips telling me to be quiet. He twisted the handle ever so slightly before he backed away and silently signaled for me to unlock the door. With all his slinking about, I must have been nervous because I dropped my key ring with a clatter loud enough to wake the neighbors.

"So much for sneaking up on them," Jimbo said in his normal voice. He picked up the keys, opened the door, and went in. I didn't know when he drew the pistol, but he had it at the ready when I entered the room. He motioned for me to wait at the entryway.

I did, silently watching while he checked each room.

"No one here," he said as he put his pistol into a holster under his jacket. "And, once again, no signs of a break-in. These people are good." In the next second, he was gone just as quickly as he had appeared, with not so much as even a good-bye or so long.

My cell phone rang, causing a tinge of fear. "Hello?"

"It's me," Tex said. "Jimbo called and said the place is clear."

"Yeah. He just left. Thanks. I'll check the video and tell you about it tonight."

As soon as I hung up the phone, there was a knock at the door. I assumed it was Jimbo coming back for some reason, but when I opened the door, I saw a gray-haired man in a peach-colored polo shirt and beige slacks.

"Chris, I'm a friend of Andrew's. May I come in?"

"You're Andrew's friend? How am I supposed to know that?" After being broken into twice, I was beginning to suspect everyone.

The gray-haired man reached around to the back of his pants, and for a second, I thought he was going for a gun. My body froze, and I knew that wasn't good. I needed to run, but I couldn't even walk fast because of the gunshot wound in my leg.

He must have sensed my fear. He held an opened left hand out to me. "Please, don't worry. All I want to do is show you my ID."

My body stayed on full alert even though my mind said everything was okay. Fear was new to me, and I didn't like it.

He pulled out a brown leather billfold with a badge and a photo and pushed it toward me. I scanned it quickly and saw MI5 and some other stuff. The ID said his name was Tim Jenkins.

"So, you're a friend of Andrew's?"

His put his billfold away. "Not only that. I was a friend of Sarah's as well. We grew up together in Somerset, England, and to be frank, I thought the two of us would end up together someday. She had different ideas, but we remained friends."

An old boyfriend of Sarah's—that's just what I needed. He seemed a bit old for her, but who knows. "Why are you here?"

He looked around the room. "May I sit for a minute?"

I motioned toward the sofa. He brushed off a spot on my clean sofa before sitting on it. I took the easy chair across from him.

"Let me get right to it," he said. "I have reason to believe you'll be in danger if you continue to search for Sarah's killers, and more importantly, I knew Sarah well enough to be absolutely convinced revenge is not what she'd want." He folded his hands and waited for me to respond.

I knew Sarah wouldn't approve of vengeance. I was doing this for me. I'm the one who let her die.

"How could I be in danger? No one knows my plans." Before I finished saying it, I remembered the break-ins. "Are you suggesting the burglaries I've had are related to Sarah's killing in some way?"

Tim cleared his throat. "Burglaries? To be honest, I'm the one who was here two weeks ago. Sorry, chap. I didn't mean to knock you down with such force. I remembered too late you were on crutches."

"That was you? But why?" I felt angry, but mostly curious. *Why would he break in and then tell me he did it?*

"All I had to work on was Andrew's word. I had to see for myself who you were."

"You could have asked." I wondered if I could trust this guy, even with his ID. "Was it you who broke in earlier today?"

He might have been a good actor, but the surprise look

he offered appeared genuine. "No, that wasn't me."

"Why am I in danger? Who killed Sarah?"

He bowed his head for a second or two before responding. "I'm here out of respect for Sarah. She planned to marry you, so I care about you. But I'm here unofficially. What I say to you cannot be repeated, not even to one of your law enforcement agencies. Understood?"

"Okay." I wondered how much he knew about Liz and Tex.

"What you're dealing with is a terrorist cell bent on another nine/eleven." He rubbed his hands together slower and stared at me.

"Is Homeland Security aware of this?"

"They've been told, but they don't believe us. They think the gang members are Mexican drug smugglers who have turned to robbery because of increased border security." Tim shook his head.

Could I believe anything this guy said? "If you're a classmate of Sarah's, how come you look so much older?"

He wiped a hand across his head. "You mean the gray hair?" He laughed. "It's part of my disguise. I hope you can tell up close I'm about your age. I'm thirty-six."

Something he'd said bothered me, but I couldn't remember what. He could have a fake ID for all I knew. "Well, thanks for letting me know." I was itching to check that video as soon as he left and had convinced myself I'd be looking at his gray hair when I did. I thought briefly about telling him I had a video just to see his reaction, but decided against it. I still wasn't positive who he was.

He walked to the door. "I'm serious. Forget this idea of vengeance. Let us take care of it. That's what Sarah would want." He went out the door, then turned back to face me. "You're not going to give up, are you?" Then he was gone.

Tim wasn't the star of my homemade movie after all.

That pleased me in a way. I guess I wanted to believe him and like him because he seemed sincere when he talked about Sarah. Besides, I wasn't sure, but he may have given us our first clue.

As I reviewed the video, I couldn't help but wonder why someone so beautiful who looked as if she were a business executive had the guts to break into someone's home. It was the dark-haired beauty I had spotted coming down the stairs while I sat in my car waiting for Jimbo. As I had watched her walk across the parking lot, I never would have taken her to be a burglar. Or was she something worse—a killer, perhaps? I hoped not.

Three separate spy cams with sound and motion detectors had been set off while she was there. The first was hidden in a wall hanging. The lens was the size of a shirt button, and I'd worked it into the design so that it was almost invisible. That one showed her calmly walking through the living area toward the bedroom. What was strange was that she didn't look frightened or concerned about being there. The second camera recorded her time in the bedroom, where she glanced around before she looked in the closet and the chest of drawers. She didn't take anything, just looked. The third camera was in the office, hidden in the computer speaker. She sat at the computer and went to work. I had installed a key-capture program so I could look at it later to see what she had done, but I looked at the computer enough to know she left it exactly as I had. She obviously knew computers. After reviewing the videos, I spliced them together and copied the movie to a DVD.

CHAPTER FIVE

The Austin History Center is in downtown Austin on the corner of Guadalupe and Ninth Streets, facing Ninth. The main library, named after John Henry Faulk, is behind the History Center, facing Guadalupe. I parked on Ninth in front of the History Center and took in the view of the massive cream-colored limestone building, which matched the Travis County Courthouse that faced it. Between the buildings was Wooldrige Park, a full city block in size, with a sunken gazebo.

I climbed out of my car and looked up at the building—and I do mean up. There were three massive flights of steps leading from the street to the three arched doors. I shuddered thinking about the climb since I hadn't gained complete use of my right leg since the shooting.

Tex worked in this building, so I knew there had to be a wheelchair entrance somewhere. I looked around, but didn't see any other way to get to the entrance looming high above me. I didn't want to make the climb with my wounded leg, but I trudged on anyway, making liberal use of the handrails along the way, stopping when needed, and vowing to ask Tex for a better way to get in next time. Tex had been after me to exercise more. Perhaps that's why he didn't tell me about the many steps.

I stopped to rest and read a plaque near the top of the second group of steps. It said the building had been the Austin Public Library from 1933 to 1979: "The Italian Renaissance Style features work of some of Austin's finest craftsmen, including ironworker Fortunant Wiegle, wood-carver Peter Mansbendel and fresco artist Harold 'Bubi' Jessen."

I kept climbing and didn't stop again until I reached the front doors.

Inside the building, there was a large area, which didn't seem to serve much purpose other than to lead to the other parts of the building. Before I had time to look around more, Tex rolled toward me with his usual beaming face.

"Hi, Doc. You okay? Looks like your limp's worse." He rolled on past me without waiting for a response. "I reserved the O'Henry Room for us. Follow me."

My leg did feel worse, but only because of climbing all those stairs. Next time, I'd know better.

At the end of the hall, he turned into the last door on the right and closed the door after I entered. It was a large conference room with a table near the door and walls covered with books. There were comfortable chairs around the room. We were the only ones there.

"Have a seat," Tex said. "I can't wait to see the video."

I reached into my coat pocket and pulled out the DVD. "I had two visitors today. One you can see on the video, and the other one I'll tell you about."

The door opened, and a flamboyant women in her sixties sauntered in. "Howdy!" she said with a Southern accent, which wasn't Texan, and the biggest smile I'd ever seen.

Not knowing who she was, I slipped the DVD into my coat pocket. Her plus-size dress wasn't quite large enough, and her straight, gray hair flopped about in all directions as she walked. But her smile was hypnotizing. The longer I looked at her, the more familiar she looked. I turned to Tex to see his reaction to this strange-looking, but familiar woman.

"Evening, ma'am," he said. "Liz, this is Doc McCowan—the guy I was telling you about."

She looked at me over the top of granny glasses that badly needed a cleaning. "Sure. I recognize him from the news."

She pulled me into a bear hug so quick it scared me. You'd think I was her long-lost son. I just stood there, hoping she hadn't broken the DVD in my side pocket, while I waited for her to free me.

Tex smiled in a way that made me think he was quietly laughing at me. "Chris, this is the librarian I've been telling you about...you know, the one who's gonna help us find those killers."

I managed to back away from her, feeling angry. "Tex, can I talk to you alone?" I was going to do the search solo if he continued to pull stunts like this. The trap I set at the apartment had caught someone, probably not one of the killers, but it proved I could work alone. I didn't need Tex and his gray-haired bureaucrat grandmother. I knew who she was.

"Sure. Excuse us a minute, Liz." Tex started rolling toward the door. He made it sound serious, but he was still grinning as I fumed.

"Wait," she said, "it'll be easier for me to leave while the two of you talk. Five minutes? Ten?"

Tex looked at me for a response, but I just stood there with my arms crossed and didn't say a word. For me, it might as well be ten hours. All I wanted to do was say good-bye and get out of there.

"Better make it ten minutes," Tex said, sounding more serious. Perhaps he finally recognized how angry I was.

When she was gone and the door shut, I let him have it. "What are you thinking bringing her here like this? Didn't we agree not to involve more people in our plans?"

Tex rolled back a foot or so. "Whoa. Don't get yourself in a tizzy. We need her. She's great at research, plus she's got contacts, people who can help us with information and money." He moved closer to the table and picked up a stack of file folders. "See these? These are police reports she got for us. We could never get these on our own. Just talk to her and then make up your mind."

I looked through the files he handed me and had to admit I was impressed. Every time I'd talked to the police, they ignored me. Of course, being a fiancé wasn't like being a husband or a relative. Even so, getting more people involved was risky.

"I don't need to talk her. I recognize her. She's not a librarian; she's the director of the whole library system here in Austin. I've seen her on TV."

"Well, sure, but that just makes it better." Tex looked puzzled.

"I can't do this if she's in on it." I turned to leave. That's when the pain hit me. It might have been from the climb up the long flight of stairs to the History Center or the way I twisted the muscle around the wound in my haste to leave the room. If I'd been alone, I would've let myself fall to the floor to take weight off my leg in hopes of alleviating the pain. Instead, I winced as secretly as possible and continued toward the door. A man never wants to let another man know he's in pain.

But Tex had noticed. "Are you all right, sir?" Tex rolled up next to me.

Instead of walking out, I fell into the chair nearest the door and took a deep breath. "Fine. It's just my leg. I don't know whether I turned it the wrong way or if it's worn out from all those steps out front."

He laughed. "Do what I do. There's a wheelchair lift just out this side door." He pointed toward the side door opposite from where I had entered. "There's only a few steps that way. Sorry, I forgot to tell you."

"Thanks. I'll try it on the way out. Just let me rest a minute."

"You know, this could be a sign for you to stay." Tex smiled, but I knew he believed in signs—signs from God.

"Don't be ridiculous. I was shot, remember? It's a sign I haven't healed yet. The doctor said I may always limp." I didn't tell Tex the doctor also said the pain should be gone by now.

His eyes narrowed as he focused on me. "I understand you not wanting to get more people involved, but Liz is different. Talk to her, and then if you don't agree she should stay, I'll never bring it up again."

"What's the use? I already know she'd never condone what we have planned."

"Oh, I see." Tex laughed aloud. "You thought I meant we should tell her what we plan to do after we find the killers. No way. She'd have us both in cuffs. All I want to do is get her to help us find them. The rest is just between us."

"Why didn't you say so?" I wondered if I could trust him.

Tex rolled toward the door. "I didn't think I had to. It's obvious we can't tell her everything. She knows we're searching for the killers and assumes we will turn them over to law enforcement when we find them. She'd never be part of a revenge killing."

"Are you sure she won't find out?" I was relieved, but still doubtful the arrangement would work. This wasn't the first misunderstanding Tex and I'd had since joining forces.

Tex grinned. He looked toward the door. "Not from me she won't. You don't think I would tell my boss I was about to commit a crime, do you?"

Crime. I hadn't thought of what we were planning as being against the law. Maybe it was wrong according to societal rules, but it certainly didn't seem like a crime to me.

"And you believe she can help us? I mean, besides contacts. We shouldn't need any money. After all, she's management, probably has an office in the ivory tower next door. She's probably too busy to help us."

Tex laughed again. "Actually, her office is in this building. This used to be the main library. She likes it better here—says it's more like a real library. Even so, she hasn't been the boss lady long. I met her on a bookmobile." Tex looked away and took a big breath. "It hurts to remember that time in my life, but you need to know you can trust her. She's responsible for getting me off the streets. She took me in, made me eat, and gave me a place to sleep." He slapped the armrest on his wheelchair. "That was before I decided to ride in this thing. She helped me get sober."

"She did that for you?"

"Yep. That's just a part of the story. I'll tell you more about her later if you decide to keep her on the team."

I held up the DVD. "What about this? Do we show her the surveillance video?"

"Sure. That's part of the investigation. She needs to know everything—except what we plan to do after the killers are found. Can I call her back now?" Tex wheeled to the door, but waited for my answer.

I thought for a long time and couldn't think of a way it would work with Liz in on it, but I decided to take Tex's word for it. I nodded. "Sure, let's do it."

Tex pushed the door open and waved at Liz, who stood across the hall talking to someone. She came in grinning, and I thought for a second or two she might hug me again, so I quickly sat down at the conference table.

She put an arm around me. "Y'all okay now?"

"Yes, ma'am. Have a seat. Chris has something to show

us." Tex closed the door behind her and opened the laptop he'd borrowed from me the last time we met. He opened the CD/DVD drive and held out his hand.

"This is the woman who broke into my apartment today," I said as I tossed an eight-by-ten color print of the dark-haired woman on the table for all to see. It was a still I had grabbed from the video, which I handed to Tex.

He put the DVD into the drive on the laptop, and after a whirling sound, the burglary came on the screen. As I watched it again, I still couldn't believe how the dark-haired woman walked around so casually in my apartment. She didn't look cautious or scared. If anything, someone watching this would think she lived there. The video I had edited for Liz and Tex ended with the burglar sitting at my computer.

"Too bad we can't see what she typed on the computer. That might tell us what she was looking for and whether or not she added anything to your computer," Tex said.

I smiled. "We know what she typed. In addition to the video, I also installed a key-capture program like the one some parents use to monitor their kid's computer use. It stores every keystroke.

"Oh yeah," Tex said, "you told us about that in class."

Liz's eyes got big. "I didn't know you could do that. Hope no one ever checks what I do on the computer. They'd see all my goof-ups. What did you find out from that key thing?"

"I found out she knows her stuff. She checked to see what I'd been doing. She opened Windows Explorer, sorted the files by date modified, probably looking for recent activity, and then she put them back the way she found them. She also looked at the browser history and checked the browser cache. She didn't learn anything, but she knew where to look if there had been anything to find. With what she apparently knows about computers, I'm surprised she didn't locate the surveillance software I had installed. But it is pretty well hidden from all, except the few highly trained experts."

"I have no idea what you just said, Son, but it sounds so interesting." Liz looked like she meant exactly what she said.

Tex laughed. "Liz has a master's in library science she didn't get until after her sixty-fifth birthday. How she got by without learning computers is beyond me—must have been her charm that got her through," he quipped, winking.

Liz laughed so hard her whole body shook. "Now, don't go telling everyone how old I am. But what you said about computers and me is nearer the truth than you might think. I memorized how to do what I wanted to do with a computer. The problem is the 'how to' keeps changing."

Tex reached over and turned the screen so he could see it more directly, then clicked on the play button. "You know what I see here? Beyond the fact that she's a real babe, she knows what she's doing. She's highly trained. See how quickly she checks everything without pausing and looking around."

I had thought the same thing when I first watched the video and was glad to hear Tex agreed.

Tex continued to watch. "You know what else? This isn't the same person who broke in before. She's not back to see what's new. She's too thorough for that."

I hadn't told Tex about Tim yet. "So?" I asked. "What good is the video? We still don't know who she is or whether or not she broke in because of Sarah. I should've followed her while I had the chance. I might have been able to get her license plate number."

"You saw her?" Liz asked.

Tex looked up with raised eyebrows. "What do you

mean?"

"Yes, I was sitting in my car in my apartment parking lot waiting for your friend to come when I saw her leave. Of course, I didn't know she was the one who had set off the alarm that called my cell phone. She doesn't exactly look like the common burglar."

Liz's eyes popped out. "The alarm called your cell phone? You can do that?"

Tex smiled. "This guy can do anything with computers. He's my professor, remember?"

I shook my head. "Still, what good is it?" It technically worked, but it didn't tell us anything that'll help find the killers.

"You said you had two visitors today," Tex said. "Is the other one on this video?"

"No, the second one knocked on the door, and I let him in." I looked at Tex before continuing. "Turns out, he's the one who broke in a couple of weeks ago. The one you found out had an English accent."

"No kidding!" Tex's eyes opened wide.

"So, who's this British fellow?" Liz asked.

"Tim Jenkins. He showed me his badge and ID. I saw his name and some official stuff, including MI5. Bottom line is he's an old friend of Sarah's and the London friend Andrew mentioned."

"MI5? That's British intelligence. What'd he say?" Tex rolled in closer, and Liz moved her chair toward me as well.

"He told me to quit looking for Sarah's killers. He said they're terrorists and dangerous."

"I knew it!" Tex laughed. "We got ourselves another nine/eleven."

Liz looked stern before turning toward me. "Do you believe what Tim said?"

I tried to be as honest as possible. "I'm not sure. I do

know that, no matter what, I'm going to continue with the search. He did say he grew up with Sarah and knew she'd want me to be safe and let law enforcement handle the investigation."

Liz put her hand on my shoulder and rubbed gently. "I understand, Son. I'm so sorry about your fiancée. I've been praying for you since I first heard about it, even before Percy said he knew you." Then she pursed her lips as tears formed in her eyes.

It took a few seconds for me to remember Tex's first name was Percy since everyone called him Tex at school.

Tex rolled his chair to the table, ejected the DVD, and handed it to me. I placed it in my coat pocket. When I looked back, he had his investigation facts database on the screen.

"Look at this, Liz," he said. "This is everything we know about the case. We'll add to it every time we learn something new and then watch for patterns. Let's start by seeing what we can find in the police files you brought."

She scooted in closer to the table, wiping her tears away as she moved. "I'm impressed, Percy. Looks like you got a good start there."

Tex popped his chest out a bit with that simple praise from Liz.

"There's more," Tex said to Liz. "Doc here is going to do his magic on the computer by searching for similar incidents around the country."

"Yes," I said, "I'm watching for high-tech crimes in smaller cities." I hadn't told Tex, but I'd already initiated several Google Alerts, so the search engine was looking as we talked.

"So, you think the fact that this happened in Round Rock is important?" Liz asked.

I rubbed my leg near the wound. The skin had healed,

but the throbbing came back at the strangest times. "It might not be important since Round Rock is part of a larger metropolitan area, but still, this type of military-like robbery could happen anywhere."

Tex cleared his throat. "I agree. The way they used that helicopter was unexpected. I don't think that's been done before."

"You're right," I said. "I'm watching for that to happen again. It may not. This gang's technique may be to do something different every time so that the cops don't detect a pattern."

Liz leaned back in her chair. "Hmm. What do you plan to do if you find a suspicious incident?"

"We'll go there," Tex said.

"Yes. We'll investigate every place that appears promising and look for clues or patterns." I hadn't considered how this investigation would affect my teaching. I might have to take a leave of absence, but I hoped I wouldn't since money was still a problem. Ten years of student loans were now due.

The police investigation files Liz had borrowed included a report from Camp Mabry, where the helicopter was stolen. The person who took the helicopter that day had all the correct paperwork and didn't look out of the ordinary. The police had found an abandoned rental car nearby and were still investigating it. The helicopter had been found in the Big Bend National Park in west Texas along the Mexican border, but the reports didn't mention what, if anything, had been found in the helicopter to help identify the ones who had used it in the robbery.

Liz stood around 9:00 p.m. "Well, I better go home. Some of us have to get up early in the morning." She stopped when she got to the door. "Chris, there's a little leftover birthday cake in the kitchen if you'd like some. I made it for Percy, and everyone said it's quite tasty."

"Oh," I said, "is today your birthday, Tex?"

"Not mine. This is November tenth. Today's the Marine Corps' birthday. We usually have a big party, but I've been too busy lately to go, so Liz made me a cake. Pretty nice, huh? And, yes, it's delicious. Everything she fixes is to die for."

Liz smiled and left.

"Well," Tex said, "is it a go?"

"What?"

"Liz—can she keep working with us?"

I liked her. She'd asked good questions. I felt good around her. "Sure. As long as you don't tell her what we discussed."

Tex smiled. "Good. Course I won't tell her what we plan to do. She'd fire me on the spot if she knew. Now, let's talk money. She'll get her friends to cover our expenses, no questions asked."

"What do we need?" I still hadn't thought of a need for funds.

Tex rubbed his hands together. "For starters, how about a laptop so I can give you this one back? We'll both need one anyway, especially on trips."

"Okay. What else?"

"We can't fly to those places where we want to check out leads. We'll need a good van for the wheelchair."

"Why can't we fly?"

"Can't carry guns on a plane," Tex said so unemotionally it scared me.

I hadn't considered having a gun. "Can't we take guns in checked luggage?"

"It's legal, but we don't want to draw attention to what we are doing anyway. A van would be more anonymous."

He was talking big bucks. "We can't ask Liz for a van.

Why don't we fly and ship the guns separately?"

"Won't work. Besides, I'll need special transportation when we get there." He pounded on the right side of his wheelchair as if I needed a reminder of why.

"Then I'll go alone. We can't ask Liz for all that."

Tex laughed. "Yeah, sure. Let's see how well you do at target practice first. I'll schedule some time at the indoor pistol range in Pflugerville. Don't worry about the cost. Liz will get all the financing we need."

I picked up my coat to leave.

"Wait," Tex said and pulled out a camera from the khaki backpack that hung behind his wheelchair, "I need a photo of you before you go. Don't ask why."

What was I getting myself into? Then I remembered Sarah and the day she died in my arms. More than anything, I wanted to find out who killed her. But, first, I had to get my body in shape and learn how to shoot a gun.

***

Two days later, I was at the fitness center looking around for Tex and wishing I had never told him about my plan to find the killers. I didn't need exercise; I needed a gun and a map.

Years of poring over textbooks and sitting in front of computers had turned my less-than-athletic body into a flabby, older guy, not necessarily fat, just sans muscle. It would take more than a few visits to a gym to change that, but there I was at the insistence of Tex. He'd told me to think of it as one more step toward revenge. I could do that if I had to, but I find physical exercise boring.

Besides not being interested in building muscle, I started thinking about how exercise was going to take more time than I had to spare. I needed to be writing. Since Sarah's death, I hadn't added one word to the textbook I was working on. Not only that, but it was also past due, and the editor was bugging me about it. She knew about Sarah's death and said she understood my situation; however, she said she couldn't give me more time because they had a book review team lined up and ready to go. She was nice about it, but in the end, she offered to find someone else to finish the book. With a little fast-talk and a reminder of the rave reviews received from my peers for the chapters I had completed, I managed to talk her into a short extension.

I failed to tell her about the nagging fear I had that I'd never write again. Writing was a big area of my life still on hold, probably because it is lonely work, and being alone reminded me of Sarah. I wanted to tell the editor to get somebody else to finish the book, but I needed the money. I hadn't been out on my own too long, and there were student loans to pay as well as other financial obligations I had made in preparation for the wedding.

Tex bumped into me with his wheelchair, knocking me out of my reverie.

"Hey, you awake, sir?" he asked.

I jumped back, feigning a pain from the ramming he'd given me. "Watch where you're going with that thing—and quit calling me sir."

Maybe I was daydreaming. Still, it was easy for him to sneak up on people in that wheelchair of his.

"Sorry, Doc." He grinned and looked out from under the brim of his cowboy hat. "At least I didn't roll over your foot like I did that time at school."

My foot ached just thinking about it, but I shook it off. *Why was he always so happy?* Sometimes I wanted to remind him his life wasn't all that great. *Didn't he know he couldn't walk?*

"Don't call me Doc, either." I don't know why I bothered. He'd never change.

"Sorry," he said with lips pursed and sad eyes, looking like a contrite child. He could be such a ham. Tex rolled toward the locker room before he stopped and spun around. He reached into the backpack behind his wheelchair and pulled out an envelope, which he thrust toward me. "Let me give you this now so I won't have to remember it later."

I opened the envelope. "What's this?" I saw a Texas driver's license and two credit cards. My picture was on the driver's license. "Who's Ken Campbell?" I asked, reading the name on the cards.

Tex laughed. "Don't you recognize the photo? That's you."

The cards looked so authentic it was frightening. Imagine, one of my students had access to a counterfeiting mill that could do such quality work.

"I don't need a fake ID." I pushed the envelope back to him, but he didn't take it.

"You never know—hold on to them just in case. I've got five different ones. The credit cards are good, by the way. Of course, they can be tracked to the real you if someone is smart enough. And we'll have to pay the bills."

I tried again to give the cards back to him. "Here, I don't want them."

Tex crossed his arms. "Don't be silly. Keep them."

"But a fake driver's license? What if the police find these on me?"

Tex narrowed his eyes and spoke softer. "Are you kidding? What if they catch you shooting one of those killers? Do you think they'll care what ID you're using?"

That caught me off guard, and I couldn't think of a reply.

Tex had a look in his eyes I'd never seen before.

"Look," he said, "if we're going to do this, we have to do it right. Like it or not, I'm the expert in the shadier side of life we're getting into." He made the word *shadier* sound menacing.

I had no immediate response, but clearly, he was waiting for me to say something.

He looked me in the eyes and continued. "You're the student now, and I'm the teacher. Do you want to follow the syllabus or drop the course?"

I understood. I thought of Sarah and knew I needed Tex and his so-called shady experience. I wanted revenge for Sarah's death, and I wanted it at any cost.

"You're right, teach. I'm no quitter." I slipped the fake credentials into my pocket.

He smiled. "Great. Now, let's get you into shape. I want to see you here every day until some muscle appears. We'll work on the upper body one day and the lower body the next. Understood?"

"Yes, sir."

We went into the locker room and stored our coats. I changed into shorts and a T-shirt. I started to walk away from the locker when Tex pointed at my feet.

"You can't workout wearing those sandals."

The sandals he referred to were my Birkenstocks. I had my sneakers with me; I just didn't think I'd have to put them on unless we were going to run. I quickly changed and went to work out.

Tex gave me a tour of the center, introducing me to the machines he thought I should use. There was a different piece of equipment for each muscle—machines I'm sure hadn't been invented the last time I was in a gym. Tex helped me find the proper starting weight and told me to do three sets of twelve reps on each machine. It got harder for each set, so we had to lower the weights from time to time. When we finished, he handed me a workout log so I could repeat the workout even when he wasn't with me—like that was going to happen.

"Okay," Tex said, "tomorrow we'll work on your legs, but I want to find something special for that limp of yours. How's the PT going? I don't want to give you exercises that might conflict with what the therapist says."

"I'm all finished with physical therapy." I wiped off the machine with the moistened paper towels the gym provided.

"Finished? But you're still limping." Tex looked up from the clipboard that held the exercise record he'd created for me.

"Forget it. The limp is part of me now. It's a reminder of how I failed Sarah." The therapist had told me he could get rid of the limp. Later, he claimed I wasn't cooperating, so I fired him. No need to tell Tex all that.

Tex shook his head. "How many times do I have to tell you you're not to blame for her death?"

I was to blame. No question about it. But there was no sense trying to make Tex—or anyone else, for that matter—understand.

I walked toward the locker room to change and could see Tex rolling behind me in the wall of mirrors where the free weights were. Then I saw someone else's reflection in the mirror. The dark-haired woman who had broken into my apartment was standing at the check-in counter talking to the man behind the desk.

"Tex! Look, that's her. Let's grab her," I said, pointing to the woman's reflection. I turned away from the mirror and started toward the woman.

"Wait!" Tex blocked me with his wheelchair. "That's who?"

"The woman in the video—the one who broke into my

place."

Tex held my arm to keep me from moving. "Are you sure? If it's her, don't let her know you recognize her. Now that we know she's following you, we can find out who she is."

I didn't care. I wanted to go ask her why she was in my apartment. I pulled away from him, but turned my back to her when I remembered I had agreed to do what he said when it came to these matters. *Maybe he's right. If we can turn this around and follow her, we could find out who sent her and why she's interested in me.*

"You got your phone?" Tex asked. "I left mine in my coat pocket in the locker room."

"Mine's in there, too," I said. "Why?"

"I can call a friend who could be here in a hurry and follow her. We can't do it. She's probably already figured out I'm with you. Go get your phone, and I'll wait here to see where she goes. Don't let her know you recognize her."

We turned in unison: Tex so he could watch through the mirror and me to race toward the locker room.

As soon as I handed Tex my phone, he made a call.

"Hey," he said, "we're at the fitness center. The dark-haired one is here. See if you can follow her."

After he hung up, we tried to act nonchalant about what we were doing and slowly made our way to the locker room. After I changed, we walked toward the front door. The dark-haired woman wasn't anywhere to be seen.

"I guess we lost her," I said.

"Don't give up yet," Tex said. "If I were following us, I'd hide somewhere in the parking lot, probably in a dull, commonplace vehicle, and watch for us to come out the front door of the gym."

"Just like we're doing," I said, scanning the lot in front of us.

"Quit looking!" Tex said. "If you ever do see her, act like you don't know her. Now, let's slowly go to the car. Why don't you push me? That'll take us longer. Then you can help me into the car. By then, my buddy should be here to follow her."

I did what Tex said, and we were rewarded when he spotted Jimbo pull into the parking lot, ignoring us totally. He didn't even nod as he drove by, but I'm sure he saw us. *Boy, I have a lot to learn about this business.*

It seemed to take forever to get into my car, store Tex's wheelchair, and drive out of the parking lot. It would have been much easier if Tex had taken the van he drove to the gym, but it was all a ploy to give Jimbo time to tail our tail. Tex once again demonstrated his acting skills when he pretended as if I didn't know what I was doing and made me reload the wheelchair. I just hope the dark-haired beauty was watching. It was a great act.

When we finally left the parking lot, I saw a black Chevy pull out and turn the same way we did. I kept watching through the rearview mirror until I saw Tex's friend pull out, too.

"Well, he's following her. What do we do now?" I asked.

"Just keep driving. Don't do anything that'll let her know we know she's following us."

"Okay, I can do that. I'll ignore her. So, where are we going? How long do we drive around? What about your van?"

Tex slapped the air with a hand and laughed. "We'll get that van later. Now it is time for your next workout."

"Workout? Now?" I asked. "I thought you said my muscles needed to rest overnight."

"This isn't the same. This is a special type of workout."

Following Tex's directions, we stopped at a rundown

storefront on Guadalupe Street with "Tiny's Gym" painted on the window. The sign needed a touch-up or replacement, as only half the letters remained. With my need for symmetry and neatness, I had to resist fixing the sign with the markers I carried in my teaching bag. But as soon I we walked in and I smelled the place, the sign was the least of my problems. The odor reminded me of a pile of dirty underwear my high school gym teacher found in his locker one day. Not that I had anything to do with the prank, but I happened to be close enough to get a good whiff of it. Ugh!

Several older guys were rapidly punching bags with boxing gloves on. Sweat poured freely. Off to the right of the entrance was a raised boxing ring. I'd never seen one in real life before and was apprehensive about why Tex had brought us there.

"Tell me we are here to flush out the dark-haired woman who's following us," I said, trying my best to look at him hopefully.

Tex laughed so hard I thought his wheelchair was going to shoot backward. "What's the matter, teach, you're not afraid of getting hit in the face are you? Don't worry, I won't let them mess up that beard of yours."

Tex's laugh was beginning to irritate me. Probably because it was usually me he was laughing about. I looked around the gym thinking of all the reasons I should turn around and leave.

"You're kidding, right? Is this another way of telling me I'm not prepared to go on this mission? Well, I am. Just give me a gun, and I'll shoot them. They're not going to stand still while I put on boxing gloves."

"Look," he said, turning suddenly serious, "you're right. Boxing isn't gonna help catch the bad guys. I looked for a place that taught hand-to-hand combat, street fighting, or something close to what the military teaches, but this was the closest thing to it for now." He stared at me without a humorous wrinkle anywhere on his face. "This is life and death we're getting into. If you can't take a few hits with boxing gloves, we might as well find out now. Here, put these on."

The gloves he handed me were huge. I couldn't believe a jab in the face with pads this thick could hurt anyone. I slipped them on, and Tex tightened the ties. My opponent, a toothless guy twice my age with a skinny chest and flab around his waist, was in the ring jumping up and down jabbing the air.

I climbed into the ring and tried to imitate the older guy's dance and jabs. Then a bell rang, and he started punching me in the shoulder, arm, and head. *Weren't we supposed to wear head guards?*

The gloves were harder than I thought they would be. I got tired of being hit and started striking back, but every time I got a good lick in, he'd hit me back twice as hard. I'd only gotten a few jabs in before he hit me so hard it knocked the breath out of me. That's when Tex stopped the fight.

I was still panting while Tex helped get the gloves off me, but I was thinking I could have done a lot better with a little training. Unfortunately, I wasn't able to talk yet to tell Tex how I felt.

As we left Tiny's, I had a strange feeling about the experience—strange because I actually enjoyed it, not the getting hit part, but the part that said I wasn't afraid to fight.

CHAPTER SIX

A week later, we still hadn't learned who the dark-haired woman was. I hadn't seen her since pointing her out to Tex at the gym. He'd told me not to scare her off by looking for her while his friends were following her, but that made me even more conscious of everyone around me. I'm sure I was doing just the opposite of what Tex had in mind. Who knows, maybe she was no longer following me.

Tex and I talked a lot since we saw her, but we'd accomplished little. He added to the clues database when a bunch of crooks in military garb made the news, but the incident wasn't similar to the Round Rock one in any other ways. I have to admit, though, it helped to be doing something, even if it seemed we weren't progressing at all.

The workouts helped; I felt physically better each day. Tex increased the weights on the machines and had me on vitamins and a balanced diet. Before the exercise regimen began, I usually ate a sausage McMuffin for breakfast, or skipped it altogether, a greasy hamburger for dinner, and a Snickers candy bar between meals when I felt hungry. Now Tex had me on a regular schedule of three healthy meals plus two snacks every day. I was eating more and losing weight—weird. I didn't have anyone to brag to, but if I did, I would say I felt better than ever before—physically, anyway.

But Tex wasn't satisfied with diet and exercise. He wanted me to run as soon as my leg would let me. In the meantime, I walked in the indoor pool at the gym. It wasn't aerobic, but it helped. He said I had to be ready to run the Capitol 10K in the spring. The Austin American-Statesman sponsored an annual 10K race that attracted runners, walkers, and athletes in wheelchairs from around the world. Tex had won the wheelchair division twice. In recent years, he'd been beaten out by the younger racers, but he still competed every year.

We also went to the pistol range in Pflugerville. I didn't see the need for it, but Tex insisted. We rented a variety of pistols so I could select the one I liked best. I went through them alphabetically—Beretta, Browning, Colt—and stopped when I got to the Glock 19. This was the one.

I emptied the fifteen-round magazine so fast it shocked me. I'd never held a gun in my hand before, and never wanted to, but this weapon felt so right in my hand it was frightening.

Tex's eyes opened so wide I feared they might pop out of their sockets. "Wow," he said. "This must be the one for you." He pulled the target in to check it, examining it for a minute before he howled. "I thought you had only hit the target once, but I believe you put them all through the bull's-eye. Outstanding!"

I knew I had.

"Beginner's luck. Let's see if you can do it again." Tex put up a new target.

I loaded another magazine, aimed, and fired. "Check that," I said, knowing where every bullet went.

Tex checked the results. "Wow! Okay, you're a natural. We'll get you a Glock 19."

It was good to know I could shoot accurately, but I knew there was more to shooting than putting holes in a stationary paper target. Shooting at a human, especially one who might be moving around and who might be standing near an innocent person, would be completely different.

Frankly, I didn't think I could shoot a person—moving or stationary. Maybe we wouldn't have to find out.

Tex still couldn't believe my marksmanship and made me try a number of different targets before he gave up and said we could go.

We were in the parking lot, ready to go home, when Tex's phone rang. All I heard him say was, "No kidding," but the way he looked at me as he put his cell phone away told me it wasn't a personal call.

"What's up?"

He held his hand over his mouth for a few seconds before answering as if coming up with a way to say what he had to say. "They caught your stalker."

"What do you mean 'caught' her?" I asked. "I thought your friends were going to follow her and find out who she is and where she goes. They don't have authority to hold anyone—that's kidnapping." Tex and his so-called friends were going to get us all arrested. I'd never gotten myself into anything like this before, and I was having serious thoughts about how to kill the project and distance myself from all this illegal activity.

"They followed her. They had a GPS on her car so they wouldn't have to stay close to her, but she must have found it and removed it. When she did, they were afraid she'd make a run for it."

"Tell them to let her go. We can't be grabbing people just because they don't want us to follow them." I was still curious about who she was. "Did they find out who she is?"

"Not really. She claims she has no identification on her. They checked the license plate number on her vehicle and turned up nothing. Jimbo thinks she could be a pro since she found the GPS and has no ID on herself or her car."

"Pro? What does that mean?"

We had stopped outside the pistol range door for Tex to take the call. Now he turned his wheelchair and rolled into the parking lot.

He kept moving as he answered. "She might be a cop or an assassin. Either way, she knows what she's doing."

"Did she say anything?"

Tex stopped abruptly and looked into my eyes. "She won't talk to anyone but you."

"What? She wants to talk to me?"

He turned and rolled farther into the parking lot, and I followed, stepping lively to keep up.

"Yeah. You up to it?" He hollered it over his shoulder.

"Sure. Where is she?" I wanted to find out why she had broken into my apartment. I wanted to know whom she worked for. I wanted to know who killed Sarah.

"Right over there." Tex stopped and pointed to a black Chevrolet. "And she's not going anywhere—the guys snatched her car keys."

I spotted her at the end of the parking lot and walked toward her, leaving Tex alone in the parking lot. She had seen me, too. She locked her eyes on me and followed me without emotion. I wondered what I'd gotten myself into.

"We meet at last." After I said it, I thought how silly it sounded. She knew who I was, but I didn't know her name. I'd been thinking of her as the dark-haired beauty for so long that was her name to me. Up close, it was her brown eyes that stood out. Her eyes could bore a hole in me, but still, I couldn't turn away.

After taking in her eyes for as long as possible, I noticed she was dressed in jeans and a white blouse—both tasteful, but both emphasized her beauty. There was no way she could be an assassin— maybe a cop, but she couldn't be a cold-blooded killer.

She had her hands on her hips and her mouth pursed in

a way that told me she wasn't happy with the situation she was in. In addition to her body language, I could see she was breathing heavier than was probably normal. That was understandable since she'd just been kidnapped.

"Yeah, we finally meet," she said. She relaxed her posture, but I could see her looking around me, keeping an eye on Tex, who had joined his friends fifty yards away from where we stood. She turned to me. "How long have you known I was following you? I was being careful."

"If it makes you feel better, we didn't spot you following us. I have a video of you inside my apartment. We didn't know you were following us until we saw you in the gym." I checked her reaction before continuing. "I watched as you left my apartment and walked out of the complex. Of course, I didn't know you were the one who had broken in and triggered the alarm. If I had, I would have stopped you."

She shook her head and grinned. "Video? Alarm? Ouch, that hurts. I should've known better than to try to covertly investigate Jason's son." Her eyes stayed locked on mine.

"You know my dad?" I didn't understand what was going on, but she was talking and she knew Dad's name.

"We work together from time to time. He asked me to keep an eye on you. Can you give me a good reason not to arrest those goons you hired to kidnap me?"

"Are you FBI? The guys said you didn't have an ID."

"I don't have to show my ID to them or to you." She continued to periodically glance toward Tex and his friends.

She didn't answer my question, so I tried another. "So, you're following me as a favor to my father? Why'd you break into my apartment? You could have talked to me."

"Why should I explain anything to you? Call off your posse, and leave the criminal investigation to law enforcement."

"Like you?" She hadn't said if she was FBI or not.

She looked toward Tex again. "That guy in the wheelchair with the ten-gallon hat—what's his involvement in this?"

I laughed. "Tex? He's the ringleader."

She raised her eyebrows. "Really? I thought you were."

"We might be amateurs in your eyes, but we're not the ones who got caught." I said it as nicely as possible with an attempt at humor—no sense making her angrier than she was.

She relaxed for the first time since Tex's friends had nabbed her, and the smile on her face showed how beautiful she was. "Touché," she said.

"Maybe we should join forces," I suggested. I still didn't know her name or whom she worked for, but I liked her style. I would prefer to have her on my side than have her following me at a distance.

"Okay, get my car keys from those thugs, and I'll think about it." She stared at me as if daring me to prove myself.

"I'll get your keys if you promise to work with us."

She didn't answer immediately, and I couldn't tell from her expression if she was considering it or thinking I was crazy to make such a demand. Finally, she smiled. "Deal."

"We meet at the Austin History Center every Monday night at six."

"I'll be there."

"What's your name?"

"Angela."

"Angela what?"

"Just Angela."

I got the keys from Tex and handed them over to our latest Vengeance Squad member. She jumped in her nondescript black Chevy and left without saying good-bye. As she drove away, I made a mental note to call Dad and ask what he knew about her.

***

The following Monday, Tex and Liz were already there when I arrived at the Austin History Center a few minutes early for our weekly meeting. That was odd since Liz usually busied herself nearby until the time the meeting started and came scurrying in at the last minute, flustered and apologetic. Tex was late for everything.

"Hey, teach, come on in," Tex rolled his wheelchair back from the table and swiveled it toward me. "I was just telling Liz about how we apprehended Angela."

Liz's eyes opened wide. "Is it true? Does that woman we saw on the video work for the Federal Bureau of Investigation? My, my, it's a wonder we're not all in jail."

I didn't know Liz well, but she seemed mildly excited with apprehension rather than afraid of the consequences of kidnapping a federal agent.

Tex beamed. "No need to worry about that. She'd be too embarrassed to arrest us." Tex proudly described the scheme he'd dreamed up to catch Angela, forgetting to mention that none of it would have been possible without the video of her and my spotting her at the gym. Tex rolled back to the table and adjusted his chair so that he faced the computer.

"Besides, teach here," he said, nodding his head my way, "smoothed everything over with her. She didn't seem all that mad after he talked to her."

Tex's grin was suddenly replaced by a look I hadn't seen on him before. If I'd had to guess, I would have called it fear. I followed his focus and saw Angela standing in the doorway with her hands on her hips. Tex gulped and then stared at me.

I hadn't told him I'd invited her to join us, mainly because I didn't think she'd show. Now I bet he thought she'd come to arrest us. The look on his face said he'd jump out of his wheelchair and race out of the room if he could.

"Come in, Angela," I said, trying not to laugh at Tex. "We were just getting started. Liz, Tex, this is Angela. I invited her to join the Vengeance Squad. I hope you don't mind."

Liz looked at Tex, then Angela. "Don't mind at all. Welcome, Angela. We were just talking about you. Is it true you're an FBI agent?" Liz was back to her usual jolly self.

"All I can say is I work in law enforcement," Angela said as she held out her hand toward Liz.

Liz never shook hands; she was a hugger. Liz had her arms around Angela before she knew what was happening. In the short time I'd known Liz, I'd grown to love her. She reminded me of my grandmother on my mother's side, the one who never met a stranger. Liz certainly didn't act like she was the director of library services for a major city, but from what I'd heard from Tex and read in the newspaper, she was good at what she did.

Tex's eyes bulged. "Yes, we're glad to have you." Ever the gentleman, he rolled over and pulled a chair away from the table for her. "Have a seat."

Angela took the chair he offered. "Thanks. Chris convinced me we should be working together. I'll give it a try; however, please don't expect me to share classified information with you, and don't tell me anything you don't want my bosses to know. I'm only doing this out of respect for—"

"My anonymous FBI contact," I said before she could mention Dad.

She looked at me and nodded. "Right." She turned toward Tex with her hand extended. "I understand you're the brains of this organization. Do we have a deal?"

Tex blushed—another look I hadn't seen—and shook her hand. "Certainly." He sat a little higher in his wheelchair as he looked around the table. Liz and I nodded in agreement before he moved back to his computer. "Okay. What do we know? Anything new to report, Liz?"

Liz sat at the table and waved a stack of papers in the air. "I got a report from a contact at Camp Mabry where the helicopter was stolen. He said it was a sophisticated heist. The guy who flew the helicopter out was in a military uniform and had all the proper IDs and documentation to pick up the helicopter. It wasn't a last-minute deal. The whole thing was routine and scheduled months prior to the robbery."

"If they're so organized," I asked, "why didn't they have their own helicopter?"

"Good question," Angela said. "I'd say right now, in the wake of nine/eleven, it's probably easier to steal a helicopter than to buy one."

Tex cleared his throat. "Sounds reasonable. Anything more, Liz?"

"Afraid not. There was a description of the guy, but no one saw anything unusual about his appearance—clean cut, Hispanic, with excellent military bearing." Liz turned her papers over as if looking for more to report. "That's all I have."

We'd been waiting on this report from Camp Mabry and had hoped for a major breakthrough, but, clearly, there wasn't enough information to move the investigation forward. The Round Rock police had also chatted freely with Liz, but we didn't learn anything new from them.

I didn't want to believe it, but I wondered if we'd hit a

dead end. We had nothing and nowhere to turn. I thought again of Sarah and the way she died helping the wounded security officer and wished there was a way to make it up to her—a way to avenge her death. *But what?* The killers came out of the sky, left death and destruction, and flew away without a clue.

Tex closed the computer. "So…the police reports are disappointing, but we're no worse off than we were before. Something will break; I can feel it. Now, let's consider some administrative issues." Tex paused as if waiting to get everyone's attention. "Chris and I went to the pistol range yesterday, and he picked out a gun. Liz, do you think your benefactor will spring for the cost of a pistol for Chris?"

Liz's eyebrows went up so high she straightened the wrinkles around her eyes. "Why on earth does he need a weapon? He's our technology expert, not a cop. Besides, the poor man is still limping."

"Yes. Why do you want a gun, Chris?" Angela asked.

I shrugged.

"For self-protection, of course," Tex said. "His fiancée was murdered, and he was shot. His apartment's been broken into twice." He glanced at Angela. "And even though we know who broke in, he's still in danger. Once we find out where the bad guys are, we're gonna have to prove it before law enforcement will do anything. If we get too close, they may come after us. We have to be ready."

Angela turned to me. "You can't count the so-called apartment break-ins as a reason for arming yourself."

Liz frowned. "Besides that, we have no leads. No matter how optimistic Percy is, we have to be honest here and consider whether to terminate the search. I find it difficult to believe there's more we can do."

"I know," Tex said, "you might be right. But what if something turns up and we get a clue? It takes time to get guns, licenses, and such."

"Plus some time at the practice range," Angela said.

Tex laughed. "You'd think so, wouldn't you? But, no, it turns out Chris has the magic touch with a pistol. He couldn't miss yesterday."

"Really?" Angela said as she looked at me. She sounded impressed.

"So, what about it, Liz?" Tex asked.

She sat straight in her chair with hands together on the table, almost in a prayer position. "I guess. The money's no problem. I just don't want either of you getting hurt. If Chris is as good with a pistol as you say, then perhaps he won't accidently shoot the wrong person or himself."

"Good," Tex said. "Now the biggie—we're going to need a van with a wheelchair lift and Internet access."

"Internet access? What are you talking about?" It was my turn to be surprised. We hadn't talked about the need for Internet in the van.

"Our number-one weapon is your computer savvy, sir." Tex pushed back from the table and faced me. "And it would be nice if you continue to research while we're on the road—you know, while I'm driving."

Liz smiled. "The computer's not costly. If I didn't know you, Percy, the way I do, I'd think you were making a fuss over the computer and Internet connection so I wouldn't notice the big ol' vehicle you're asking for. What's the matter? Did your van break down again?"

Tex looked down and shuffled some papers. "No. Really, I think we need a special vehicle for this project."

"Okay, I can swing it. I have a friend who owns a car dealership—he'll help."

"Thank you, Liz," I said. "I hope we can justify your faith in us. Now, let me give my report."

I pulled out the map of the United States I'd been using

to mark where unusual crimes had occurred in the past year. I spread the map out for all to see. "This is all I've learned from my research. See the cities circled?" I pointed at the seven cities on the map, including Round Rock, Texas. "These are places we should check out, but it won't be easy. We won't have the cooperation of the local law enforcement agencies in these other cities the way Liz has here."

Angela couldn't take her eyes off the map. *What was she staring at?*

Tex waved a hand in the air. "No problem. We wait them out; they'll mess up somewhere. That raid on the mall in Round Rock was brazen. Somewhere along the way, they'll leave some clues, and we'll be ready."

Angela pulled the map closer. It was as if she had laser vision, and I could see the orangey red beam on New Mexico.

"Maybe so," I said. "I'll keep looking for other locations and watch these to see if anything else happens. That's all we can do for now."

"And get my new van and your pistol." Tex rubbed his hands together. "Also, we can't go chasing around the country until you're in shape. You need more PT and lots of exercise."

The meeting was coming to a close.

I turned to Angela. "You're not going to keep following me, are you? If you are, I can make it easy for you and tell you my plans for tomorrow." All I wanted to do was stay home and figure out why New Mexico was so important to her.

"Old habits are hard to break," she said. "But, to be honest, I'm leaving town for a while."

I wondered if we could trust her. "Where are you going?" *Probably somewhere in New Mexico*, I thought.

"Don't ask. I'll call you when I get back in town."

As she walked away, I still had the image of her staring at the map. It was almost as if she wanted to tell me something about New Mexico and couldn't say it in words.

***

I taught two classes the next day after the meeting at the Austin History Center, but skipped office hours and went home early. My mind was on Sarah. Today would have been her twenty-fifth birthday. The automated date reminder on my computer had gone off a week before, which would normally give me time to buy a card and a gift and prepare for the big event, and the reminder sounded again today, knocking me through a loop once more.

What's worse, I didn't delete it. Erasing the reminder would be like erasing my love for her. I couldn't delete the birthday alert any more than I could get rid of the email messages from her.

I'd read enough about grieving from the pamphlets given to me by well-intentioned people to realize I could leave those reminders of Sarah on my computer for as long as I wanted to. The experts said everyone passed through the steps of the grieving process at different speeds, and I was in no hurry to move on. To be honest, I hadn't studied the grieving process yet, but with my crazy so-called photographic memory, I picked up enough information by glancing at one of the pamphlets to feel I was doing okay.

Still, today's reminder of Sarah was more than I could take. About the time I thought I would toss the computer off the third floor landing of my apartment to shut up its constant nagging, Mother called.

"Are you okay, Chris?"

It was scary the way she knew when I'd reached my

limit and could no longer cope.

"I'm okay." I couldn't tell her how un-okay I really was.

"No, you're not. Talk to me, Son." There was love in her voice even though she sounded a lot like my nagging computer. "I know what today is. I had Sarah's birthday marked on my calendar. I know it's hurting you to think about it."

Then why'd she bring it up? "Really, Mom, I'm okay."

"Well, you can say that as many times as you want, but I know my boy."

Wouldn't she be surprised if I told her how I really felt? Depressed because of it being Sarah's birthday, yes, but I felt worse because there was nothing I could do about her death. How do you tell your mother that you're obsessed with finding your fiancée's killers and that you plan to shoot them one by one until they're all dead and their loved ones suffer as much as you do? If I told her that, she'd have me committed.

"Really, Mother, I'm doing fine. I'm getting grief counseling and learning to deal with this." Thanks to Tex, I was getting good at lying, too.

"Still," she said, "today is one of those days when you're reminded of Sarah. It's okay to feel worse than usual. There will be other dates you'll have to face, but this is one of the hardest. The day you met, the day you were to be married, even holidays like Christmas and Thanksgiving will all be difficult."

And I'm sure Mother would call to remind me on each one of those dates.

She sounded as if she were going to talk for a while, so I carried my wireless phone into the office and sat in front of the computer. I might as well do some work while I listened.

"I know. I've studied the grieving process, Mother."

I'd set Google alerts to send me an email when there was a robbery similar to the one in Round Rock. There were three messages from the search alerts in my inbox. I'd been doing this for so long without finding anything that three alerts were routine, not cause for celebration. I was beginning to wonder if everything I did was simply part of the grieving process and that I shouldn't expect to find those responsible for Sarah's death. It made me angry to think the killers could get away with it, but I had to be realistic. I had a textbook to finish, I had classes to teach, and I had students counting on me. I had a life to live. *But what did any of that matter without Sarah? Was there really life without her?*

"Chris? Are you listening to me?"

"Uh, yes."

"I asked why you're home. I called your office, and they said you were working from home today. Is that because you're too depressed to go in, or what?"

"I met my classes today. I'm doing office hours from home. The students are used to online chat. Some professors teach from home as well."

I straightened a stack of bills I'd been tossing on my desk for the past week or so. I hoped there wasn't anything past due in the now neat stack.

I didn't care if I taught or not. With Sarah gone, work didn't mean as much. Only, I did need to pay those bills and the student loan. Do we only live our lives because of the people we love? I had heard a news report that more people in the armed forces die from suicide than from the war in Afghanistan. The report went on to say most of the suicides were due to broken relationships.

That report surprised me. I hurt from losing Sarah, and I couldn't see a future for me without her. But, even so, I hadn't once thought of taking my own life. I wasn't sure how I was different other than having been a devout Christian. I couldn't face going to church now. I couldn't talk to the priest. To be honest, I thought I still believed in God, but I was mad at him. And, again, being completely honest, if my plan to wipe out the killers succeeded, I didn't think God was going to be too happy with me.

"Teach from home? Daddy would never do such a thing. Are you sure you're okay, dear?"

Mother just wouldn't give up. I was glad I didn't live in the same city as my parents. She'd probably come over every day to check on me. I opened the first alert message and linked on the news item it contained. The article told about a cruise ship robbery in the Gulf of Mexico with a pirating angle. It fit the profile I was looking for because the ship was attacked by a team of men in military uniforms.

"I'm fine, really. I'm on the Internet right now responding to a student who has a question about an assignment." Lying was easier than I thought it would be.

I opened the second message, and the word *Albuquerque* stood out like an animated GIF. I caught my breath as I remembered how Angela had stared at New Mexico on my map at the meeting the day before. I knew there was no such thing as true photographic memory in adults, but I had a natural inclination to see things on paper. The spot Angela had focused on matched the area described in this alert. *This could be something.*

"Chris, are you there? What's going on? Answer me, now. If you don't get past this depression soon, I'm going to move in with you until you do."

Her threat brought me back to the phone call, but I couldn't take my mind off the page on the screen.

"No need for that. I'm doing fine. Just check with Paul and Ann. They'll tell you. We're all getting together for a party to celebrate Sarah."

I opened the third alert, and there it was again—Albuquerque. It was another news source for the same incident. I scanned both stories, not caring what Mother thought about my lack of response. A bomb had gone off in the Apple Store in the ABQ shopping mall. Two people were killed, and a truckload of computers was missing. One witness said he saw bearded men in army uniforms loading boxes into the back of a UPS truck shortly before the blast. This was just weird enough to be similar to the robbery in Round Rock. I'd found the trail to Sarah's killers!

"Mother, I love you! Gotta go. Thanks for calling. You've made me feel great!" I hung up before she could say anymore.

This could be the break we need. I read everything I could find on the news stories before calling Tex.

"We need to make a trip. Is that van you ordered ready?" He'd be proud of me for not saying more on the phone.

"Not yet. It's taking longer because of the Internet link you wanted. We can still travel, though. Meet me at the office in fifteen minutes, and we'll work out the details. Okay?"

The "office" was code for Denny's in Round Rock.

CHAPTER SEVEN

Two days later, Tex and I checked into the Albuquerque Marriott Hotel on Interstate 40, an easy cab ride from the airport they called Sunport and walking distance to the ABQ Uptown Apple Store.

We checked in and took our luggage up to our rooms, taking time to freshen up after the flight. When I was ready to go, I knocked on Tex's door and was shocked when he opened it. I saw an old man sitting in his wheelchair.

He laughed. "Gotcha! I could tell by the look on your face you thought you had the wrong room."

He was right, but I didn't let him know. "What on earth are you thinking?"

I looked closer and could only imagine he had put makeup on his face and hands to make himself look older. Instead of his usual ten-gallon hat, he wore a British driving cap, with scraggly gray hair poking out from under it. And the way he slumped before hollering "Gotcha!" made me believe he really was an elderly man.

"Why are you dressed like an old man?"

"Simple. People talk to old geezers in wheelchairs more easily than clean-cut young men like you, sir—especially with that blond beard of yours."

"I thought I could talk to Apple employees because I have a PhD in computer science."

"I don't think your credentials will work here. Trust me," Tex said, pointing to himself with both hands, "this will get us the information we need."

I shook my head and walked toward the elevators.

"Sir, I hate to ask this, but will you give me a push when we get close to the store? It'll enhance my character."

Tex usually did not let me push him around, as he said it made him look like an invalid. I hoped this worked. If it didn't, we made the trip for nothing.

The Apple Store was a few blocks from the hotel in ABQ Uptown—one of those lifestyle centers designed to look like main streets of yesteryear. I pushed Tex most of the way. For some of the older intersections, he had to take over. When we got there, I peeked through the plate-glass windows and couldn't see any indications that it had been bombed recently. The sign on the door said they were closed, but I counted five people inside.

We'd discussed the objective of the trip while we were on the plane. We wanted to learn more about what was stolen. A list of the stolen computers would help us track the killers. Serial numbers would be nice, but I didn't see any way that was going to happen.

"I don't know why you went to all this trouble to look old," I said.

I saw someone inside walking toward the door. "Should I leave? I don't want to scare them away with my youth and fair-haired beard."

Tex doesn't get sarcasm at times. "Nah, you can stay. Just keep your hands on the back of the wheelchair like you're doing and act like you don't care what's being said. They'll think you're my aide. Lots of older wheelchair dudes have aides—especially the ones as rich as I'm supposed to be."

I did as I was told, but I didn't think his plan would work. People aren't as trusting as they once were, even of old men in wheelchairs. I had to admire the way Tex looked, though. He could easily pass for my grandfather.

A young woman opened the door. "Sorry, we're closed. Come back Tuesday for our grand reopening."

She started to close the door, but Tex reached over and blocked the door. His other hand shook ever so slightly as he pointed a crooked index finger toward her. "Pardon me, miss, I'm not here to buy. It's just that...well, I heard about the unfortunate robbery you had." His voice sounded old, too. "I was so upset when I read about it I had to come see for myself. Were you here at the time?"

She nodded. I did what Tex had told me to do and acted uninterested. I glanced in the store without appearing to focus and saw employees unpacking boxes and setting up equipment on display tables.

"What's this world coming to?" Tex asked in his old-man voice as he swayed from side to side in his wheelchair. "Did you actually see those hoodlums?"

The woman's eyes sparkled. "Yes, I was in the back of the store helping a customer. I saw everything."

Tex pushed his hat back and scratched his forehead. "It is so hard for me to comprehend acts like that. I don't mean to disturb your progress in getting the store reopened, but can you tell me what the robbers were like? I must be getting too old. I don't understand how people can treat others this way. In my day, people were polite."

The young woman didn't respond. I tried to grab a look without focusing on her.

"Oh, I'm sorry." Tex swung his head to the side as a signal to me that we should leave. "We'd better go, Chris." He looked back at the store employee. "I'm sorry, miss, I didn't mean to remind you of that awful day. I'm sure it must be painful for you to talk about it."

She came outside and shut the door behind her. "Oh, that's okay. You're sweet to be concerned. I can't tell you much, though. We're not supposed to say this, but they looked like the terrorists you see on TV—you know, the ones who attacked on nine/eleven."

Tex's eyes were wide open. "You don't say. Do the police know this?"

"Oh yes, I told them, but they think the robbers are Mexican drug smugglers dressed like terrorists."

"And you don't think they were?" I asked, even though I was supposed to keep my mouth shut.

"Well, duh. I'm Hispanic. I know a Mexican when I see one."

Tex laughed so loud and sounded so much like himself I was afraid he'd blown his cover, but the young woman smiled and nodded in agreement with his response.

Tex turned his head back toward me. "Can you believe that? Our government can't tell a person of Mexican descent from a member of al-Qaeda. Scary, huh?" He turned to the woman and leaned into her slightly. "Miss, if you're allowed to say—I surely don't want to get a pretty thing like you in trouble—but, if it's okay, can you tell me what kind of computers they took? I'm just curious."

"Computers?" She looked puzzled. "They didn't take any computers."

"Really?" Tex asked. "The news reports said they set off a bomb and went out of here with a bunch of computers." Tex acted dumbfounded, as if the reports were the gospel truth.

She grinned. "Yeah, we all got a laugh out of that." Then she turned serious. "They came in the back door. One wore a delivery uniform, so the door was opened for him. The boss said the others rushed in behind the first. They ran in, and one of the bunch tossed a grenade to the front corner of the store—right over there." She pointed to her right.

"A live grenade?" Tex asked.

"Yes, two people were killed, several hurt. Everyone else ran out of the store. I was stuck back over there." She pointed to the corner opposite from where the grenade had gone off. They knew where we kept the iPhones and took our whole inventory. Luckily, we only had about fifty of them at the time."

Tex turned toward me. "You see, Son, I told you we should never trust those newspapers you read to me."

The young woman looked at me as if she hadn't noticed me before.

"The police didn't recover the stolen phones, did they?" I asked.

"No," she said, "but they found the stolen truck up near the Petroglyph National Park."

Tex rubbed his hands together and rocked slightly in his chair. "You don't say...interesting...Petroglyph, huh? That's near here, isn't it?"

"Yes," she said, "it's about fifteen miles from here."

He threw a kiss toward the Apple employee. "Young lady, thank you for helping a curious old man."

She smiled.

I shook my head. "Thank you, ma'am," I said as I pushed Tex down the sidewalk toward the hotel. When we were a block away from the store, he started turning his own wheels, and I took that as a signal not to push him anymore.

We met in my room to review what we'd learned. I sat at the desk, and Tex sat in his wheelchair next to the bed.

"Where did you learn to act?" I asked. "I was beginning to believe you myself."

Tex laughed. He tossed his cap on my bed and pulled off his wig. "Learned it the hard way, sir—on the streets," he said as he scratched his head.

"What do you mean?"

"I used to panhandle. It's not easy to get people to hand over cash. I had to play a part. I had to learn to be someone who touched their hearts, and that someone was different for each person." He checked me, with his eyes twinkling as if looking for understanding. Just as fast, his youthful eyes looked older as he turned away. "One day I'd play the wounded marine, which was partly true. At other times, I was an electrical engineer who'd lost his job because of economic downfall. I had to convince the marks I'd use the money to find a job and they'd give me enough for booze to make it through the night." Tex pushed his hair back on his head, exposing the beginning of baldness. "I'd do what I had to."

"You'd do anything?" I turned on the laptop and connected to the Internet. Even though ACC was closed for Thanksgiving, I could expect one or two panicked students with questions.

He eyed me for a few seconds. "I stopped short of doing anything illegal. I grew up in a family with strong religious beliefs. I just meant I would act and say whatever it took."

"I know you haven't talked to your parents in years, but do you know where they live?" I asked Tex as my fingers told a student what she'd missed at the last class.

Tex's voice was muffled as he rolled toward the window. "No."

I twisted toward him in my chair, letting go of my keyboard long enough to give Tex my full attention. "You don't even know what town they're in?" I asked.

"Nah, they moved while I was in prison and didn't leave a forwarding address. That was a neat trick, huh?" He looked out the window.

"Have you tried to find them?"

"It'd be easier for them to find me. I'm the one who's

still in town."

I pulled up a search page. "What're their names? I'll see if I can find them."

"Forget it." He sat at the window, staring silently at the sky as the sunlight gradually diminished.

I could tell he meant it, so I didn't pursue the matter. Lately, I'd been wishing for a little less contact with my parents, especially Mom, but only because I've had to lie to her so much. Even so, I loved having them in my life. I made a mental note to call them tonight after Tex left. I wasn't sure how to explain to Mom where I was, but I'd think of an innocent lie.

Tex wheeled around toward me, scratching where his fake sideburn had been. "Did you keep the business card that cabbie gave us today?" he asked.

The cab driver who drove us from Sunport to the hotel was a friendly sort. He'd told us to get a room on the east side and to be sure to look out at sunset. I checked the window and could see it was almost time.

"Yes, I've got it here somewhere. What do you have in mind?" It didn't matter if I couldn't find it because I had it memorized. Being able to see objects for days after looking at them was easy for me. I used to think everyone could do it. The card was clearly homemade, not one provided by Yellow Cab Company. It said, "J.R. Grey, Author, Physical Fitness Trainer, and Tour Guide," followed by his phone number.

Tex's voice was business-like. "Call him and see if he'll take us out to that park where the stolen delivery truck was found."

"I'm sure the police searched the area thoroughly." The trip to the Apple Store had been beneficial. We had talked to an eyewitness and learned what the robbers took and how they looked. We knew they used a grenade instead of a bomb. I didn't know if that was significant or not, but we added it to the database. *On second thought, maybe we should search that park.*

"I guess you're right," Tex said, "probably nothing left out there for us to find."

"Hold on a minute," I said. "Let's go with your instincts. Maybe we can find something the investigators missed." I picked up the phone, looked at J.R.'s business card in my head, and dialed the number.

After making arrangements to meet J.R., it was time for the sunset.

I stood at the window, and Tex sat in his wheelchair next to me. We didn't say a word until the sunset was over because we were both mesmerized by the view from my fourteenth-floor room. The funny thing was, since our room faced east, we couldn't see the sunset. What we saw was its reflection. As the sun set, we saw how the Sandia Mountains got their name—*Sandia*, Spanish for watermelon. The sunset in the west reflected off the bare rocks of the mountain to our east, giving them a dark-pink appearance, and the dark-green conifers that outlined the base of the mountain and slightly up the left and right side appeared to be the watermelon's rind.

***

The next morning, J.R. picked us up at the hotel and drove us to the Petroglyph National Monument, where the police had found the stolen delivery truck used in the Apple Store robbery. The trip took us west on Interstate 40 to Highway 345 and the entrance to the park. It was only about thirteen miles from the hotel.

J.R. was happy to get us as a fare, especially when we told him we wanted him to wait for us there while we looked around the park.

"What are you guys looking for at Petroglyph?" J.R. asked.

I wasn't sure how much we should say to him, but Tex answered him before I had time to consider it further.

"We're doing some research for a book," Tex said. "The doc here is an author and may do a book on the Apple Store robbery."

"Really?" J.R. sounded excited.

"Do you know about the robbery?" I asked.

"Sure. Everyone in Albuquerque knows about that. A group of men in costumes stole a bunch of computers and then dumped the delivery truck at the park."

The huge parking lot for the Petroglyph National Monument was near a residential area. There were very few cars in the parking lot, and we could have parked anywhere; however, J.R. drove around the circular parking lot until we were at the entrance to the monument, where he parked in a disabled parking spot.

I looked at Tex, who shrugged.

"I'd like to look around some," I said.

J.R. climbed out and grabbed Tex's wheelchair from the trunk and started setting it up. He turned to me as he worked. "Say, when you're done writing your book, maybe you could help me with my story. I'm kinda stuck and can't seem to write it."

"What's it about?" I asked as I helped Tex into his chair.

The cab driver smiled. "It's about when I was dead."

I shouldn't have asked. "Sounds interesting."

J.R. sounded like a nut, making me wish Tex hadn't used the writing story as a cover for why we were there.

J.R. laughed. "I know, you're thinking I'm nuts, but it really happened. I was in a car wreck and banged up so bad they declared me dead at the scene. But I wasn't dead. I woke up in the morgue." He laughed again. "They told me later that, when I hollered, several morgue employees about jumped out of their skins." He laughed again.

I was glad he survived, but all I got out of the story was the fact that we had been riding with a man who had been in a serious car wreck, and we needed him to get us back to the hotel after our search there.

"Are we safe riding in your cab?" I asked.

"Not to worry," J.R. said, "I never hit anything I didn't intend to hit."

That wasn't as comforting to me as he probably meant it to be. I was tempted to ask more, but instead went to where Tex was looking at the volcanic-appearing rock behind the visitor center.

"We're not going to find anything here, are we?" Tex sounded gloomy.

I shook my head as I looked out at the view of Albuquerque. "I doubt it. But we had to see for ourselves."

"What y'all looking for?" J.R. asked.

Tex rolled around to look toward J.R., and I stood behind Tex, surveying the area.

"We don't know what we're looking for," Tex said. "Anything to do with the truck would make the doc's story more realistic."

J.R. nodded. "I get it. Yeah, makes sense. Follow me." He walked past the entrance to the visitor center to the left. When we reached what looked like a restroom, he stopped and pointed beyond it. "Right here is where the delivery truck went through the wall. They found it about a hundred yards down there—behind that hill."

"How do you know it was that particular part of the mountain?" I asked. "They all look alike to me."

"Because—See that house there?—that was in the

newspaper photo I saw." He was pointing to a house a couple hundred yards beyond the park restroom.

Tex smiled. "I bet there's a clue out there." He wheeled around, then stopped. "How do we get to it?"

J.R. looked at the wheelchair and shook his head. "I don't think we can. The truck's wheels were destroyed going over the rock. I'm sorry, but you'd never make it."

"I'll go," I said. I was itching to get close to where the killers had been.

"Want me to go with you?" J.R. asked.

"Have you been there before?"

"No, but I wouldn't mind helping."

I thought about it for a second. "I'd really like you to stay here with Tex."

Ten minutes later, I was behind the pile of rocks J.R. had pointed out. My leg hurt as I walked along the uneven trail cluttered with rocks and shrubs, but I didn't care. Behind the hill I found two possible routes. I went about fifty feet down the left one. Seeing nothing unusual, I backtracked and took the trail to the right. Around the next turn, I came to a small burned-out cabin with what looked like a pile of garbage next to it. Smoke odor was in the air. I searched the debris outside the shell of the building, but nothing appeared promising. I went to the garbage pile outside and poked through it. It was mainly empty tin cans and food packaging. I continued to search until I found a computer—the disassembled parts of one, anyway. I looked for the hard drive, but didn't find it.

I didn't like leaving empty-handed, but there wasn't a clue there, so I turned to go back to the parking lot. I hadn't gone five feet before I saw a reflection of light coming from an object leaning up against a large volcanic rock off the trail to my left. I climbed to it and laughed aloud when I saw it was a hard drive—perhaps *the* hard drive. The connecting cables were seared, but the housing for the drive itself appeared to be intact. Someone must have purposely thrown the drive away from the rest of the computer.

I stepped more lively on my way back to the parking lot where the cab was while holding the hard drive close to my chest. It might not be related to the robbery, but there was a chance it was. When I got close to where Tex and J.R. waited, I held the drive high. Tex gave me the thumbs up, and I could tell by his smile he was glad we had something to take home.

"Great," Tex said.

"Don't get your hopes up," I said. "Based on what I saw of the rest of the computer, they may have been smart enough to wipe this clean before tossing it."

Tex rubbed his hands together. "Let's hope not."

J.R. stowed the wheelchair in the trunk, and we were on our way. We got him to drop us off at the hotel to pack and then come back to take us to the airport for our flight home.

**

The nonstop flight got us into Austin around 9:30 p.m., so it was near midnight by the time I dropped Tex off and got to my place. Even though it was late, I wasn't thinking about sleep. What I wanted to do was find out what, if anything, was on the hard drive. Of course, it could have been wiped clean or not left by the killers at all. Learning what that disk contained was the only thing on my mind when I got to my front door.

I quickly forgot about the drive when I realized I'd had another visitor. Worse yet, someone could have still been there because the door was left ajar. To add to my concern,

I remembered my new pistol was inside and could have very well been pointed toward me at that very moment. I put my suitcase and computer case on the landing, quietly pushed the door the rest of the way open, and walked in.

The only light in the apartment was from the windows, but it was enough to keep me from bumping into furniture. Once inside, I froze and waited long enough for my eyes to adjust to the darkness. Standing there, I gradually relaxed because I didn't feel anyone was in the apartment. It was just a feeling, not anything scientific, but the time I walked in on the MI5 guy, I'd had a strong sense someone was there. I took a chance on my intuition and flipped the switch to light up the living room. All the inner doors were open, and the rooms were dark. No one was there.

I retrieved my suitcase and computer case from the landing and shut the door. The lock clicked into place, and there was no sign of forced entry. Then I looked around to see if anything had been disturbed. If someone had been in my apartment, there would be a video recording. Then it hit me—the intrusion system should have called me. I looked at my cell phone and checked for missed calls. There it was. A single call from my computer came in during the flight back to Austin while my phone was turned off. Someone had been there—perhaps someone who knew I was out of town. *Or was that being paranoid?* I headed to the office to check the video and see who it was this time.

I turned on the light in the office and found a dust ring where the computer used to be. The whole system was gone, including the monitor, keyboard, and my favorite mouse. My first thought was this time the burglary had nothing to do with the case we were working on—probably some druggy looking for something to pawn who knew I was away from home overnight. But after I searched the rest of the apartment, I knew it wasn't simply a burglar.

A druggy would have taken the brand new Glock 19 in the drawer next to my bed. A druggy surely wouldn't have bothered to take all the webcams hidden around the place, because they weren't worth the effort. A druggy would have taken the three $100 bills in the unlocked fireproof safe in my closet rather than the backup flash drive sitting in there next to the bills. Someone was looking for information. That didn't explain why they took the hidden webcams— probably to let me know how smart they were.

It was late, and my plans were blown. All I'd wanted to do was check what was on the disk we brought back from New Mexico, but I couldn't do that without a computer. To make matters worse, all our research was gone as well as the textbook I was writing and the backup on the USB flash drive. Tex had some of the data on the new laptop Liz bought us, but he didn't have any of the textbook files. Even so, his search data would be incomplete since we hadn't kept our files in sync on a regular basis. We would from now on. I tried to remember when I last printed the textbook. If I could scan it in from the last printing, I could recover most of it. I looked around and realized the scanner was gone, too.

What data remained? I wondered. I touched my neck, and tears came to my eyes, not because the flash drive I used to wear was not there, but because it reminded me of Sarah. The drive wasn't there because she used to tease me about wearing my computer—not a hurtful tease. It was all in fun. I missed her so much.

I'd learned a few things from studying grief that came to me now. One, as silly as it sounded, was losing an object such as a computer could bring on the same strong feelings of loss most often associated with the death of a loved one. I hated that my computer was gone, and I'd probably never see it again, but, after all, it was just a thing, and it could be replaced. What made me the maddest was that I knew someone had been in my home again. Still, the loss of stuff and the fact that someone had been there again didn't explain why I felt sad. It was Sarah. It was how easy her image and voice popped into my head. Remembering the flash drive did it that time. *What would it be next time? Would I ever be able to live without her?*

Suddenly, I was so tired I decided to forget it all and hit the sack. The next day would be soon enough to call Tex and the police. *What could they do about it anyway?* I realized I should call Angela, too, but then remembered I didn't know her number. She knew about the webcams, and she hadn't seen them when she was there, so I knew they were well hidden. Perhaps she'd told someone about the webcams. As I lay in bed in a drowsy state, I contemplated how little I knew about her.

I dreamed my cell phone was calling to let me know there was an intruder in the apartment. I tried to answer it, but I was shackled to the bed, unable to move. If I could only move, I could save the files, finish the textbook, and catch Sarah's killers before they killed again.

I sat up and listened, but there was no sound in the room. It was late for a phone call. Perhaps the ringing was part of my dream. But it wasn't. It began again. I reached over and grabbed the phone.

"Hello."

"Is this Chris McCowan?"

I didn't recognize the voice.

"Yes."

I was glad it wasn't a wrong number, but still, it was an odd time for anyone to call. I rubbed my eyes with my free hand and wondered what the clock would say if it were light enough to read it. My body was stiff, and my mind was groggy. I wasn't supposed to be awake yet.

"Sorry to call so early in the morning, but we've got a bit of an emergency here."

My first thought was Sarah, and then I remembered she was gone. My second thought was something had happened to my parents—a car wreck or something terrible like that. I couldn't stand to lose anyone else.

"Emergency?" I braced myself for bad news.

"Yes. This is Sergeant Newman, Albuquerque Police. We found your name and phone number in an abandoned cab and wondered if you could help us."

"Abandoned?" I was awake, but I didn't understand what this man was saying. My parents were safe, though. I turned on the lamp and saw by the clock on the bedside table it was nearly 6:00 a.m.

"Yes, the driver—a Mr. J.R. Grey—is missing. Do you remember anything unusual while you were with him? The log says you rode in his cab three times in two days, and one of the trips was for more than two hours."

I wanted to talk to Tex and Liz. We needed to discuss this. If it wasn't Angela, someone was following us. J.R.'s disappearance was too much of a coincidence to be unrelated to our investigation. But J.R. didn't know anything. *Why would someone kidnap him?* There had to be another explanation.

"That's right. He drove us around while we were there, but nothing out of the ordinary happened."

The voice on the phone sounded surprised. "We? Was there someone with you?"

J.R. must not have listed Tex in the log. "Yes, a friend was with me. We're writing an article together, and J.R. drove us around so we could do some research. That's all."

"Article? What about?" Sergeant Newman sounded interested. I wondered if I would be able to continue with this lie under oath—if it ever came to that.

"The Apple Store robbery. We had heard about it in the news and thought it was unusual enough to make an interesting story." I hoped he didn't ask if I'd ever had anything published. Textbooks probably wouldn't count.

He grunted. "Oh, that. Should have known. That's the fed's case now—not for the lowly police investigators." He clipped his words, clearly bitter.

"Sorry I can't help. The cab driver seemed okay when he dropped us at the airport."

"That's okay. Just thought I'd better check on all his passengers. Give us a call if you happen to think of anything that might help us find him."

He gave me his phone number and hung up. That's when I remembered the apartment had been broken into and my computer was gone. I looked out the front window and watched the sunrise. Someone out there had all our research. While it didn't mean much to us, a trained person might see something we missed. That person probably had his or her dirty fingers on my keyboard right now, searching through my files. I didn't want to believe it was Angela, but it was hard not to consider her a suspect. I didn't care how early it was; I picked up the phone and called Tex.

He agreed when I told him how the missing webcams—devices Angela had missed when she searched the place—made her look suspicious. She either took the webcams or told someone else about them. Tex reminded me not to talk about it on the phone, so we made plans to get together to decide what to do next. He told me Liz would get her benefactors to pay for replacing my stolen equipment. He also told me to get an online backup system like Carbonite this time.

The following Monday, I called Dad. Since Angela knew him, I wanted to find out from him if I could trust her.

"Hi, Dad." We'd been talking more frequently since the shooting, either by voice or email, but we had yet to talk about the search I was engaged in. "I want to ask you about a friend of yours—Angela?"

"Who?" he asked.

"Angela. I don't know her last name. She mentioned you had sent her to keep an eye on me because of—"

"Son, Son, I don't know whom you're referring to, but I can't talk right now—school stuff, you know. Bye."

I stared at my phone, and sure enough, I had lost the connection. *Wow. We never had such a short conversation before.*

While I was looking at my phone, a text message from Dad appeared: "F2F DEN Baggage 12/2 noonish."

What on earth? Was he telling me to meet him in Denver? I texted back, "AYS?"

"Yes" was the reply.

I paused forever before typing, "K."

I called Liz for financial help. A last-minute round-trip ticket to Denver wouldn't be cheap—at least more than I could afford. And a waste of money if I had misunderstood what Dad was saying. But the request didn't seem to faze Liz. As it turned out, a plane ticket wasn't needed. She had a friend with a private plane going to Denver that Tuesday morning and coming back Tuesday night. All I had to do was be at the Georgetown Airport, where her friend and many other Austin pilots kept their planes. She told me to ask for Matt.

I got a sub for the day and met Matt at his King Air 350 at 7:00 a.m. I learned Matt was the owner of the Quarry Restaurant, and a number of others, in Austin. Sarah and I had eaten there once and were amazed by how the quarry had been made usable again. Matt was going to Denver for a quick check of a restaurant he was building there.

We landed at the Rocky Mountain Metropolitan Airport, and I took a cab to Denver International. I still didn't know what to expect and was actually surprised to see Dad smiling at me when I walked into the baggage area.

"Hi, Son," he said. "Sure glad you could make it."

We hugged.

"I hoped I understood you correctly. This espionage stuff is new to me."

Dad laughed and, with an arm around my shoulder, turned me away from the baggage area. "Let's grab a coffee and talk. I'll explain it all to you then. When's your flight back?"

"I came up in a private plane and need to get back to the airport by six tonight."

Dad's eyebrows arched. "Private plane? How'd you arrange that? I was going to offer to reimburse you for the flight, but maybe you don't need my help."

It was my turn to chuckle. "If I'd had to pay the last-minute flight fare, a little financial help would have been welcomed. As it is, we have some financial backers who are interested in our research—good Americans who believe in justice."

"We?" Dad asked.

"I told you about the Vengeance Squad, didn't I? Tex, one of my students who has the street smarts I don't, and Liz, the librarian who has lots of influential friends."

"Sounds like a great combination of talents. What's your contribution again?"

I laughed even louder this time as we took seats in the airport coffee shop. "Naturally, I'm the group's computer geek." I should have told him about what I'd done to keep the investigation going as far as it had. I should also have told him about my success at the shooting range. But I wanted to get to Angela and find out what Dad knew about her. I couldn't continue to work with her as long as I suspected she was responsible for the latest break-in at my apartment.

Dad ordered two coffees. "I notice you're still limping. What do the doctors say about that?"

I slapped the air. "I'm okay. It comes and goes. Just sitting on the plane for the trip up here made it worse." Another little lie.

I pulled out the photo of Angela and gave it to Dad. "This is Angela. Do you recognize her?"

He stared at it for a minute, moving it closer to his face and then away again. "How come she's in your apartment?"

"This is a still from a video taken automatically while she searched my apartment."

Dad handed the photo to me and took a sip of coffee. "Nice. Does she know you have the video?"

"Yes, I had to tell her when we kidnapped her. She wanted to know how we knew she was following us. When I told her about the video, she said she should've known better than to try to outfox Jason's son."

Dad smiled.

"So, do you know her?"

He grabbed the photo back and looked at it again. "Actually, I don't know her. I don't recognize her, and I don't know anyone named Angela."

"I was afraid of that. My place was burglarized again, and this time they took my computer and the hidden cameras."

"Oh no," Dad said. "I can see why that makes her look suspicious, but don't let my not knowing her cause you to believe she's the one who did it. First of all, I don't see all my contacts. I only talk to some of them on the phone. For others, the only contact is by email or through another person. Besides, field agents don't always use their real names."

"I understand, Dad." I wished he had recognized her.

That would have simplified things so much. I wanted to trust her.

He sat up, grinning. "But I do have some information for you. I met with a friend here in Denver last night, and we talked about the Round Rock robbery. He didn't know I was your father. We were actually working on another case of white-collar crime. Anyway, it was a sort of shoptalk thing that should never happen in this business, but probably happens more often than we think—between agents, of course."

"So? Tell me what he said." Maybe this trip would be worth the effort after all.

"This guy I talked to was joining a team that was investigating ways to stop Mexicans on the Texas border from assisting Middle Easterners in getting across the border into the United States. He was leaving here to go to El Paso today. I don't know if this helps or not, but from what I've read in the news media, most people believe the Round Rock robbery was done by Mexican illegals dressed as soldiers with Arabic beards."

"He's heading for El Paso? Should we go there, too? What do we look for?"

Dad shrugged. "He said he was flying to El Paso, but who knows where he'll go from there. I don't know what to tell you except to continue what you're doing. Collect all clues, and look for patterns. If you see anything about El Paso, jump on it."

"Thanks, Dad. You made the trip worthwhile, even though I still don't know if I can trust Angela."

"Worthwhile? The trip was worthwhile because I got to see my son."

I laughed. "Oh, yes. That, too."

Dad had to be in Denver another night, so he gave me a ride back to the Rocky Mountain Metropolitan Airport.

CHAPTER EIGHT

The following Saturday, I parked my car next to the barn at the Eason Farm where Sarah used to park. This little spot on earth brought back precious memories of her—simple recollections I wanted to always have available even though they made my heart ache. After getting back from Denver, I bought a new computer and spent the day installing software. Tex was right; Liz offered to ask her money people to finance the purchase, and I took her up on it. The money was available the same day. Even so, it wasn't until the next night that I found enough time to examine the hard drive I'd found in Albuquerque.

I didn't like the idea of going to a party, but Sarah's mom hadn't actually asked if I wanted to come. She'd said something like, "Sarah would want you to make new friends. You are coming to the party." The idea of celebrating Sarah's death was so foreign to me I wanted to hang up when Ann called But I didn't. I had to go to the party because Sarah would've wanted me to and because I didn't want to hurt Sarah's mother, but I didn't have to enjoy it.

As I walked from my car to the front door, I thought about how this was another role for me, like the part I played in Albuquerque digging for clues. That wasn't the real me any more than this was me getting ready to attend a party at the Eason's place. Teaching wasn't me, either. The real me preferred to sit alone with my computer and dig into secrets of discarded disks. I hoped what I found had been left by the killers.

Having parked so far from the front door, my leg was hurting more than usual. At the airport in Denver I'd seen several men and women in uniform. That made me think the limp I had was not too different from that of the wounded veterans home from Iraq or Afghanistan. My wound gave me a new respect for those who served our country. I also noticed how some people nodded at me in public places in a way that made me wonder if they thought I was a war veteran myself. When they did, I had this weird mixture of pride and guilt because I hadn't served. The military probably wouldn't take me now.

The front door opened before I knocked. "Come in, Chris, dear." Ann's words almost fizzled out before she took a deep breath and continued. "There's someone I want you to meet."

My leg ached more than it had during the walk from the car when I saw Ann was leading me toward a brown-haired beauty across the room. By the time I was halfway there, my limp was more pronounced. The sight of the guest caused me to gasp. She wasn't supposed to be there.

"Angela, this is the young man I told you about— Sarah's fiancé." The way Ann said fiancé made it sound as if Sarah were alive.

I felt Ann's eyes on me, but I looked to Angela for how to play this introduction. *Had she told Ann we'd met?*

I didn't have to wait long.

"Chris, isn't it?" Angela asked. "It's nice to meet you. I've heard so much about you." She reached out to shake hands.

I took the hand she offered. "Nice to meet you, too," I said, thinking how I was adding another make-believe role to my list of acting accomplishments. It's funny what weird thoughts pop into one's head in these awkward situations. All I could think was, *her hands sure are soft for a spy.*

Ann took a huge breath and grinned. "Wonderful, then. You two will get along famously, I'm sure. Ta ta." She was gone.

"What are you doing here?" I whispered. I didn't know if she had anything to do with the last break-in at my place or whether or not I could trust her. After all, the webcams were missing, and she knew about them being there. *How had she worked her way into the Eason's family like this?* If this was a con, I had to let them know before it was too late. I had to know. "Did you break into my apartment again?"

She looked shocked, but I knew her well enough to know she was suppressing her amusement. "Excuse me? I've been out of town for nearly two months."

If she was being honest, she wasn't my latest intruder. *But could I trust her?* After all, she was a trained liar. She lied to Ann about not knowing me. Besides, she didn't actually say she hadn't broken into my apartment. I took her elbow and walked toward a table with cold drinks. I smiled all along the way. *Boy, this acting is beginning to become a way of life for me.*

"Didn't you notice I was gone?" she asked.

I picked up two soft drinks and handed her one. "I noticed."

Her smile was friendly once more. "I see you still have your limp."

"Only when I see you." I don't know why I said that.

She smiled. "Like a pain in the—"

I took a sip of my soda. "Where have you been?"

"You know I can't talk about that." She stared at me over the top of her glass for a second and then moved it toward her mouth.

"Were you in Albuquerque?"

"Why do you ask?" She turned and walked to the nearest chair and sat.

I took the seat next to her. "I thought we were going to work together. I didn't know where you were and didn't have a way to contact you. I asked Dad if he had your phone number, but he'd never heard of you."

She looked at me with a fierceness I hadn't seen before. "I told you the rules. I'll work with you, but I can't give you official information. Your father wouldn't know me by name. He does some computer work for us. There's no need for him to know me."

"He didn't recognize your photo, either," I said.

"Photo? Oh yeah, from your video, I bet. I've never met your father, but I know of him. His work for me was always handled by an intermediary. If it becomes important, I'll give you a name your dad will recognize."

"It's already important," I said.

"No," she said, "it's not. We agreed that I wouldn't be able to tell you much."

I didn't like it, but she was right. That was our agreement. "So, what are you doing here?" I swung an arm around the room.

"I'm an old family friend."

That angered me more. She could lie to Paul and Ann, but I knew better. "No, really, why are you here? What did you tell them to get in here? And why?"

"I told you why I'm here." She clipped her words.

"You knew Sarah?" This was too much of a coincidence. My mind wouldn't let me believe it.

Angela wiped the moisture off the bottom of her glass with a paper napkin. "Not Sarah—she'd already moved to the states before I met the family."

"Andrew? You know Andrew?" *How could an FBI agent be friends with Andrew, whose best friend was a British agent of some type?* I wondered what her reaction would be if I tossed out Tim's name. *Something is fishy here.*

"Yes, I met Andrew when I was in Great Britain on holiday." She sounded as if she wanted me to believe this fantasy.

"You're an American, right?" I was still suspicious of everything she said.

She looked at me with a frown. "Of course."

I checked my watch. It was 7:50 p.m., which meant it was nearly 1:00 a.m. in England—too late to call Andrew and ask him if he knew Angela. I didn't know what to believe. I thought she was helping us with the research. After all, she'd been responsible for us going to Albuquerque by the way she stared at the map the last time I saw her.

"Do you have to be somewhere?" She motioned toward my watch.

"I'm sorry. It's just that I don't know whom to trust anymore. If it weren't so late I would call Andrew and ask him if he knows you—that's how confused I am."

She pulled out a cell phone. "Call him. His number's on my favorites list." She pushed the phone toward me. "I'm sure he won't mind being awakened for a good reason."

I paused—long enough to let her know I didn't trust her and too long to change my mind and take the phone.

She pulled it away and held out her hand. "Give me your phone." The palm of her hand was much lighter than her arm. Her skin tone reminded me of an Italian girl I once knew.

I handed her my cell phone, and she tapped on the keys for a few seconds and gave it back to me. "Now you have my cell number. I won't always answer when you call, and I won't always call you back, but you can always leave a message. Why did you need to call me? Was it while you were in Albuquerque? From what I heard, you and Tex where successful."

"I don't know. It's too early to tell." A chill covered

my body. *Were we being watched? No one could have seen us at the Petroglyph National Monument parking lot.*

She smiled. "But you found something there that made you plan another trip, right?"

She was right, but I hadn't even told Tex about that yet. I only discovered it myself a few hours before while examining the hard drive. I wanted to trust her. "Maybe. We found a clue in New Mexico, but we don't know if it belonged to the killers."

"You still have to check it out." She drained her glass and chewed on a piece of ice.

What would I do if she asked about the clue? "I guess so, but what worries me is that the cab driver who drove us around in Albuquerque has disappeared."

"Yeah, that's unfortunate." Angela stood. She took my empty glass and put it with hers on the table, walked back, and stood in front of me, speaking softer than before. "They found his body in the trunk of a car at the Albuquerque airport—not his car, but a car that belonged to someone who had been away on a trip."

"Are you sure it was the same person?" My stomach knotted up. *Why would anyone kill J.R.?*

"Positive. Sorry."

"But why? Is his death related to our investigation?"

"Sorry, can't say anymore. What's that hanging around your neck? That's new, right?"

I was surprised she noticed since I had stuffed most of it under my shirt. I pulled out the flash drive and held in up for her to see. "It's a backup drive for my computer."

She grinned and tapped her chest. "Neat. I wear one, too. You're using Carbonite, too, aren't you?"

Tex had told me the same thing. "Well, not yet, but I plan to."

"You should. So, where are you going next?" She said it

nonchalantly, smiling in a way that the other guests might think we were having a charming time together.

I didn't want to tell her, not because I didn't trust her, but because of what happened to J.R. and what could happen to Angela. But I finally realized I had to tell her. She was the professional, and I needed her help. She'd told me about the cab driver. Besides, she'd probably find out anyway.

"We're going to Rowe, Massachusetts."

"Hmm. Never heard of it." She sounded more professional. This was business as usual for her. "Why are you going there?"

"I'm not sure. I found a hard drive in Albuquerque around the area where we think the Apple Store robbers were hiding out."

She looked interested. "And?"

"Whoever owned it was researching this little town in Massachusetts—not much of a clue, but it's all we have."

"You going in that private plane you took to Denver?"

I probably gasped, but quickly recovered. "You must still be following me." All the doubts I'd had about Angela before I got to the party came tumbling back into my head. *Could I trust this woman?*

She laughed. If she were as evil as I wanted to think she was, she probably wouldn't have told me she knew I'd gone to Denver.

"Don't get paranoid. I wasn't following you. I just learn things."

Paul and Ann had left us alone most of the evening, and now it was time to go. I left Angela with Ann while Paul took me around the room introducing me to everyone who was there. These were Sarah's friends and coworkers, some of whom I had met before, some for the first time. Everyone asked how I was doing, and many of them seemed to care.

I got back to Angela as soon as I had made the rounds of the other guests, feeling some pangs of guilt thinking how much I enjoyed talking to Angela. She was like Sarah in two ways: She was easy to talk to and said what she thought. I liked that about them both.

When we left together, Ann nodded in a way that made me wonder if she thought Angela and I would continue talking to each other somewhere else. There was no way I was ready for that. I didn't think I would ever date again. I walked Angela to her car and told her goodnight.

J.R.'s death was on my mind as I drove home. He mentioned having a daughter away at college somewhere, not my school, but a young woman like one of my students. What a terrible way to lose a parent. J.R. was the typical nice guy. *How could anyone kill a person like him?*

***

Two days later, we were on our way to Rowe, Massachusetts. The van was ready for a trip, but we didn't have time to drive all the way to Massachusetts and keep our jobs. Even flying, I'd have to miss two classes, and Tex had to take off work for the trip. I'm sure Liz's friends, who provided the funds for our chartered flight to North Adams, Massachusetts, and the special rental van, would provide financial assistance for Tex if asked. Liz hadn't said who our benefactors were, other than to say they were people interested in justice, but after talking to Matt on the Denver flight, I knew he was one of them. He also mentioned Brian, Phil, Ron, Tony, Richard, and the Combine as if I knew who or what he was talking about—funny how I remember all the names like that. Everyone envies me because of my ability to easily recall stuff, but sometimes I feel all the little details keep me from seeing the big picture. Most people didn't know about my other thing—my need to keep my world in order. Sarah knew, and she still loved me, so I guess it's not so terrible—a bother sometimes, though.

We had our weapons with us, but I didn't feel too confident with mine. Although I continued to practice and consistently knocked the center circle out of the paper targets, I knew shooting a person wasn't the same.

As we descended into Harriman-and-West Airport, I glanced out the window to see a winter wonderland. Snow was everywhere. Back home in Central Texas, everything shuts down with less snow than I could see there. But as we got closer to earth and saw traffic moving on the cleared, dry roads near the airport, I relaxed.

Once on the ground, we talked to the pilot about the return trip, agreeing to leave around noon the next day. The van was ready and waiting for us at the car rental office. I looked back at the airport as we drove out of the parking lot and could see a mountain range rising above the buildings, a majestic whiteness magnified by sunlight.

We had printed Google Map directions for the twenty-mile trip to Rowe before we left Austin and selected the shorter route on Massachusetts Highway 2E, or what was also called the Mohawk Trail.

It was supposed to take about forty-five minutes, but it was more like an hour and a half, partly due to the weather, but mostly because I was awed by the view. Snow piled high on both sides of the road, not white, but golden from the sun. Melting ice surrounded the barren tree branches, giving them an eerie effect that reminded me of slender, misshaped, monster-like fingers sheathed in glass that shimmered as the ice melted from the sun's rays.

Tex sat in the passenger seat with his wheelchair stored in the back of the van. I could tell he was looking around at the sights, too, but he was unusually quiet.

"Nice, huh?" I asked. "Everywhere I turn, I feel as if I'm looking at travel postcards—beautiful. Wish we were going to be here long enough to look around more."

"Beautiful? It's terrible. I'm sure this snow's already covered up what we came here to find."

I didn't know what to say to that. Tex complained so rarely. He was the one who usually saw the good in everything. I slowed the vehicle as we went down a steep hill that ended with an S-shaped curve. All we knew was whoever owned the hard drive I found in Albuquerque had been researching the Rowe area. We didn't know if the drive belonged to the killers or some innocent person, perhaps someone who had had a computer stolen. Still, I hoped we'd find something useful there to lead us to the bad guys.

"Terrible mess," Tex said. "All the clues—if there ever were any—are hidden for the winter."

I almost slipped into my old way of thinking and started to say something about God putting us there for a purpose. Tex would understand that, but I wasn't sure I believed it anymore. Regardless, I knew God wouldn't be happy with where this trip would eventually take us—not if it took us where I hoped it would. Hadn't Father Jesse reminded me, "Vengeance is mine," saith the Lord?

"Look, Rowe's not huge. Let's check around. Maybe someone saw something unusual."

"Maybe." Tex sat with his hands in his lap staring straight ahead. "I think it's a big waste of time."

Rowe was smaller than I thought. The Internet listing I'd checked before we left said the population was 350, but still, we almost missed the town.

I was gazing at a woman standing in the snow on the shore of a frozen pond when Tex hollered, "This is it."

I pulled into a church parking lot near the pond and got

out. I set up Tex's wheelchair and helped him into it.

"Not much here, is there?" I asked.

"Nah, we won't find anything here." He sat with his arms crossed.

"There's a woman across the road there near the pond. I think she's taking pictures."

"Yeah, I saw her. How do you know it's a woman? With that big coat and hat, it could be a man." Tex didn't move.

"Wait here, I'll go check." I crossed the street and walked toward the photographer.

He rolled along behind me. "What'd you mean 'wait here'? I'm not some invalid, you know." But as soon as he got across the street and to snow that would come up to his lap, he stopped. "Yeah, you go check on that guy or gal. I'll cover your back from here."

I followed the path cut through the snow by the person with the camera. It was a woman. She looked me over, nodded silently, and continued shooting. You could tell she was a professional by the size of the camera and the way she handled it. After several more clicks, she lowered it and turned toward me with a pose that told me she was ready to talk.

"Good morning," I said. "Nice view you have here."

"'Tis. And the lighting is perfect. So, if you don't mind, I'm going to go ahead and shoot while you talk. Are you lost?" She turned back toward the pond and brought the camera up to her face again.

"Oh, no, we're doing research for a magazine article and wondered if you've seen anything unusual around here in the past two months or so." I couldn't keep my eyes off the scene I knew must be in her lens finder. I'd never seen anything so stunning. From this viewpoint, the morning sun was bouncing off the ice. The limbs of trees beyond the

pond hung low from the weight of the ice. The snow sur-
rounding the pond was the perfect frame. The color of the
snow was whiter than I'd ever seen.

She snapped a shot. "Unusual how?"

That was the problem with what we were doing. I never
knew how much to say about the people we were looking
for. "Have you noticed any groups of men in the area who
seemed out of place? Especially military types with beards?"

Something I said got her attention. She jerked around
so fast I thought she might fall. Her mouth was open, but
no words came out. She unzipped her coat and dug into the
camera bag that hung on a strap inside her coat and pulled
out a card. "Meet me at this address at six tonight," she
said. "I may have the information you need. I must finish
these shots while the sun is right."

She didn't say good-bye, but I felt dismissed. However,
I had her address and an appointment for 6:00 p.m. When I
got to where Tex waited, I showed him the card. "Photos
by Mary Simpson," it said. Back in the van, I entered the
address from the card into the iPhone map feature and saw
it was nearby. I memorized her phone number in case I
needed it. While I had my iPhone out, I snapped several
photos of the area.

I felt we'd accomplished something, but the appointment with Mary didn't improve Tex's attitude. It was the
look on her face as she handed me her business card that
convinced me we wouldn't go home empty-handed. Tex
continued to whine the rest of the day, while I basked in
the delightful scenery. Growing up in Southern California
and then living in Central Texas, I'd never experienced a
place like this.

To kill time while waiting for our meeting with Mary,
we drove around making random turns and ended up in an
interesting place called Shelburne Falls. I made a note to go

back there someday when it was warm enough to enjoy.

The Potter Road address on Mary Simpson's business card took us up a dirt road not far from the pond where we had seen her earlier. The road, as well as the long driveway leading to the house, had been plowed. We parked on a circular drive closest to the house, and Tex climbed into his wheelchair. He smiled when he saw a wheelchair ramp leading to the front door. It was the first time he'd smiled all day.

I rang the doorbell.

The door opened quickly. "Come in," Mary said, holding the door open wide. Without the bulky cold-weather clothing, she was slender and quite attractive. Her brown hair was cut short, and up close, I could see the marks of age on her face. She was probably in her sixties, maybe seventies.

"Thank you for seeing us," I said. "My name is Chris, and this is my friend Tex."

Tex rolled right in and held out his hand. "Howdy, ma'am. So nice to see a house with a ramp."

Her smile was warm and real. "Yes, I'm sure." She closed the door. "That was for my late husband."

"Sorry," Tex said.

"I don't have many visitors who use the facilities, but I'll never get rid of them. They remind me of my husband. And, who knows, I might need a ramp myself someday." She walked toward a hallway. "Come with me, Tex. You can use his elevator, and we'll meet you upstairs. No one has used it since Tom died two years ago. I prefer the stairs for the exercise. Besides, it's a small elevator—just about room for your chair."

Mary and I climbed the stairs and met Tex as he exited from the small elevator. I could see his attitude had improved.

"Neat," Tex said, "I'm gonna have to get me one of these."

Mary led us to a well-lit room across from the elevator. "This is my studio. I've set out some photos that may interest you." On the table in the center of the room were a dozen eight-by-ten photos of mostly snow, with snow-covered trees on a mountain range. Looking at one of the photos closer, I saw eight men in a military-like formation dressed in white from head to toe and with rifles on their shoulders.

"Where were these photos taken?" I asked.

"From my patio." She looked at me carefully as if checking my reaction. She picked up one of the photo enlargements and handed it to Tex.

"Do you know who they are?" I couldn't believe what I was seeing. Surely the killers wouldn't walk around in plain sight. These couldn't be the soldiers we're looking for.

"No, I took these photos in moonlight with a high-power lens—not because of the soldiers. I wanted a picture of the way the moon reflected off the snow and didn't know there were soldiers in the shot until after I made these enlargements."

The brightness of the moon on the snow had made me think the photos were taken during the daylight hours. Knowing they had marched through at night was easier to believe. I stared at the photos trying to find something we could use. "Do you have a magnifying glass?"

"Of course." Mary pulled open a drawer and handed me a large magnifier.

I leaned over to examine the photos with the lens. "Interesting." I wanted to yell it out, but said it as mildly as I could. Instead, I nodded slightly toward Tex as I put the magnifying glass down on the table. "Did you tell anyone about this?"

She nodded. "Yes, for all the good it did. I showed the photos to the police, even gave them copies. I never heard back from them, so I assumed it was nothing to be concerned about."

I pointed at the soldiers in the photo. "Could you show us where this is exactly?"

"Sure. It's too dark tonight. Will you be in town tomorrow?"

"Yes," I said, "we can be here in the morning."

As soon as we were in the van driving away, Tex asked, "You saw something, didn't you?"

"It's them." I was still calm on the outside, but inside was a different story.

"How do you know?" Tex's excitement was clear.

I drove out of Mary's long circular driveway onto Potter Road and turned toward the center of Rowe before I told him what I had seen.

"With the magnifying glass, I could see all the soldiers had long black beards."

His smile let me know he agreed it was them.

We were on track. All we had to do was find their hideout somewhere in the hills behind Mary's house.

***

Before we left Austin, I'd researched the area around Rowe and found it was close to Marlboro College in Vermont, where a friend taught computer science. Brett Barnes was a study partner during my undergraduate days in California. I hadn't seen him in years, but we'd stayed in contact by email. At my insistence, my publisher had added him to the textbook review team for my books.

When we got to the campus, I thought how strange it

was for me to be there without seeing Brett. Perhaps it was silly not to, but thinking about J.R. made me wary of who I talked to. I didn't tell Tex about Brett, just that I knew a place where we could stay for the night. He looked at me funny when I told him my plan, but smiled knowingly when he heard the details and the reasons. I think he, too, was thinking about J.R. and how we were better off staying away from hotels for a while.

We went to a dorm on the campus after checking the map and finding the largest one there. We used the common shower area to clean up, and found a couple of blankets which we borrowed. Afterward, we found a public park nearby where we slept in the van. Once during the night I woke up so cold I turned on the engine for a few minutes to warm up. Tex slept through the warm-up time.

At daylight, we went back to campus to shave, return the blankets and change clothes. Well, Tex shaved; I trimmed my beard. We ate breakfast in the student union and checked our email using the campus Wi-Fi before driving back to Rowe. We were both so at home on a college campus I'm sure no one noticed us.

Mary had coffee and homemade sweet rolls ready when we got to her house, making me wish we'd skipped the college breakfast. She seemed to enjoy having company, and this made me think about what it was like to lose a partner the way she had—the way I had. It could be lonely.

After eating, Mary showed us some of the many photos she had taken around the area, not just winter scenes, but photos taken during other seasons. Photography had started out as a hobby for her, but now she sold picture postcards to businesses around the world. She was especially proud of the close-ups she had of wildlife. There were deer, rabbits, frogs, and birds, just to name a few. One that caught my eye was a photo of a black squirrel reaching for a bird feeder while hanging precariously from a tree limb.

She took us out on the back patio, recently shoveled free of snow, and pointed to the place where she had taken the photos of the men in white uniforms. I could see the row of dark-green fir trees that were in the photos, so I could picture where the soldiers were and in what directions they were headed.

Back in the house, she showed us a map of the area, pointed out where she thought the men might have gone, and offered to take us there. I shook my head, again thinking about what'd happened to the cab driver in Albuquerque. We thanked her and said good-bye, promising to let her know what we learned.

When we got to the place she'd indicated on the map, my crazy intuition kicked in stronger than usual. I could tell we were on the trail. I stopped the van at the bottom of the hill, not wanting to scare away anyone who might be there.

I turned to Tex. "Will you be okay here?"

He pulled his pistol out of the backpack that hung behind the wheelchair and flipped it from hand to hand. "Of course. The question is will you be okay up there alone?"

"I don't think we have a choice. We can't call the police, and we must find out who is up there. Who knows, they could be gone." I climbed out of the van, zipped up my coat, and pulled my cap down over my face for protection. It wasn't snowing, but it was colder there on the side of the mountain than it had been down in the valley where the center of town was.

I started to walk away, but went to Tex's window first. "Look, we aren't prepared for this. This van isn't designed for you to drive it. That means you're stuck here if anything happens to me. We should've let Mary come with us to add a level of communication for us. The problem is I was worried about her safety after what happened in Albuquerque."

Tex nodded. "Yeah, I was thinking the same thing. I'd hate to be the cause of anything bad happening to that sweet lady." Tex looked at his phone. "There's no signal here, but I can get out and into my wheelchair, then make my way down to the main road and flag down help."

"Are you sure?" I was still reluctant to leave.

"Yeah, but that doesn't mean you should do anything foolish. Just look around and then we can call for help if we need it. If you're seen, don't engage the enemy—run. Understand?" Tex sounded more like the ex-marine he was than he had before.

"I understand."

While staying close to the tree line to block anyone from easily seeing me, I was on top of the hill in a matter of minutes, feeling more alone than I had in a long time. I thought of Sarah when I was alone, which isn't bad, but not then. I didn't want to be distracted. That was the time to focus all my attention on what was going on around me.

I scanned the area, but saw nothing out of the ordinary, and all I could hear were the sounds of nature. The top of the hill turned out to be a valley at the base of an incline to an even larger hill, invisible from the road down where Tex waited. Maybe we had parked too soon. Getting up to the place where Mary told us to look was going to take longer than Tex and I had thought. *Would Tex worry when I was gone longer?* We hadn't set a time limit on when he'd roll down the hill for help. As all this went through my mind, I considered giving up the idea of vengeance, and going home, all the way back to Georgetown, Texas. Instead, I walked across the valley toward the next mountain and started climbing. Soon, a large cabin came into view. I jumped behind a tree and listened for movement. I pulled my pistol out of its shoulder holster, feeling exposed in the clearing.

I stood still for several minutes, listening before I

moved from one tree to another, each one nearer the cabin. When I was close enough to smell chimney smoke and see footsteps in the snow, I moved with more stealth toward the cabin. The hand that held the pistol was cold, so I held it against my chest for body heat. When I got to a window, I looked in. For a brief time I thought how I could have been arrested for this—peeping Tom. The occupants of the cabin could have been innocent, unrelated to the soldiers we had seen in the photo. But, still, I scanned the room.

There was no furniture in view. But, as I searched left to right, a flash of light came into view, followed by some motion and the closing of a door. Someone had left the cabin on the right side of the building from where I was. They could have been heading this way. I lowered myself silently to the ground and made my way along the edge of the cabin toward the right. There wasn't an opening under the cabin to hide. Besides, I wanted to see who exited the cabin.

When I got to the corner of the cabin, I looked around with my pistol at the ready. But, when I saw two people in the white uniforms I'd seen in Mary's photo and heard the sound of their voices, I withdrew from their sight and listened.

"Talk English," one said with a British accent. "How come you're still here, anyway? Aren't you supposed to be at the next station?"

"I clean up here. Man came…see me. I took care of him."

"So, you've finished with the cleanup?"

"Yes."

"Then let's get out of here."

When I could no longer hear their voices, I peeked around the corner of the house to see if they were coming toward me. I saw the two men walking in the opposite direction. I waited a few minutes before getting up and going to the front door.

I turned the knob and walked in. The furnishings were sparse, and the large room was littered with trash. There was a fireplace at the far end, and I could tell by the smell that it had been used recently. I looked for clues while watching the door. It didn't take long to find exactly what I was looking for. I stuffed the piece of cardboard into my pocket and walked toward the fireplace.

I froze when I saw what looked like someone sleeping near the fireplace. I raised my pistol silently. Tex had said not to confront anyone. I was supposed to run if discovered, but I couldn't move. Whoever or whatever was there was completely covered by a khaki-colored blanket. I had to see what was under there. I pointed my gun at the bulk and gently pulled the blanket away.

I gasped and jumped back from what I saw. There was a man with an open wound in the center of his forehead. *He must be dead.* I shifted the pistol to my right hand and reached down with my left hand to check for a pulse. Before I reached his neck, both his hands came up and grabbed my left hand at the same time his eyes opened. There wasn't a sound in the room, but I had a strange sensation I was surrounded by a scream.

"Il Lasso!" the man with the bloody head said three times before he let go of my hand and slumped away from me. The silence was deafening. Even the inner scream had stopped. I waited for him to move or speak again. I hadn't been this frightened since childhood, but unlike those times, I was in control. I shifted the gun from my right hand to the left without making a sound and looked around the room. Not seeing or hearing anything, I checked the man's pulse again. Nothing.

Then I heard sounds I didn't want to hear. The two

men were back. They were talking rapidly outside. *Had they heard the man's screams?* I pointed the pistol toward the door and looked around for a place to hide.

"I thought you killed him," the one with the English accent said from outside.

"I shot him in the head. He has to be dead."

"Never mind. This'll do it."

I could smell the gasoline, and I knew then the two wouldn't come in. They were dousing the cabin and setting it on fire. I had to get out. *But what about the man on the floor? Was he really dead? Should I try to get him out?*

I felt his neck for a pulse. Still nothing.

I could see flames rising up near the door. I went to the side where I had first looked into the cabin. The window opened easily, and I jumped out into the soft snow and followed my footsteps back to the van.

Ten minutes later, I was sitting next to Tex in the van.

He turned to his left to look out the back window. "Listen," he said, "I think we should get going. The same car passed by down there twice. Maybe it's nothing, but I'd feel better if we get going."

I started the engine, then checked the rearview mirror. "It could be a neighbor checking on a suspicious-looking van." I made a U-turn and drove toward the main road. "We need to be more wary about the two soldiers in white uniforms I saw on the hill."

"Soldiers?" Tex asked.

"Yeah, and a man died while I was in the cabin. And then the two guys set fire to it. I hate for that guy to burn like that, but he was definitely dead. I checked twice. Should we call the police?" I didn't know how we could explain our presence there, but we had to tell someone.

"Did you kill him?" Tex all but yelled his question.

I wanted to pull over and tell him what had happened,

but not if someone was following us. We had to get to the plane and head home. "No, I didn't do it. One of the soldiers said he shot the guy in the head. He was alive when I found him, but just barely. He said something weird, then died. Should we call the police or not?"

"Not now." I glanced over to see Tex rubbing his hands together the way he did when he was thinking. "I still don't have a signal, but even if I did, we should wait. We could be tracked if we use a cell phone."

"So, what do we do?"

Tex looked around. "Head for the airport, and watch for a phone booth."

"Phone booth? I hardly ever see phone booths anymore." I slowed for an S-curve, then stepped on the accelerator for a race to the airport.

"I've seen a few. Keep watching. There might be more public pay phones in a mountainous place like this where the cells don't work well."

I nodded.

"Besides knowing the soldiers were there for sure, did you find any clues?"

I pulled out the small piece of cardboard I'd found in the cabin. "This is part of an iPhone box. There were dozens of empty boxes there."

"They must have come here from Albuquerque and unpacked the phones. Bet they're gonna use them to set off bombs." Tex looked out the window at the mirror on the passenger side.

"I guess, but that doesn't tell us much, and I didn't hang around long enough to find our next clue. This may be the end of the trail."

Tex turned his head side to side, probably checking for a pay phone. "Was the dead man one of them?"

"I don't think so. He was an older guy—baldheaded, no

beard." I glanced into the rearview mirror and found a dark-blue car close behind us. "What color was the car you saw on the hill?"

Tex's head jerked around to look out the rear window. "Uh-oh. Same as the one following us."

I put both hands on the wheel and pressed the accelerator down gradually until we were going as fast as the road allowed. "We've got to take a chance. If your phone is working now, call the pilot. Tell him we'll be there in fifteen minutes and that we'll need a quick takeoff."

Tex grabbed his phone, looked at it, smiled, and made the call.

"It's clear we can't stop for a pay phone, but I have an idea."

I hit the brakes as we entered a turn. This let the car behind us get close before it, too, slowed for the curve. I noticed Tex had his pistol out. I hoped it wouldn't come to that.

"What's your idea?"

We were on a straight section of the two-lane road, and the pursuing car was getting closer.

"I've got Angela's phone number. When we get to the plane, let's call her and let her notify the authorities about the body. She can call Mary to get the location. I'm sure Angela can clean up behind us without any problem."

"I hope so," Tex said. "She knew we were here, right?"

I remembered considering whether or not to tell her our plans to go to Massachusetts. "Yes. When I told her, she gave me her phone number. Listen, don't do anything rash, but the dark-blue car is getting closer. You don't think it's a police car, do you?"

I heard a sharp crack just about the time the back window shattered.

"Does that answer your question?" Tex asked. "Police

don't shoot first."

I watched as Tex turned his pistol toward the rear of the van. That's when I remembered his wheelchair and thought about how it would slow us down getting to the plane, even if we did outrun the car behind us. If we drove onto the tarmac the way they do in movies, and if the pilot had the engine revved up and ready to go, someone still had to help Tex and his wheelchair out of the van and onto the plane.

"We need to ditch this guy to give us time to board the plane," I said. "Any ideas?"

Tex had turned as far around as he could with no help from his lower body, and I saw his seat belt strap dangling toward the floor. He fired three rounds in quick succession, knocking the back window the rest of the way out, then fired more shots toward the pursuing car. I watched through the rearview mirror as the car swerved left, then right, before it drove into a snow embankment on the left.

"Does that help?" Tex laughed.

"That should do it."

We were near the airport, but not knowing how badly the pursuing car was damaged, I continued to drive as fast as I could without tilting the vehicle over. I parked the van near the tarmac and removed the wheelchair. That's when we saw the piece of lead embedded in the side of the wheelchair. We grabbed our bags and made our way to the plane. The pilot greeted us at the door, but he had the engines running.

As soon as we were in the air, I called Angela, and she picked up on the first ring.

"Chris? Where are you?" Her voice sounded shaky and deep as if she were in a tunnel or holding a hand over the receiver.

"We're in Rowe, and we need your help."

The sound of her voice, shaky or not, was calming.

"Are you safe?" She was all business. I could feel the power in her voice.

"Yes, we're in a private plane heading home, but we left some things undone. Can you clean up for us?"

"Sure. What do you need?" She sounded relieved. *Or was it my imagination?*

I hoped she'd sound as eager when I told her about the dead guy.

"First, before I forget, there may be a dark-blue car off the road near the Harriman-and-West Airport in North Adams. It was following too close and shooting at us, so we had to take action. I'll give you details later."

"Okay. What else?"

I looked at Tex, who seemed to be admiring the bullet in his wheelchair. That would give him something to talk about for years to come.

"Call this number." I brought up Mary's phone number from memory and gave it to Angela. "She can tell you where to find the cabin with the dead body."

"The what?" What did you do?" Angela's voice was much louder.

"We didn't kill him. He was almost dead when I found him."

"Was he one of them? The killers?" There were sounds of traffic in the background.

"No, he didn't look like them, but two of them were there."

Angela was quiet for so long I wondered if we'd lost the connection. I looked at the iPhone screen, and it didn't show the call had ended. Finally, she spoke.

"I can take care of this, but you've got to promise to let me know before you go on another trip."

"I told you about Rowe."

"Yeah, but you didn't tell me when you were going. I could've helped."

"This was unexpected. We thought it would be like Albuquerque, where we went to look for clues." I didn't think I'd have to check in with her every time we made a trip.

"You left a man dead in Albuquerque, too." Her voice was louder now.

"Are we sure J.R.'s death is related to our visit?"

"We're sure. What about Mary? Who is she? Is she in danger?"

"She's a local photographer. She has pictures of some suspicious characters hiking in the snow. I don't think anyone could connect us to her, but after what happened in Albuquerque, I would feel better if you check on her."

"Okay, I better get started." She spoke rapidly, with a sense of urgency. I could still hear outdoor sounds in the background.

"Where are you?" I asked.

"I'll be in Austin in about a week. Let's get together and talk then. If you learn anything new, call me." She hung up without saying where she was or saying good-bye.

Too late, I remembered I should have told Angela about the iPhone boxes, the man with the British accent, and the house fire.

CHAPTER NINE

The next night, I cancelled the meeting with Liz and Tex to stay home to work on the textbook. For the first time since Sarah's death, I was actually writing, not just holding my hands over the keys while staring at the screen, not just filling the chapter with exercises copied from what I had posted on Blackboard for my students. I was creating sentences and meaningful instructions again—finally. There was nothing better than a fast-approaching deadline and an empty bank account to awaken a sleepy muse.

I read over the digital forensics section I had just written. It was good. I couldn't see a need for changing anything. It was written from memory based on my experience with the burned hard drive I had found in Albuquerque and presented in a narrative style the students would find interesting—well, at least the editors would. *And wasn't that what mattered now?* I told how I was able to find information on the drive, what software I used, and showed examples of what the data looked like in hexadecimal. It was a near true story. All I did was change the names and places.

After that, I made it through a section on white-hat hacking based on information my dad had told me. Again, I changed enough of it so that no one could be identified. Also, I didn't tell them everything. There was enough to arouse the reader's curiosity, but not enough to help anyone break the law.

I was in my spare bedroom slash office deep in thought, typing as fast I could while the muse was with me, when the front door opened—the door I'd been meaning to oil. Every hair on my body stood at attention. Whoever was coming in uninvited this time was in for a big surprise. After being shot at in Massachusetts, I carried my weapon with me everywhere I went, even in the apartment. I had the Glock 19 out of its holster and the safety off before I climbed out of my chair.

I stepped into the hall and aimed the gun at the chest of the man who was closing the front door as nonchalantly as if he'd come home after a hard day on the job. I locked in on him the way I'd practiced so many times at the pistol range. His body started to look like the paper targets I'd so easily peppered with bullets. When he turned to face me, I'd be aiming at his heart, and my aim was perfect. All I had to do was squeeze the trigger and the man would be dead.

He turned and saw me—and the gun—and I watched his facial features change from nonchalant to fear, or at least surprise—maybe a bit of each. His right hand went into the air in the surrender posture. His left hand was in a dark-blue sling that hung close to his body. "Chris! Don't shoot! It's me—Tim."

I was so calm and steady I started to think how weird this was, even a little humorous. It was as if my heart had stopped beating long enough for me to hold a steady aim. But that wasn't the only thing that was weird. No one had ever said "Don't shoot" to me before. I took a breath, but held the gun steady, still pointing at the target for some unknown reason.

"What are you doing here?"

Tim lowered his right arm, but stood in place. "I thought you and Tex were getting together tonight?"

"So?" I held the gun steady, still aimed toward his chest.

He smiled. "So I stopped by to leave you a note." He

motioned my way with his good arm. "Can you put that thing down? I've heard how accurate you are."

I lowered the pistol, but it still felt like an extension of my arm. "You have a key?"

"Of course. I told you I'd been here before." He seemed more relaxed now that I wasn't aiming the pistol at him.

"You could have sent an email or called. You could have knocked first." What he was saying didn't make sense. No one walks into somebody else's home, with or without a key.

Tim shook his head, causing his long, gray hair to shift from side to side. "I don't trust sending messages that way." He sat on the couch. "Long as you're here, tell me what you learned in Massachusetts."

I sat in the chair across from him, surprised by his question. "What do you know about that?"

"I don't know a thing—that's why I'm asking." He stared at me in a pose that meant he was waiting for my response.

Perhaps it was a British thing, but he irritated me. Rationally, I didn't think it could be, but my suspicious mind caused me to wonder if Tim's could have been the voice I'd heard at the cabin on the hill. *Was he the driver of the car that ran off the road on the way to the airport in Massachusetts?* He could have broken his arm when his car swerved off the road. But it was hard to believe he would shoot at us the way the man in Massachusetts did, especially since one of the shots missed Tex by less than an inch. And he couldn't have been the person who set fire to the cabin with the dead man in it.

"What happened to your arm?"

He shifted around in his seat. "Nothing interesting—home repairs. Tell me about your investigation."

"We didn't learn anything. It was snowing, and if there was anything there, it was covered up." I was tired of working with agents. They took information without giving anything back. And this one I distrusted more than the others.

"Not what I heard." He cleared his throat. "I heard you found a body."

That angered me more than it should have, probably because Angela was the only person we'd told about the dead man. "Who said?" It came out childishly belligerent, but I didn't care.

Tim was on his feet, pointing at me. "Look, must I remind you I'm the one who warned you to stay out of this? If you insist on sticking your nose where it doesn't belong, the least you can do is share what you learn with law enforcement. That ragtag team you've put together is going to get some more innocent people hurt—maybe you."

He probably thought he could intimidate me, but his broken arm took away some of his power. Besides, I still had my weapon in my hand, and he knew it. I saw him glancing at it more than once. The more he demanded, the more resolute I was about not telling him anything.

"I know we look like amateurs to you, but you might be surprised to hear what we've learned. And we have shared all we have learned with law enforcement." I wished he'd leave so I could finish the textbook. The publisher had said there could be no more extensions.

Tim returned to his seat, but he didn't relax. He leaned in toward me and smiled. "Good. So, what happened?" Even though he looked friendly, he still sounded like he was demanding me to answer his question.

"I'm sorry, I don't think I should say anything about it." I leaned back and crossed my arms, making sure the pistol in my right hand wasn't pointing at Tim.

His fake smile turned into a sneer, then he laughed soft-

ly, with his good arm held out. "You remember who I am,
right? Sarah's friend. She'd want you to talk to me."

That was a low blow. "I've told the FBI what I saw.
Talk to them if you want." He was beginning to make me
angry. If he'd leave, I could still make the publisher's deadline.

His eyes popped open as he leaned back on the couch.
"FBI? I told you how screwed up they are about this case.
Why'd you talk to them?"

I stood and went to the door. "Because it's the right
thing to do. Look, I'm busy and on a tight deadline. I don't
think there is anything more we can talk about." I held the
gun close to my side, out of view.

Tim took the hint and left after he grumbled more
about the FBI and their lack of competence.

I found my cell phone and tapped Angela's name from
my list of favorites. I had to find out why she told Tim
about Massachusetts.

"Can't talk." It was a soft whisper.

I recognized her voice, but glancing at my phone, I
could see she'd hung up.

I called the apartment manager and told him to change
the lock on the door, then went back to work on the textbook.

Angela called the next day, but when I told her I suspected Tim was the one who'd shot at us in Massachusetts,
she laughed and said there was no way that could be true.
So I told her about how he broke into my apartment again.
She said she couldn't explain, but she knew him well
enough to know he was on our side.

As soon as I got off the phone call to Angela, I called
Mary. She seemed happy to hear from me, and even though
I was careful how I questioned her, nothing out of the or-
dinary had happened since we left Rowe. If I were still a

praying man, I would have asked God to protect her.

***

Austin Community College was closed for four weeks between semesters, giving me time to finish the textbook. I
passed it by Tex for a quick read and then sent it to the
publisher. The editor emailed me a few days later saying it
was perfect. It felt good to have it out of the way, but I
didn't relax as much as I had hoped. Knowing I could write
again after Sarah's death was all the encouragement I needed to start another book. In fact, my brain started without
me and kept me agitated day and night until the outline was
complete. With my so-called photographic memory, I could
already see the next book in my head.

I was pleased when the spring assignments were final-
ized. Because of my situation, I was given online classes
only. The department head did it to give me more time to
grieve, not go across the country searching for Sarah's killers, but the result was the same.

The following Monday, the Vengeance Squad met at
the Austin History Center to analyze the Massachusetts trip
and decide what to do next. As I walked toward the old
library building on December 15, I was obsessed with finding another clue. If we didn't have a clue, the search was
over or, worst case, we'd have go back to waiting for
Google Alerts to come in. We'd found good, solid leads
that took us to Albuquerque and then Rowe, Massachusetts. In Rowe, we found photos of the suspects, a dead
man, and a piece of cardboard that may have come from
the Albuquerque robbery. They were all good clues, but we
had yet to find anything that would take us to where the
killers went next. Unless someone in the group could make
sense of what we had, the search could have well been over.

When I got to the O'Henry Room, Angela and Liz sat across from each other at the table in a friendly, animated conversation. Tex was in the hall talking to a patron. I walked in and sat next to Angela and nodded.

"Liz, Angela, good to see you both."

Before I could say more, Liz was on her feet grabbing me by the shoulders. She lifted me out of my chair. "Come here, you, and give me a hug. I haven't seen you in...in...forever." She hugged me tight, and over Liz's shoulder, I saw Angela's smile, knowing she was silently laughing at me and knowing Liz had hugged Angela earlier.

Liz didn't let go of me until Tex rolled into the room and took his place at the table.

"Hey! Let's get started," he said. His laptop was up and running. "Anything to add to our database?" he asked.

The silence in the room reinforced my fear we might be at a dead end. I looked at each person, one at a time. Nothing. I was surprised by Liz's silence. She was the type of person who hated silence and would say most anything to fill the vacuum. Also, she was our cheerleader, the one who encouraged us to think outside the box when we couldn't find answers. Angela had warned us she couldn't say much about the investigation officially; however, I believed we'd gone to Albuquerque based on hints from her, and I hoped she'd toss us another clue tonight. Even Tex was unusually quiet. He was one of those people who could talk for hours on any subject when he wanted to, even though he was more analytical and concise about what he said in our meetings. Besides, I knew what he knew from our trip and there wasn't much to say.

I could kick off the conversation by discussing the incident in Massachusetts. There were the photos, the iPhone cartons, and the dead man. Then there was my meeting with Tim. I'd talked to Tex about all this, but brainstorming with the group might help. I decided to wait to see if Angela would say something first. I considered laying out a map of the country and watching her eyes—that's how desperate I was.

Liz spoke first. "Sounds like we could use some help tonight." She looked directly at me as she asked, "Okay if I pray?"

I wished she wouldn't, but I wasn't about to say so to Liz. Tex had told me how Liz helped him through some rough times with prayer. Before Sarah's death, I would've prayed myself, but now I didn't even believe in God. I nodded and bowed my head—no need to invite trouble.

"Dear Lord," Liz said, "we need your help to right a wrong. We know vengeance is yours, and we're willing to let you take care of that. All we want to do is find those responsible for the senseless killing of your servant Sarah. If it be your will, give us a sign that'll lead us to the killers. Amen."

Liz would be shocked if she knew what I planned to do to those killers. The odd thing was I didn't feel guilty about the way I felt. I hadn't been to church since Sarah's service, but everyone thought it was because it was the place where Sarah and I were to be married. But I didn't intend to go back at all. I couldn't trust a god who would let a saint like Sarah die the way she did.

I looked at Liz. "Thank you. I thought of a couple of things we can talk about."

She hollered it. "Praise the Lord. My prayer is working already."

Angela smiled, and Tex shook his head from side to side. Liz could believe what she liked, but what I had wasn't a lead, and as far as I could tell, we were still at a dead end.

I looked around the table. "First, I want to hear what you think about something that happened when we got

back from Rowe." I told them about Tim's visit, throwing
in as many details as I could remember.

Tex responded first. "Chris and I already kicked this
around some, so I know what he's thinking." He looked at
me for permission to continue.

I nodded.

"Because of Tim's broken arm and his knowledge of
events in Massachusetts, Chris wonders if Tim might be the
one who chased us to the airport and took a few shots at
us." He rubbed the right side of his wheelchair. "I've got a
slug right here to prove we were under fire."

Liz cleared her throat. "And I have the bill from the car
rental agency for the broken windows and bullet holes. But
that doesn't prove Tim was the shooter. I thought he was a
secret agent or some such thing. Chris, you saw his MI5 ID,
didn't you? Why on earth would a law enforcement agent
be shooting at you? And if he did believe he had a reason
to, why would he lie about it?" She emphasized her questions by leaning over the table toward me and furrowing
her brows.

I shook my head. "I got a quick glance at his ID, but I
don't know who he works for. He broke into my apartment
twice. He says he's my age, but looks twenty years older—
claims it is a disguise. Every time I talk to him, he tries to
talk me out of continuing the search. We don't have any
proof he was in Massachusetts when we were, but the broken arm fits." I looked at Angela. "Angela thinks we can
trust him, but I'm still not sure."

Angela pressed a fist against her lips as if attempting to
keep quiet while she was searching for the correct words.
Finally, she moved her hand away. "I can't give you any
details. I wish I could, if only to allay your fears." She
paused so long I thought that was it. But a sparkle in her
eyes told me there was more, so I waited. "All I can say is

what I already told you. That is, you have nothing to fear from Tim Jenkins. He didn't shoot at you."

I believed her, but I wasn't sure if I could ever trust him. There was something funny about him. Could it be he had conned her? "Thank you. That helps." As I thanked Angela, it occurred to me I knew less about her than I did Tim. We had taken her word she was FBI and knew my father. Dad said he didn't know her, but that didn't mean she wasn't a field agent. I shook my head rapidly, trying to dismiss the notion that she could have been anything other than who she said she was.

Tex tapped the keyboard. When he stopped, he looked at me. "Okay, that's settled. What else you got?"

"I'm confident the killers were in Rowe. There's the iPhone boxes, the photos Mary took, and the conversation I overheard. But all we have for a clue to where they went next is the dead man's last words." I didn't think brainstorming would help, but felt we might as well toss it out for everyone to think about. I could see the man staring at me after he was dead. It was an image that would be hard to forget. I looked toward Angela. "Can you tell us anything more about the dead man?"

Angela looked at the ceiling, then brought her head down slowly. "Not much. One thing I can say, even though you already guessed it, is that the man you discovered in the cabin was not one of the gang."

That was more than I expected from Angela. "Thank you. Anything else?"

"That's all I can say." Angela focused on me. "Now, tell us what he said before he died."

"It wasn't so much a word as it was a sound. I told Tex as soon as we were on the plane and heading for home. He wrote it down phonetically so we wouldn't forget." I motioned toward the computer. "You've got it in there, right?"

Tex tapped a few keys, and we heard the computer's interpretation of what I'd heard—"Il Lasso."

"Is that what you remember?" Tex asked me.

I nodded. "Yes, that's the sound I heard. It's not the same voice, of course—and not the same volume. The man said it loudly, and he repeated it a few times. If I hadn't been so frightened at the time, I could have recorded it with my iPhone." I looked around the table while Tex played it several more times at various speeds. "Anyone have any ideas about what it means?"

"Could it be Spanish for 'the rope'?" Liz asked.

"It didn't sound Spanish," I said.

Angela moved away from the table, causing the legs of her chair to scrape noisily.

Everyone turned toward her.

"I was just thinking…Two points: One, he was trying to tell you something, and two, he had a head wound that could affect his speech."

"That's right," Tex said, "he could have been saying anything."

Angela turned toward Tex and gestured for him to continue. "Now, assume he was telling you the next town to go to." She motioned again.

"Are you wanting us to guess a town that sounds like Il Lasso?" I asked.

She frowned at me. "I thought you wanted to brainstorm. I'm just trying to help." She turned to Tex. "Say the syllables. Does anything come to mind?"

I looked at Tex and wondered if he was thinking what I was. The look in his eyes said he was.

He laughed. "Il Lasso. Il Lasso. This is silly. There are thousands of possibilities. Maybe Illinois. No, that's a state. There's no way. Besides, how'll we know if we get it right?"

Angela smiled. "You'll know."

And then I knew it was a game. She knew, but couldn't tell us. Still, I didn't know how to play. I couldn't think of a city that sounded like Il Lasso.

Liz had been staring at the table all the while and probably wasn't aware of the game Angela was playing. Suddenly, she looked up. "El Paso!"

Both Angela and Tex looked stunned, and I probably did, too. Liz wasn't guessing, she was stating a fact as if it had come to her by holy intervention, perhaps even her prayer for clues. That was when I remembered what Dad had told me in Denver about the possibility of terrorists coming across the border between the United States and Mexico. El Paso was on that border.

Angela looked at me and didn't say a word for the longest time. "She could be right. I can't think of any other city that would fit."

Tex shook his head. "Yeah, but that doesn't mean there aren't other towns that match the sound, none of which come to me right now."

"No, Liz could be right." Angela was through with the game.

The meeting broke up shortly after that. Liz said goodnight and walked out with Angela, leaving Tex and me alone in the conference room.

"So, what do we do next?" Tex asked. I could tell he also felt our search could have been over.

I shrugged. "I don't know. All we have is El Paso. Rowe was one thing. What was the population there—two or three hundred? Sure, we had a good chance of running into someone who could help us. But El Paso? No way."

Tex rolled over to reach the keyboard. "Let's look it up." He clicked while I looked over his shoulder. "El Paso's population is close to seven hundred and fifty thousand."

"That's what I thought. Where would we begin?" I sat in the chair next to him.

Tex tapped the keys some more. "It's impossible, but let's take a look at the map." He scratched his head. "Hey, the Google Map for El Paso is already open. Did you do that?"

I shook my head and looked at the screen. "It wasn't me. And look at that—there's a location flag." I stood behind Tex to get a better view. Someone had marked a spot on the El Paso map.

Tex laughed. "If you didn't do it, it was either Angela or an answer to Liz's prayer. I bet it was Angela. This is her way of helping. I set up the computer earlier, then left to talk to a patron. Angela was here alone for a few minutes before Liz came in."

I wondered why she would do that. If she wanted us to go to El Paso, she could have said so. I had a strange feeling about whether or not she worked for the FBI.

"I don't know, Tex. Can we trust this?"

"Sure." Tex was smiling. "You know what's happening, don't you?"

"What?"

"We're helping them. They know that if they point us in the right direction, we'll come up with another clue for them."

He could make anything sound positive. I wasn't sure. Maybe they were trying to get rid of us. But, still, we didn't have anywhere else to look.

"Let's do it, then."

Tex shook his head as we said goodnight.

Since we had little time alone at the History Center, I called Liz when I got home and told her about the discussion I'd had with Tex about his parents while we were in Albuquerque. I told her it sounded to me as if he missed them, but was too proud to try to contact them. Liz agreed and said she'd see what she could find out.

***

The next day Tex and I were in our brand new Vengeance Squad van headed for El Paso. The specially outfitted vehicle had everything we'd asked for. It must have cost a bundle, but Liz said her benefactor didn't bat an eye when she told him the purpose for the van. It was designed so that either one of us could drive, and it had a state-of-the art computer hookup included. The navigation system was a much-appreciated extra.

Before we left Austin, I read the user's guide to learn how to use the navigation system, then keyed in the address someone, probably Angela, had left on Tex's computer. The screen flashed, then displayed a route map and a note that it would take nine or ten hours to get there. Even though I'd lived in Texas for four years, I was still taken back to learn it would take that long to drive halfway across the state.

As usual, we were going in blind, not knowing what to expect when we got there, same as in Albuquerque and Rowe. But, with ten hours to get there, we had time to talk about it and even do more research. While Tex drove, I pulled up Google Earth on the computer and found our destination was near the border with Mexico. Actually, it was about as close as you could get and still be in the United States.

We arrived late in the afternoon, early enough to see that the house looked abandoned. The lawn had not been cared for, and the house badly needed new paint and roofing. There were no curtains on the windows, and one windowpane was missing.

Tex glanced at me. "Is this the right address?"

I shrugged. "According to the info we got off your computer, it is."

Tex slammed the steering wheel with his right hand. "If there was ever anyone here, they're gone. Once again, it looks like we just missed them. I thought it'd be different this time because of Angela and the FBI."

"Yeah, me too." I studied the map again. It was the correct address. "Let's look around before it gets dark. I doubt if this place has electricity." I reached for the door handle.

"Wait." Tex held out his hand. "Shouldn't we move the van to a safer place?"

I scanned the area. It was a rough-looking neighborhood. Although most of the homes nearby appeared to be occupied, none were well cared for, and some had what looked like broken down cars and trucks in the front yards.

"By the looks of things, the only safe place for the van is right here where we can keep an eye on it."

Tex looked around, then nodded. "You're probably right."

The house was old, with a separate garage off to the right. The garage door was open, and the garage appeared to be empty.

"Why don't I go to the door and make sure no one's home? When I give the signal, back the van into the garage. Okay?"

Tex smiled. "Yeah. Good idea."

I patted my pistol and grabbed my phone before climbing out and walking toward the front of the house. As I got closer to the entrance, I knew the place had been abandoned for years. There was no way anyone could have been living in a broken-down house like this. Once white, now yellowed, paint curled away from the wood siding. A hole in the porch, probably caused by rotting wood, was ready to trip intruders. A rusty light fixture, installed long ago to illuminate the entryway, now hung from wires covered with spider webs.

I carefully tested the wooden porch until I found a part that would hold my weight, then stood still at the door for a minute listening. Nothing. I reached for the door handle and turned it. It was unlocked, and the door squeaked as I pushed it in slowly. Just then, a huge black cat jumped through the window next to the front door, meowing wildly as it flew past me, and goose bumps quickly covered my arms and neck.

Even though it was only a cat, I pulled out my pistol as I stepped inside the house.

The place was vacant all right—no furniture, no trash, no people. There was no need to park in the garage. I could search the place in a few minutes, and we could be on our way. I went back to the van to tell Tex.

"It's empty. Just wait here, and I'll look around quickly.

He thrust a flashlight toward me. "Okay. The sun's going down; take this with you, just in case."

I went back in the dwelling and made a quick survey. It was a two-bedroom house from the 1950s. The hardwood floors were water-stained, and some boards were so warped they couldn't have been used in years. The rotting wallpaper exposed mold-covered sheetrock and rotting wood. *Had Angela deliberately sent us on a wild-goose chase? Or was she just doing what she was told?*

I checked each room and closet, not knowing what to look for. When I got to the kitchen cupboard, I froze. The goose bumps returned. The floor-to-ceiling shelves on the back wall were not aligned properly, another example of the way my compulsion for neatness either paid off or frustrated me. I had to find out what was wrong. I pulled the shelves toward me and felt a gust of stale, cool air. Pulling the shelves more, I could see they were hinged on one side like a door. I pulled them out of the way and saw stairs leading down into darkness behind the pantry.

I turned on the flashlight and swung the beam down the stairs. I saw what looked like a tunnel about four feet high. Wooden supports rose from the sandy floor. Discarded fast-food bags strewn about announced the recent use of the tunnel like a neon sign.

I climbed up the steps, left the hidden door open, and ran back to the van. Maybe this trip wasn't a wild goose chase after all.

Tex leaned out the window when I got there. "Ready to go?"

"Not yet. I just came to tell you it's going to take longer than I thought. I found a tunnel under the house. Someone was in that tunnel not long ago. There's nothing else in the house, but I think I should search the tunnel and see what's going on. Just wait here."

Tex opened the driver-side door. "Uh-uh. I'm not waiting. I'm going with you. You may need someone to watch your back."

"Uh, look, the tunnel is down some steps." I wanted to tell Tex his wheelchair would slow me down more than his being there would help. "I can handle it. We may need to get out of here in a hurry."

He frowned. "I'm not an invalid. I can get myself up and down a few steps, if that's what's bothering you. Now, help me get the wheelchair out of the van."

"It's not that," I said, even though it was. "It's getting dark, and I just think we should hurry. Besides, this is a one-man job."

"If you're in such a hurry, why are you standing around talking? Get my wheels, and let's go."

Sometimes it was easier to go along with Tex than it was to try and change his mind. "Okay, but if you're sure you want to do this, put the van in the garage as we planned."

Tex shut the door and started the engine. He drove past the driveway and backed into the garage. When he was safely in, I closed the garage door to hide the van from view, set up the wheelchair, and Tex climbed into it. We went out the side door of the garage onto a sidewalk connecting the garage to the house. I helped Tex through the door and found we were in the kitchen.

"Where's this tunnel you found?" Tex asked as he rolled into the house.

I pulled the cupboard door back so he could see. "Right in here." I turned on the flashlight and pointed it into the tunnel.

"Well, looky here," he said, laughing, "a secret passageway. I bet this thing goes all the way to Mexico."

"Could be. I read about tunnels under the California border to Mexico, but I didn't know they had any here." Something Dad had said about terrorists coming over the border popped into my head.

It was easy getting the wheelchair down the stairs, but it was going to be more difficult going back up when the time came.

"Wait here in case someone comes," I said.

"Are you kidding?" Tex laughed so loud his voice echoed around the tunnel. "Look around. I'm better suited for this little venture than you are."

"What do you mean?" Very little sunlight shone in through the cupboard door. I wondered if we should wait until daylight to search this area. I guessed it would still be dark down there, though.

"This." Tex pointed into the tunnel. "Don't you see? I

can roll in the tunnel sitting down. You're going to have to bend over." He laughed again and burned rubber as he sped into the tunnel.

I followed him with my head and shoulders bent and held the flashlight to illuminate the way. My gunshot wound reminded me I hadn't finished physical therapy. I didn't like thinking about what we'd do if we had to get out of there in a hurry, but Tex was right. The tunnel was just the right height for him. Anyway, I figured the killers had vacated this place. If we could find something to tell us where they went next, I'd be happy. I couldn't get it out of my mind that this could be the end of the search, and it was probably because Angela sent us there to get us out of the way.

I heard the voices about the same time Tex came to a halt. He held up a hand, but didn't speak.

I moved up close to him and whispered. "What was that?"

"Not sure," he whispered back. "Keep quiet until we find out."

We remained frozen for a time, then I heard another sound, and it was coming from the tunnel ahead of us.

I got my mouth close to Tex's ear. "We've got to get out of here. Someone's coming."

Tex nodded and swung around and headed back the way we had come. He went faster, and I had trouble keeping up with him in the cramped passageway. I turned the flashlight away to check for sunlight to determine how close we were to the kitchen, but didn't see anything. That worried me because it shouldn't be so dark outside already.

When we reached the stairway without seeing light from above, I pointed the flashlight beam up the stairs, and all I saw was a wall where the opening had been. We looked at each other silently. I didn't want to think about why the shelves were back in place or whether or not the van was safe in the garage. I had to get the shelves out of the way before helping Tex up the stairs. I climbed the steps, but before I reached the top, I heard voices coming from the kitchen.

I stood at the top of the stairs with a flashlight in one hand and a pistol in the other, not knowing when I'd pulled out the gun. I listened, trying to determine how many people were on the other side of the cupboard shelves, but the sounds were too muffled. The flashlight's ray caught some scribbling on the wall leading down to the tunnel. I stared at the writing. It was nothing but numbers, not a phone number, but a sequence I had seen before. I memorized the numbers before quietly going to where Tex waited.

With the numbers safely tucked away in my brain, an idea hit me.

"Do you have any costumes in that magic backpack of yours?" I asked as softly as possible.

Tex's frown changed to a grin before he reached around and retrieved two hats and two serapes. We put them on and waited.

"You still look like a gringo with your blond beard." Tex pulled out an eyebrow pencil. "Here, use this to darken it."

I did as I was told, but as the voices in the tunnel got louder, I wondered what to expect. We could probably shove the cupboard shelf out of the way, but I was afraid doing that could lead to a confrontation with both ends of the tunnel. I suspected the shelf would open as soon as those in the tunnel got there, and when it did, we'd have a better chance to escape. I could tell Tex understood the plan even though we didn't discuss it. If we worked it right, those coming to the house would think we were part of the gang in the house, and those in the house would think we were coming in with those in the tunnel.

Tex swung around suddenly to face the tunnel, and I heard someone speak loudly in Spanish. It took me a few seconds to realize it was Tex. I didn't know what he said, but the response from those in the tunnel sounded friendly.

I tightened the grip on my pistol, hiding it under the serape, and waited with my hat pulled down to cover my gringo face. Tex greeted the men who were close enough to smell. One of them gestured toward the wheelchair. Tex said something in Spanish, and everyone laughed. I could hear the cupboard shelf moving out of the way as if on cue. We had made it past one encounter, but now we faced another with whoever was upstairs, and there were many ways that could go wrong. For one thing, I wondered how was I going to get Tex out of the tunnel while holding onto my serape and gun.

I shouldn't have worried. Tex motioned for me to go up the stairs just as two of the men in the tunnel grabbed his wheelchair and lifted him up toward the opening. When we got to the kitchen, it was darker, and no one seemed to notice us in the crowd coming up behind us. We followed everyone out the door, but stayed behind as they went toward the street. We went to the side door of the garage and quietly climbed into the van.

We sat in the van and waited for the others to leave. I was in the driver's seat with my hand on the key. Tex smiled at me, and I know he wanted to talk about what we had done. All I thought about was what a wasted trip it had been. We had come there to find the killers, not meet up with a bunch of illegal immigrants. Angela must have set us up. Or perhaps she was a pawn. This place had nothing to do with Sarah's killers.

"Hola!"

The voice was loud. I started the engine without consulting Tex. No use being quiet when someone is hollering at you. The voice came from someone at the side door who was shining a flashlight at us. I put the van into gear and stepped on the gas. We hit the garage doors, popping them out of the way. Luckily, these were the older type of garage doors that opened left and right, not the newer type that rise up. The headlights came on automatically, and I saw two men scrambling out of the way. I steered away, but still knocked one man down. In the rearview mirror I saw someone aiming a handgun at us. I turned right into the street just as I saw the blast and heard the sound of breaking glass. I stood on the accelerator, elated over how we'd managed to get away.

"Look out!" Tex said.

In the middle of the street was a group of men, and we were headed right for them. One had a machine gun under his arm, and we were close enough to see the grin on his face. I turned left as hard as I could, not knowing what it would take to set the van on its side. The machine gun went off about the same time as I began the turn, putting Tex in the line of fire. I kept driving.

Moments later, I straightened out the van, marveling over its ability to turn so far so fast. My foot was still on the accelerator when I realized we were in the middle of someone's front yard and heading for a huge tree. Another quick turn got us back on the street and away from the gunshots.

"Hey, are you okay?" I asked.

"I'm great," Tex said. "I think I may have another bullet notch in my wheelchair, though. But I didn't get hit, if that's what you mean. How'd you learn to drive like that, teach?"

"I don't know. I guess you never know what you can do until you're scared enough."

Tex laughed. A long, lyrical laugh—his happiest yet.

CHAPTER TEN

Well, so much for the van's maiden trip. We were headed home with dents in the front, smashed windows all around, bullet holes in the front, back, and right side, and no telling what else. I wasn't about to stop to survey the damage as long as the engine worked and continued to move us away from danger and toward home. I kept the van going as fast as I could, not caring if we got stopped by the law. We didn't pull over until we got to the first roadside park on Interstate 10 heading east, somewhere near Van Horn.

That's when the uncontrollable laughing began. I wasn't sure why. I'd never been so scared in my life. And I'd never had that much adrenalin pumped through so fast, either. It was exciting in a terrifying way. Helping Tex with the wheelchair, we climbed out to check the damage.

"Wow, look at the bullet holes," Tex said.

The passenger side and the back of the van were littered with holes. It is a wonder none of the bullets had hit Tex or me.

"Yeah," I said, "we're lucky to be alive."

The engine worked fine, and the tires looked good, so we climbed back into the van. That's when I remembered the sequence of numbers I'd found in the tunnel and why they looked familiar. I'd seen a similar series of digits on the van's navigation system screen. They were probably latitude and longitude numbers used by the tunnel diggers to help reach their destination. First, I opened the notepad on my iPhone and recorded the numbers so I wouldn't forget

them. Next, I entered them into the van's system as a destination to verify my theory. What I expected to see was a
map of the house in El Paso with the tunnel under it.

"Where we going?" Tex asked.

I kept typing. "It's not where we're going; I think it's
where we've been. Just checking on some numbers I saw
on the wall in the tunnel near the exit to the kitchen." The
navigation system took the numbers, marked the spot on
the map, and asked if we wanted guidance to get there.
"Whoa."

"Hey," Tex pointed at the map, "we haven't been to
Galveston."

I could feel my whole body relaxing. A clue. We'd
found a clue after all. I looked at Tex, and he was grinning,
and I knew I was, too.

"Nope. That's *where* we're going next. Another clue."

Now we could go home. But before I put the van in
gear, my cell phone rang. I looked at it and saw it was
Mother or Dad.

"Hello."

"Chris! Is that you? This isn't a recording, is it?"

I looked at Tex. "Mom? Yes, it's me."

"Thank God you're okay. Where are you?" she asked.

How did she know about the danger we'd been in? "Uh, I'm on
the road." I didn't want to worry her more with the details.

She didn't respond immediately. I looked at my phone
to see if I still had a connection.

"You don't know, do you?" she said, finally.

"Know what?"

Her words were choppy. I could tell she was upset.
"Your apartment was bombed. There was a body. The college called and said we should come." She sobbed.

"A body? In my apartment?" I pressed the speaker button on the phone so Tex could hear. "Mother, I'm okay. I

didn't know anything about it. I've been out of town. Have they identified the body?"

"Evidently not. They assumed it was you. Who else would be at your apartment? I'm so glad you're safe. We're coming anyway. Daddy has nonrefundable tickets for the flight, and you know how he is about not wasting money. I called your cell number by mistake. I was trying to call Millie, my next-door neighbor, to get her to watch Muffin. I was so upset about your death I must have hit the wrong button. I'm not used to these new-fangled phones. Oh, I still need to call Millie." She sobbed. "You're really okay?"

"I'm sorry, Mom. I should have told you about my trip." It was painful hearing her crying.

"I'll call the college and my apartment manager and tell them I'm okay." I had no idea who would have been in my apartment. Tim had been my only visitor lately.

"Good. When will you be back to Georgetown?"

"I'll be there by morning." I looked at Tex, and he nodded.

"Okay, call me when you get a place to stay. We arrive tomorrow around noon."

We said good-bye. I hadn't thought about having to find a place to stay and wondered what all had been destroyed.

***

When we got to Georgetown, Tex dropped me off at my apartment and took what was left of the van to his house. If I hadn't lived on the third floor, or if my apartment house had an elevator, I'm sure Tex would have wanted to come up and see the damage. I bet he wanted to get home and get some decent sleep. We had taken turns napping on the drive back from El Paso, but it wasn't the restful kind of sleep you get in your own bed. I suspected it would be a long time before I got a good night's sleep—I didn't know if I had a bed or not.

I climbed the steps to my apartment and found the door blocked with yellow plastic tape. I could see a man inside, though, with a pencil and notepad.

"Hello," I said loud enough for him to hear me.

"Who are you?" he asked as he walked toward me.

"I'm Chris McCowan. I live here." I looked around at the damage in the living room. "At least I used to live here."

He showed a badge. "I'm Detective Gonzales, Georgetown PD. You got any ID?" he asked.

I pulled out my billfold and passed my driver's license to him.

He looked at it, then me, and then back at it again. Finally, he returned the license. "Come in," he said, holding the tape out of the way. "We thought you were dead. Lucky you were out of town."

"Yeah, lucky. Do you know who it was?"

"Yes." He looked at the notepad he carried. "Name's Tim Jenkins. Friend of yours?"

Tim! Poor Tim broke in once too many times. "Friend? No, not really. I know who he was. He'd broken in twice before."

"Really, that's weird. Based on our investigation, he seems legit. Seems he's a sales rep for a Brussels-based automated brush manufacturing company. According to his home office, Jenkins was in the States making sales calls. The police found his rental car in your apartment parking lot, with product brochures and sample brushes." He looked at me as if waiting for me to explain what I knew about Tim. When I didn't respond, he continued. "According to his home office, he was staying here at this address—

your address. He had a key to the apartment in his pocket. Did you give him a key?"

"No," I said, "I asked the apartment manager to change the lock after the last time Tim Jenkins broke in."

"So," the investigator asked, "you found the guy in your apartment before? Did he say why he was here?"

I was so tired, and all I wanted to do was get this over with, grab some clothes if possible, and go find a place to sleep. But I had to tell him what I knew.

"I'm not sure who he is. He flashed a badge the way you did when I got here. I didn't have time to read it. He said he was law enforcement from England."

I decided not to tell him Tim also said he was a child-hood friend of Sarah's. It didn't matter. If he was a spy, the other agents would probably cover it up anyway. If he wasn't, everything he told me was probably fabricated as well.

"Hmm" was all he said as he rapidly made notes. When he stopped writing, he looked at me. "Can I see your cell phone?"

It was on my belt. I pulled it out of the holder and handed it to him.

He didn't take it. "That's okay. Just wanted to make sure you still had it."

"Why?" I asked.

"The bomb was ignited by an iPhone just like yours, and I wanted to rule yours out as the cause. Now, can you tell me where you were last night?"

Being on a covert mission in El Paso wasn't the best al-ibi in the world. But I could tell him where I was, and I had Tex to substantiate it.

"I was on the highway coming back from a business trip."

"Anyone with you?"

"Yes. Percy Thompson." I gave him Tex's phone number and address. "Can I look around now?" I asked. "I need to pick up some clothes and other necessities."

"Sure, we've taken photos and analyzed the damage—nothing left for us to do. I'll let the apartment manager know it's okay to start repairs."

"Thanks."

There was a chalk outline of a body in the hall near my office. The once beige walls were blackened in that area. The computer didn't seem to be damaged. I was surprised the floor wasn't more littered with debris. Perhaps the police had taken the bomb residue with them. The bedroom didn't seem to be damaged at all. I packed a suitcase with enough clothes for a week and grabbed the cash I had hidden away. I logged onto the computer long enough to make sure Carbonite had recently backed up. I could get to the files remotely with my laptop from the hotel.

I stopped by to talk to Joe, the apartment manager. He promised to have the place repaired and ready in a week, but I wasn't sure if I wanted to live there or not. I still didn't know if the bomb had been meant for me or for Tim.

When I got to the airport to pick up my parents, Mother hugged me forever. Once she knew for sure I was alive, she probably could've turned around and gone home, but Dad insisted they use the return tickets he'd purchased. He wasn't going to pay premium prices for last-minute tickets and not use them. Besides, he was out of school for break between semesters.

I dropped them off at a Holiday Inn near my apartment in Georgetown and got a room for myself. When they were settled in, I headed to Austin for the weekly Vengeance Squad meeting.

Liz and Tex were waiting when I walked into the conference room at the Austin History Center. I hoped they had a suggestion for what we should do next. I didn't. We had the clue, or possible clue, from El Paso, but I had this nagging feeling the FBI had orchestrated everything we'd done so far. If so, that meant Angela was involved. I'd talked to Dad on the way back from the airport about what I'd found in El Paso, even though Mom got upset. Dad said the tunnel fit with what he'd heard. He didn't know anything about Galveston, though.

Liz had her arms around me before I had a chance to sit. "Chris, dear, I'm so sorry about your apartment. We thought you were deceased. I'm glad no one called me to identify the body. I couldn't stand it if anything happened to you. You're like a son to me." She gave me a big kiss on the cheek to prove it.

I knew from what Tex'd told me that Liz had a grand-son she'd raised as her own who'd gone to prison for a bunch of DUIs. I moved away from her loving arms as gently as I could, wondering how anyone she'd mothered could have strayed from the straight and narrow enough to serve time.

"Thanks. I'm okay. My parents came anyway since they already had plane tickets."

Liz brushed her gray hair back with her hand. "Good. It's nice to have family with you during a crisis. So, have you found out who died in your apartment?"

Tex looked up from his computer. "Yeah, was it anybody we know?"

"We knew him all right." I scooted up to the table and moved my notepad to the center of the space before me, making sure the tablet lined up with the table's edge. "It was Tim." I glanced at Liz, then Tex, to check their reactions.

Liz gasped and sat in her chair. "That secret agent from

London?"

"Really?" Tex pushed away from the table and rolled over closer to me. "Did the police wonder why he was in your apartment?"

I shook my head. "I tried to tell them who he said he was, but I don't think they believed me. They think he's a salesman. And his home office in Brussels said his home address was the same as mine. From all they told me, maybe he was."

"Are you thinking he really wasn't an agent after all?" Liz asked.

I shrugged. "He showed me an ID that said MI5, but it could have been faked. He must not have had the identification on him when the police found his body. Of course, the killer could've taken it. In fact, whoever killed him could have switched his badge for the salesman ID. We don't know who he was for sure and probably never will. Only thing is, Angela vouched for him after our trip to Massachusetts. I wonder if she was duped, too."

"We'll have to ask her," Liz said.

Tex laughed. "That guy was always breaking in to your place. Too bad, huh?" He rolled back to his place at the table.

"Yeah," Liz said, "but whoever killed him may have thought it was you, Chris. Have you thought of that?"

"Yes I have," I said. "No way of knowing, though. Anyone heard from Angela?"

"Not me." Tex didn't look up from his computer. "Don't know about you, but after the last trip, I think we're better off without her."

Liz's brows rose quickly. "What do you mean? I thought she'd been helping with the investigation."

"We thought so, too," I said.

"So, what happened?" She looked at Tex.

Tex popped his eyes up from the computer screen just long enough to nod at me. "Tell her, Doc."

I checked to see if my notepad was still lined up parallel with the edge of the table, and of course, it was. I placed my pen next to it and twisted it recklessly to one side just to prove I could.

"We don't know for sure, but it seems the FBI might be dropping hints to send us out on these trips as a way of getting us out of the way or to do their dirty work. Either way, we're not making much progress, and we're beginning to feel like puppets. Do you agree, Tex?"

He didn't look up. "Yeah, mostly."

"I see," Liz said. "But finding that tunnel in El Paso was important, wasn't it? When I told my INS friend about it, he acted surprised and thanked me for letting him know."

I straightened my pen. Reckless wasn't me. "Yes, but is that tunnel related to Sarah's killers?"

"I sure don't see a connection," Tex said, typing as he spoke.

"The FBI may have wanted us to find the tunnel and tell INS. Meanwhile, we're off in El Paso and out of the FBI's way," I said.

"You didn't find anything to connect the immigrants to the killers?" Liz leaned in toward Tex as if she were trying to catch his eye.

He continued typing without looking up.

Liz focused on me and threw her hands in the air. "Well? Did you find anything at all?"

I shook my head. "All we found were those coordinates of a place in Galveston."

"We've got to go where the clues tell us," Tex said, looking up from his computer screen to focus on Liz. "But we don't know why—as usual."

"Hi, y'all," Angela said as she walked in sounding more like a Texan than usual. "Sorry I'm late."

I looked at Liz and held my forefinger in front of my lips while blocking the gesture from Angela with my other hand.

Liz didn't turn my way, so she missed the signal to keep quiet. She was on her feet hugging Angela. "I guess you heard that Tim guy was killed in Chris's apartment? Don't know why. They may've been trying to get Chris. Guess what? We're going to Galveston next."

There was a silence in the room for the longest time before Angela slammed her purse on the table, then stood next to where I sat, loudly addressing her comments to me. "Galveston? Are you crazy? Of course they're trying to kill you. You've got to stop this nonsense—now."

In the midst of her emotional outbreak, all I thought was how she all of a sudden had a British accent.

Liz sat with her hands clasped on the table, quiet for a change, and Tex closed his computer and leaned back in his wheelchair, both staring at Angela.

Angela had never sounded so angry before. "We looked the other way because you were grieving, but now it's over. They've found you and tried to kill you. If you continue with this stupid search, you're going to end up dead just like Tim. You're not going anywhere else. You're off the case."

"Off the case? What are you talking about? I don't work for you." I was close enough to feel the heat of her body and close enough to see the beginning of tears. She was upset, and I didn't think it was because of my safety.

She stared at me as if I were the only other person in the room.

"You know what I mean," she said. "I'm not going to help with your search anymore."

"Help? You call what you've done helping? If anything,

you've been sending us off on wild-goose chases." I looked to Tex for help, but both he and Liz remained silent.

Angela grabbed her purse. "Well, good. If that's what you think, you won't miss my help at all."

I was always surprised to see how fast Liz could move. She was up and standing between Angela and the door before I could say good-bye. "Angela, dear, I know you're concerned for Chris's safety, but I feel there's something else happening here. Surely, in your business, you can understand his need to pursue the killers, can't you?"

Angela didn't try to get past Liz, but she didn't answer right away. She lowered her head as if praying. We all waited until she looked up and spoke. "You never get used to people getting killed, even in my business."

Liz pulled Angela into a hug. "I know, dear, I know. This Tim—did you know him well?"

I couldn't hear Angela's response because Liz's shoulder muffled the sound, but I saw Angela nod affirmatively.

Liz patted her back. "Dear Lord, please comfort your child Angela and help her through her grief. Be with her as she goes from here back to work, and keep her safe. Dear God, also be with Tex and Chris as they try to solve the mystery of Sarah's death, and keep them out of harm's way."

"Amen," Tex said.

"Thank you," Angela said, "I appreciate that. Now, if you'll excuse me, I have to leave."

Angela's eyes focused on mine briefly before she turned and left the room. The anger I'd seen before Liz talked to her was gone. It felt like a silent "I'm sorry." Sarah had that look just before she died. My gunshot wound throbbed as I remembered.

Angela closed the door behind her and was gone. I had to talk to her to clear the air. I stepped toward the door to catch up with her, but before I reached the door, I tumbled to the floor.

"What the...?" Tex's voice boomed.

He rolled up to me, and Liz stood over me.

"I'm okay. My bum leg gave out."

"That's not supposed to happen," Tex said.

I sat up. "Well, I'm sorry, it did."

Liz held my hand. "Do you want me to call for help?"

"No, I'm fine." I stood up to prove it. "Sometimes the pain is so bad it is best to give in to it—that's all." I shook my leg. "See, it's okay."

They looked at me warily.

Tex rolled back to the table. "I thought you were over all that. You better get back into PT."

Liz was standing close by as if ready to catch me if I fell again. "Chris, you need to see a doctor about this. You shouldn't have to put up with pain for this long."

But I did have to suffer. The pain reminded me of Sarah's death, and it was my punishment for not protecting her.

"I know. But, really, it doesn't happen often."

Tex closed his computer. "I guess there's no sense in going to Galveston."

I was still stretching my leg. "Because of this? I told you—it's not serious."

"Not because of your leg," Tex said, "because of Angela. From what she said, we're not going to find anything there."

"On the contrary." For the first time since we began the search, I felt in charge. "She doesn't want us to go because of what we might find."

"We're gonna need the van," Tex said. "Will it be ready soon enough?"

"I forgot about that." I thought a minute about going

there alone, but I needed Tex.

"I'm afraid it's still in the repair shop. You guys messed it up pretty bad. I'm surprised you made it home. My financial backer asked if we wanted to get it armor-plated while it was in for repairs."

I looked at Tex. "What do you want to do?" Perhaps we should forget about going. We had no idea if we'd find anything in Galveston anyway.

"Hey, I've got an idea," Liz said. "How about a book-mobile? It has a wheelchair lift and Internet connection."

Tex smiled. "Why not? Should work. You don't need it?"

"It's not being used right now," Liz said. "This is one that doesn't belong to the city. I wouldn't be offering it if it did. A friend of mine owns it, and he's going out of town for the Christmas holidays. I'm sure he'd let us use it."

"Let's do it," I said.

We started planning our trip right then. We checked the coordinates on the map and found they pointed to the shipyard area in Galveston where the cruise ships were. We studied Google Earth and Google Maps and checked street photos in the area, looking for possible terrorist targets. Besides the cruise ships, there were several refineries in nearby Texas City.

My leg no longer bothered me, so I headed out. As soon as I left the Austin History Center, I pulled out my cell phone, intending to call Angela. I stared at the device for a long time before I put it away. I had no idea what to say to her.

***

Three days later, on Christmas day, Tex and I were in Galveston. Liz tried to talk us into waiting until after Christmas to go, but neither of us wanted to put it off. Tex had to leave his family alone, but he said his wife understood and supported his decision. My parents had already returned to California because Mom said they had several holiday obligations. Dad explained what she meant by that: They had tickets for a between-semester trip to Virgin Gorda she was dearly looking forward to. So we managed to get away without too much of a fuss. To be honest, I hadn't wanted to stay home for Christmas anyway. I didn't want to be there with all those memories.

The bookmobile Liz commandeered for us worked perfectly. It had everything we needed, plus the added feature that no one would suspect us of any vigilante activity while driving a vehicle like this one. Tex complained it wasn't set up for him to drive by hand, but I didn't mind doing all the driving. It had a state-of-the-art computer with Internet connection, so we were able to do research on the road.

We got to Galveston without a hitch. The beach and the smell of salt water reminded me of where I grew up in Redondo Beach, California, and I made a mental note to come back when I could enjoy it. Even in December, it was pleasant. The nice thoughts didn't last long. Memories of happiness reminded me of Sarah, and I knew life would never be enjoyable again.

The coordinates we found in El Paso led us to a warehouse a few blocks from the cruise ship terminal. The sign in front of the tall metal building said, "Westlake Moving and Storage Company." We parked in the empty lot and climbed out. Even though the bookmobile had a wheelchair lift, we didn't use it. Tex's arms were strong enough for him to climb out of the vehicle and into the wheelchair I'd setup for him.

The temperature was in the low seventies and quite comfortable. I wore a light, black London Fog jacket, mainly to hide the pistol I carried in an underarm holster. Tex had his gun in the backpack hanging behind his chair, where he carried everything else he might need. His weapon might seem out of reach, but I'd seen him practice drawing it, and he could have his gun out, cocked and ready, as fast as I could mine.

The sign on the door announced they were closed, which didn't surprise me since it was Christmas Day. I knocked on the door in case someone happened to be there and waited. We didn't have a plan, but we'd learned to work together easily when some playacting was necessary. This location was the only clue we had, and for all I knew, the series of numbers I'd found in the tunnel that led us there could mean any number of other things to the person who put them there.

No one opened the door, so I turned the knob and went in. Tex rolled in behind me.

If the moving storage company was still in business, they were lacking for customers. The place was empty.

"Anyone here?" My teacher voice seemed louder in the vacant space of the building as the sound bounced off the metal walls.

A rapid movement in the opposite corner, fifty yards or so away from where we were, caught my eye. I flipped off the strap that held my pistol in place.

"Did you see that?"

"Yeah," Tex rolled toward the place where I'd seen the movement. "Looked like a rat scurrying away—a human rat, that is."

I had to run to keep up with the wheelchair. When we got there, all we found was a door opened to the outside. I went out and looked in all directions. No one. There were several buildings nearby, and a person could have ducked behind one before we reached the door.

When I reentered the building, Tex had rolled up to a table close to where we'd seen the movement.

"Well, looky here, there's enough explosive in front of me to sink Galveston Island."

I had never seen a bomb, but what Tex pointed at reminded me of what I'd seen in the films featuring mad bombers. There were red sticks, wires, and clocks strewn about the table. It looked more like a supply cache than a bomb. None of the individual parts were connected together as far as I could tell, so I didn't feel we were in danger.

Then I saw something that did scare me.

"Tex, look at this. This is an ID card for a cruise ship employee. Do you think they plan to blow up a ship?"

"Sure looks like it." He rolled over to the wall and pulled a coat from the hanger. "This uniform matches the ID card."

I dreaded the thought of being tied down in a lengthy police investigation and having to explain why we were there, but we didn't have a choice. We had to report this—and the sooner the better.

"We have to call the police. There could be bombs on the cruise ship already."

Tex rolled toward the door we had entered. "I know. I was just thinking the same thing. But let's do it from the bookmobile. I want to put away this gun first."

I pulled out my iPhone and took photos of the bomb ingredients and everything on the table. I also took shots of the rest of that end of the building, making sure the cruise ship coat was included. Before putting away my phone, I emailed the images to my computer.

"Freeze!" The command came from one of the dozen or so police officers who appeared suddenly at both ends of the building.

Tex was halfway across the warehouse. He stopped and

raised his hands.

I was surprised to find myself on the floor with my hands cuffed behind me before I had a chance to raise them. *How silly*, I thought, since we were on our way to call the police.

"We're not the bad guys here," I said, with more indignation than I should have for a person trussed face down on a dusty concrete floor.

"Shut up!" A burly guy in a black uniform patted my chest. "He's carrying," the man yelled out. "Watch that guy in the wheelchair. He probably is, too."

I felt the weight of my Glock 19 holster lighten as the gun was jerked away from my body, leaving me feeling more vulnerable, if that was possible.

"Hey, I have a permit for that. Check my ID." I reached for my billfold with my shackled hands, but it was gone. I looked around to see one of the police officers holding my billfold in one hand and my driver's license in another.

The guy holding my wallet leaned into a microphone on his shoulder. "Anything on a Christopher J. McCowan— Texas driver's license number five-five-five-three-four-six-seven?"

Tex was thirty or forty yards away, so I couldn't hear what was going on with him, but I suspected he was getting the same treatment I was getting. It was a bother, but I wasn't worried, because as soon as the police checked us out, we'd be free to leave.

The guy with my driver's license turned his attention to me. "Okay. If this is really you, you have a permit for the piece."

"Of course it's me. That's my photo, right?"

He pulled out another driver's license. The one I had hidden in the bill section of my billfold and forgotten about.

He held it up as if examining it. "And this one looks like you, too. Only thing is, the name on it is Ken Campbell. And you've got credit cards under both names. Now, who are you, and what are you doing in here?"

Yikes. I wish I hadn't let Tex talk me into that fake ID. Of course he had told me not to carry both IDs with me at the same time. I was glad he'd made me get that concealed weapon permit. As soon as I explained I was getting ready to call the police, I was sure they'd let us go.

They hadn't taken the cuffs off—probably just forgot.

"We knocked on the door, and when no one answered, we walked in. Some guy ran out the back door, so we looked around. That's when we saw the bomb stuff and decided we better call the police." I nodded toward the table behind the policeman.

The cop glanced at the table, and then two of them pulled me to my feet.

"Let's get out of here," the burly one said as they ushered me toward the front door.

When we were outside, he pushed the button on his microphone. "Possible bomb here. We're evacuating. Please send the bomb squad to investigate."

"Can't you take these handcuffs off now? I was just getting ready to call you when you got here," I said to the policeman who was still holding my billfold.

Instead of a key to free me, he pulled a crinkled card out of his pocket and read it: "You have the right to remain silent. Anything you say can and will be used against you in a court of law. You have the right to an attorney. If you cannot afford an attorney, one will be appointed to you. Do you understand these rights as they have been read to you?"

What was he talking about? Why was he reading me my rights? "You're not arresting me, are you?"

"We're arresting you for breaking and entering."

I still had the cuffs on when they loaded me into a black van and drove off. I didn't know where Tex was.

CHAPTER ELEVEN

They put me in a small holding cell at the Galveston Police Station without booking me. One of the guards said I'd probably be released soon since he'd heard they had no reason to hold me. But then he came back and said there'd been an explosion of a cruise ship, and they decided to book me. I was photographed, fingerprinted, and moved to a larger, private cell alongside other prisoners.

I started to call Angela when I was offered a phone call, thinking she might have more pull with the police, but I called Dad instead. He was in an airport in Los Angeles and wanted to cancel his trip and come to Galveston. I talked him out of it by telling him the police would learn I had nothing to do with the cruise ship bombing. They would find out that Tex and I had helped the investigation by discovering the place where the bomb was probably made. Dad's voice was more serious than I'd heard in some time while he was probably making his decision about coming or not. Finally, he said for me not to worry because he'd take care of everything.

I didn't know if all the jail scuttlebutt was accurate or not, but based on what I'd heard from jailers and inmates, the bomb had exploded in the crew's quarters on the cruise ship. The ship's name was the same as the name on the ID card Tex and I had found in the warehouse. Since the explosion was below the water line, the ship sunk quickly. No one in the jail rumor mill knew how many people had been lost, but I heard there were other ships in the area picking up survivors.

Sitting alone on the steel bed, I couldn't help thinking the bombing could have been prevented if we'd found the cruise ship uniform sooner and acted faster. I had this nagging feeling of responsibility for what had happened. Maybe I shouldn't have tried to do anything about Sarah's death. I was clearly in over my head. And then there was Tex. He could have ended up in prison again for helping me. I didn't know if he was still on parole or not, and I wasn't sure if he had a permit to carry a weapon. What he'd said in the warehouse about putting his gun away before we called the police made me doubt it. They probably don't let ex-cons have permits.

I stretched out on the small metal bed to ponder what to do next. This was one of those times I wished I could pray—or had someone to pray to.

I may have drifted off. I'm not sure, but I felt as if I were waking from a deep sleep when I heard a voice call my name. I sat up and saw a tall black man standing outside my cell.

"Hi, Son," he said. "It's Christmas. I thought you might like a little company."

I stared at him with what I knew must be hate as I walked to the bars where he stood. I could see the word *Chaplain* on a bright-red badge attached to the left lapel of his dark-blue coat. My stare didn't faze him. His smile warmed the cell. I didn't care. He was the last person in the world I wanted to talk to. *Christmas. Hmph. Christmas without Sarah. I'd never celebrate Christmas again.*

"Didn't you read my booking form?" I said it loud enough for the other inmates to hear. "I wrote atheist on it where it asked about denomination." Atheist may have been too strong. Maybe I was agnostic. Maybe I didn't know. That made me laugh—the not knowing part.

"I read it. Doesn't matter what you wrote—I can see in your heart that you love your Lord and God and always will."

I laughed. "That's funny. If you could look into my heart, you might be surprised at what you'd see. You might have to run tell the guards what you see there." I turned and walked to the back of the small cell to put distance between us.

"I know, Son. That's why I'm here—to help you get beyond your loss so you can feel the love of God once more."

When he said the word *loss*, I turned around quickly to face him. Then it hit me, he was just guessing. He didn't know about Sarah.

I laughed again and sat on the edge of my cot.

"I'm praying for you, Son," the black man said. "Here's a Bible for when you're ready for it."

He was silent after that. I couldn't resist looking to see if he had left, and when I did, he was nowhere in sight. He'd placed the Bible just inside the bars on the floor. I wanted to leave it there and let him find it sitting in the same place after I was out of there, but I couldn't. There was a piece of paper sticking out of one side, and it was crooked. Sometimes I hated this obsession of mine for neatness. I wasn't tempted to read the piece of paper, yet I couldn't resist straightening it.

I stood and quietly walked to the bars. I looked as far as I could to the left and then the right. No one was in sight. I picked up the Bible and grabbed the paper to make it line up with the pages of the Bible, but it wouldn't move. It was stuck inside somehow. I opened the Bible to release the skewed paper, and when I did, I saw the slip of paper was blank. There was, however, a Bible verse highlighted in yellow. I was compelled to read it. The verse marked was Romans 12:19. I knew it because of my so-called photographic memory: "Beloved, never avenge yourselves, but leave room for the wrath of God; for it is written, 'Vengeance is mine. I will repay, says the Lord.'"

I felt a chill, but shook it off. It was just a coincidence. That verse would probably apply to most of the guys there. I flipped through the pages of the Bible looking for more yellow ink. I found two more. The first was Colossians 3:13: "Bear with one another and, if anyone has a complaint against another, forgive each other; just as the Lord has forgiven you, so you also must forgive." The third verse I found marked in yellow ink shocked me even more. It was Matthew 28:20: "…and teaching them to obey everything that I have commanded you. And remember, I am with you always, to the end of the age."

A strange feeling surrounded me, and I knew the Bible readings were for me. God was with me, even there.

I knelt on the concrete with my elbows on the cold metal bed and bowed my head. Nothing happened, but I didn't give up. I stayed there for several minutes, feeling the coldness of the cell, smelling the odor of previous occupants, and trying not to think about the pain in my leg that was worse when I knelt. I wanted to pray, but couldn't. "Help me" was all I could say, so I repeated it over and over again until a sense of comfort enveloped me. That's when I knew God was with me. I felt His strength surround my body. Even the throbbing in my leg from the gunshot wound was gone. I was at peace and pain free for the first time since Sarah's death. It was then I realized God had always been with me. He hadn't abandoned me although I'd doubted His love and even His existence. Now I could pray.

"Dear God, thank You," I said aloud. "I feel Your power and know You're with me here in this cell. I don't know what to do, but I know I will look for your guidance. Forgive me, Lord. Forgive me for my doubts. And, please Lord, help my friend Tex. Amen."

After my prayer, I was so relaxed I stretched out on the cot and rested.

I woke up the next morning energized for the first time since Sarah's death. Even my leg felt better. I walked around the cell trying to find the pain that had plagued me for so long. I did deep knee bends and twists, but nothing I did caused the pain to return.

I saw the Bible setting on the floor near my cot. I thought about my conversation with the chaplain and felt a need to apologize to him for the way I'd treated him.

"Guard," I called out.

"Yeah?" A beer-bellied guard appeared.

"I'd like to talk to the chaplain."

"Okay. We don't have a staff chaplain, but I'll put in a request, and they'll send someone over."

"I don't want just anyone; I want the guy who was here last night. I need to talk to him."

"Last night? There weren't any chaplains here last night."

"Yes, there was—black guy in a dark-blue suit. I talked to him myself."

"Sorry, don't know anyone like that. Do you still want a chaplain or not?"

That's strange. "No, I guess not."

A while later, another guard showed up and took me to a conference room, where I met with two men dressed in business suits, complete with white shirts and solid-colored ties. One held out a welcoming hand.

"Hello, Chris," he said as he shook my hand. "I'm Charles Morris. This is my partner, Nathan Bitely." Morris pushed an opened billfold toward me showing a badge and an ID card—FBI.

"Thanks for coming. When can I get out of here?" I wanted to find Tex and get back to the search.

"We're working on it," Bitely said. "You doing okay?"

"I'm good. What about my friend Tex?" I sat at the table in the center of the room, and the agents joined me.

Morris responded this time. "We were told to get you out—that's all. The paperwork for your release is being processed as we speak. We're just here to let you know not to worry. You'll be free soon."

"I can't leave without Tex." I was calmer than I'd been in so long that it was weird.

"You'd better," Morris said. "If you're talking about a Mr. Percy Thompson, your friend is an ex-con, and the state wants to check him out a little closer. It didn't help that he was carrying a gun without a permit."

"See what you can do. Did my father call you?"

"We have orders to get you out of here," Bitely said. "We don't know where the orders come from. Suffice it to say you have some pull from on high."

Both agents rose, and Bitely moved toward the door.

"Just a minute," Morris said to his partner, and then he turned to me. "Chris, we know what you're doing. We understand your need to find those who killed your fiancée, but let's be honest, you're not going to succeed no matter how hard you try. If you continue the search, you're going to either get yourself killed or cause the deaths of others. I know you mean well. It's just that you're dealing with some characters who are so bad they'll kill anyone for any reason. Let us take care of the revenge you're seeking. Go home. Enjoy your life. Oh, and by the way, we're destroying your fake ID and credit cards."

I never wanted the fake ID and stuff anyway, but, for some reason, I started thinking of ways to get some more.

What was happening to me? I was starting to think like Tex.

Shortly after I got back to my cell, I was released. While I was getting my personal property, I asked about Tex.

"The guy in the wheelchair?" the desk sergeant asked. "He's out on bail. Some fancy lawyer from Austin showed up this morning and checked him out already. His attorney asked about you, but by then the feds had sprung you. Who are you guys, anyway?"

I wasn't surprised. If Tex had called Liz, she'd probably sent the attorney for us.

"Nobody," I said. "Nobody important. Thanks for your help." I took my stuff and turned to leave.

"Your friend in the wheelchair hasn't been gone long," the guard said. "He's probably still out front."

I found Tex near the front entrance talking to a man in a gray suit.

When Tex saw me, he swung his chair around to face me with his usual infectious smile. "Hey, what took you so long?"

Liz was there, too, which I learned as soon as she hugged me.

"What are you doing here?" I asked. I could understand her sending an attorney, but I was surprised to see her there, too.

"Where else would I be when my friends are in trouble?" She leaned back to look me in the eye, and I saw hers were moist.

We hadn't been separated long, but it was a relief to see them again—especially Tex. I didn't want to be the cause of his going back to prison.

I nodded to the man in gray. "Who's your friend?" I asked Tex.

His friend spoke for himself as he held out his hand toward me. "Hi, you must be Chris. I'm T.H. Worthington.

Ms. Siedo asked me to get you two out of jail, but I understand you have some federal friends."

"Nice to meet you," I said. "My father works for the FBI. That comes in handy from time to time." Tex raised his brows at my admitting who my contact was, but I didn't care. No need to keep that secret anymore. I didn't need any secrets—not now, not with God back on my side.

I faced Tex. "Are you free to leave this place?"

He looked at Worthington, who answered for him. "When you walked up, I was just about to tell him he could leave town as long as he comes back for the arraignment."

"When's that, boss?" Tex asked.

"Two weeks from today—unless we can get them to drop the charges. Once they investigate the cruise ship bombing, I think they'll learn you two actually helped them find a clue to the bombers and may have prevented other ships from being damaged. If I'm right, they'll set you free."

Tex laughed. "Yeah, we led the police to the bomb factory, didn't we?"

"Did anyone get killed in the cruise ship bombing?" I asked. "All I heard in jail were rumors. What really happened?"

Worthington cleared his throat. "Well, I don't know if the news media are being told everything at this point, but what we're hearing is that the bomb may have gone off prematurely. Some crew members are missing—presumably, the bomber is included in the missing—but no passengers were killed. Luckily, they were still in Galveston bay when the explosion happened, and the other ships were able to quickly assist in picking up survivors."

I was thankful for that. I still felt some responsibility for the cruise ship explosion, but I didn't know what I could have done differently.

I turned to Worthington. "Did either you or Tex hear

anything about how the cops knew we were in the warehouse?" I was thinking about clues. Even after all that had happened, I still wanted to continue the search.

"Yes," Worthington said, "some woman called the police. She didn't tell them anything except it was critical for them to go the warehouse. The call couldn't be traced."

Angela. Was this something she'd do? "A woman, huh?" I looked at Tex and could tell by his nod he was thinking the same thing I was.

"Can I give you a ride anywhere?" Worthington asked. "I need to get back to the airport."

I moved behind Tex's chair to help him over a curb. "Where's your car, Liz?" I asked.

"Car?" She looked at me as if I were crazy. "I'd never drive all this way."

"So, how'd you get here?" Tex asked.

She crossed her arms and planted her feet in place. "Greyhound bus."

I turned to the attorney. "Yes, we need a ride. Our vehicle is at the warehouse where we were arrested, unless the police impounded it."

The bookmobile was where we'd left it in the parking lot of the moving and storage company. I helped Tex climb into the backseat, where the computer was, and offered the front passenger seat to Liz. I wished I could have been in the back with the computer to see if I could learn more about the cruise ship explosion, but that wasn't possible. The bookmobile wasn't set up for Tex to drive, and I didn't want to consider letting Liz behind the wheel.

This trip had brought us closer to the killers, but we were still far from finding them. We had another indication of what they were capable of doing, and I was more determined than ever to stop them. But the situation had changed. With God back in my life, I was confident for the first time about what I was doing.

As I stood outside the van folding the wheelchair, a woman came up to me. She appeared to be in her forties, plainly dressed, wearing a bulky black coat. Tears moistened her cheeks, and she shook slightly. I couldn't help thinking she wasn't merely frightened, but afraid for her life.

"Please, sir," she said, "will you help me find my boy?"

Liz was out of the van and by my side in a wink, and the next thing I knew, she had the stranger in her arms. The woman sobbed more, but she was no longer quivering. "There, there," Liz said as she patted the woman on the back.

"They killed my husband. Now they have my son." Her lips shook when she finished speaking.

I suspected a drug deal gone bad and didn't think there was much we could do except call the police for her. I wished we could do more to help, but I didn't want to be stuck there any longer than we had to. Still, I felt compelled to do what I could for this poor woman. We had nowhere to go. We could take a little time to listen. I held her hands to comfort her and get her attention.

"You're safe with us. Tell us what happened, and we'll see what we can do to help."

She looked at me for several seconds before she responded. "Thank you, sir. I thought I could trust you. I've been waiting for you to come back for this…." She pointed at the bookmobile, evidently not sure what to call it. "I called the police yesterday. I didn't mean for them to arrest you. I wanted them to arrest my husband and my son, but they both sneaked away before the police got here."

"Just a minute," I said. "Let's step inside to talk." I wanted to include Tex, and it was easier for us to climb aboard than to have him join us there. When we were inside the bookmobile, I said to Tex. "She's the one who called the police."

"You called the police?" Tex asked. "But why?"

I turned to Tex. "She said she called them to stop her husband and son, but they got away before the police arrived. That's probably who we saw leaving the warehouse when we got there."

"Why did you want your husband and son arrested?" Tex asked.

She held her head down. "To keep them alive."

Liz rubbed the woman's shoulder. "What do you mean?"

"The cruise ship…you know, the bomb. My husband did it. They made him do it. Now they've got my son, and they're going to kill him, too," she wailed. "Help me. He's just a boy. He doesn't know what he's doing."

I pointed at the warehouse. "Your husband and son worked here?"

She looked at me and nodded.

"Who did they work for?" Tex asked.

She shrugged. "I didn't know. But after what happened to the ship, I think they might be one of those suicide bombers you hear about in the news."

I looked at Liz and saw the anxiety in her eyes. I turned back to the woman. "Where's your son now?" I asked.

She opened her purse and pulled out a piece of paper. When it was unfolded, I saw a drawing.

"What's that?"

"I'm not sure. I found it in my son's room. Maybe this will help you find him?" She pushed the drawing toward me.

I took the paper and looked at the map and recognized it was a rough diagram of downtown Houston. This was where they were going next, and we had to find them fast.

"Do you have a picture of your son?"

She smiled, dug into her purse, and pulled out a picture of a young man, kissing it before giving it to me. "This was taken last year. He's seventeen."

I took the photo from her, looked at the innocence in his eyes, and wondered how he'd been convinced to join in such evil as a suicide bombing.

"What else can you tell us? Is he wearing anything unusual?"

"He took his violin. He plays in the high school orchestra and is quite good. They told him to take it. He carried it separately, making me wonder why he didn't put it in the case. He took the case, too. You need to hurry, though. He left an hour ago and acted as if he was in a hurry."

I focused on the woman and made sure she was looking at me. "Okay, we'll look for him and try to stop him. But you have to tell the police everything you told us. Will you do that?"

She nodded slowly while maintaining eye contact, and I knew she meant it.

After the woman left, I shut the door, Liz took her place in the passenger seat, and I sat behind the steering wheel. We waved at the woman left standing alone in the empty parking lot.

"Where can we drop you off, Liz?" I asked as we headed toward Houston.

She laughed. "You're not getting rid of me. There's something powerful cooking in Houston, and I want to see what it is."

Bits of information were beginning to fall into place in my head, and if my suspicions were right, I didn't want Liz to go with us. But once she picked up the scent of something exciting, I knew from experience it was next to impossible to distract her.

I waved the paper the woman had given me in the air

where Liz could see it. "There's no telling how long we're going to be searching for this kid. This drawing covers a lot of downtown Houston. You can't sit in the van all day waiting for us to search the area." Actually, the map focused on a tunnel in one building, but I didn't want Liz to know that.

"I don't intend to sit around," Liz said. "I'm going with you. I can help."

She didn't have any idea what we were getting into. None of us did, really, but I knew I didn't want to worry about her safety while we looked for the killers. It was enough to have Tex with me, but at least he could help in his special ways.

"Liz, I'd feel more comfortable if you took the bus back to Austin. We could be here for days."

Liz shook her head. "I don't care. I'm here; I'm staying. God must want me here, or it wouldn't have happened this way."

"That reminds me," I said. "I prayed last night for the first time since Sarah died, and it felt right. It wasn't what I expected from God. I felt loved and encouraged to continue the search."

"Welcome back, teach," Tex said with laughter in his voice.

"Thank you, Jesus," Liz said.

Liz was right. We were all there at this time and place for a reason, but I still didn't like taking her into what was sure to be a dangerous situation. Tex and I needed to concentrate on finding the kid and following him to the gang leaders. Liz was agile for her age and size, so I wasn't concerned about her keeping up. What worried me most was that she might try to talk the killers into giving up, or worst yet, hug them into submission.

"Liz, how would you feel about setting up a command

post in a nearby hotel? We all have our cell phones, so Tex and I can give you status reports and keep you up-to-date on what's going on. You can coordinate with the police if it is needed."

Tex spoke loudly to be heard from the backseat. "I have a suggestion: Let's split up when we get there so we can cover the area in less time. Liz can go with me."

"Are you sure?" I asked.

Liz snorted. "You don't have to worry about me. I can take care of myself. I feel like the kid neither team wants."

"I just said I want you to go with me," Tex said. "You're my first choice."

"Only choice," she corrected, feigning hurt feelings.

I concentrated on driving. If she went with Tex, I'd still worry about her, but I could do my job better that way.

"Okay," I said.

As we drove into downtown Houston, I followed the hand-drawn map the woman had given us, seeing it clearly in my mind. After parking near the Wells Fargo Plaza, about where a large X had been drawn, I went to the back of the bookmobile where Tex sat and turned the computer around so I could see it. I found a map of the downtown area of Houston and matched it to the landmarks on the drawing.

Then I switched to *Wikipedia* to learn more about the area. That's where I learned there was a seven-mile tunnel about twenty feet below the streets in downtown Houston that connected many of the buildings. Employees of the businesses in the area as well as customers used the tunnels to protect themselves against rain and hot summers.

I held out the hand-drawn map and matched it up with key buildings along the tunnel's route. "Look at this," I said. "See how the X on the map is right where we are?"

"What's here?" Tex asked.

"It's a bank. According to the Internet, there is a street-level opening to seven miles of tunnels. Our map shows a big X about where the entrance should be. After that I'm not sure where we go. We can split up when we get in the tunnel, like you suggested."

"Sounds good," Tex said.

"I'll go with Percy," Liz said, looking at me for a reaction she wouldn't get. She was the only person I knew who called Tex by his real name, and every time she did, I wondered whom she was talking about.

With somewhat of a plan in place, I picked up the phone to take care of another matter.

"Hello," she answered on the first ring.

That surprised me. I'd already planned to leave a message since Angela usually didn't answer her phone.

"Hi, I'm glad I caught you. You've heard about the ship bombing, right?"

"Yes." She spoke confidently, but with little volume and enthusiasm. Perhaps she was not at a place where she could talk.

"Tex, Liz, and I are following a lead we got in Galveston, and we are going into a tunnel near the Wells Fargo Plaza in Houston."

"Why?" Angela asked.

"We learned the son of the ship bomber is here, possibly with explosives in a violin case."

"Oh no!"

Click.

I looked at my phone and saw the call had ended.

***

When we got to the tunnel below the Wells Fargo Plaza, I turned to the right for no particular reason. Tex and Liz took the left route.

"Wait," Tex said, "did the cops give you your weapon back?"

I turned back to face them and patted by chest holster. "Yes. You?" I thought about the time I'd spent with Tex at the pistol range in Pflugerville and wondered what would happen if I had to use my gun there in the tunnel. I knew I had a knack for shooting, but I also knew it'd be different aiming at a human instead of a paper target. "Thou shalt not kill" smacked me in the face.

"Nope, they kept mine."

"We don't need a gun," Liz said. She pushed the wheelchair down the corridor to the left, not waiting for the conversation to be over.

"I can do it," Tex said, grabbing the wheel handles.

I watched as they moved away. "Stay in touch by phone, okay?"

When they were well on their way, I turned and walked in the opposite direction. It wasn't long before I heard the violin music. It was beautiful, lilting music—sad in a way, but full of force. It wasn't the music you'd expect from a seventeen-year-old kid bent on blowing himself to bits.

I walked toward the music, planning to go past the violinist when I got there so as not to alarm him as I studied the situation. When I got to where he was, I tried to keep my head aimed down the passageway while turning my eyes toward him. When I saw who was with him, I couldn't go through with my plan. Instead, I stopped to verify that it really was Angela standing next to the kid. There was an accordion hanging around her neck, but I couldn't see her hands.

Angela nodded toward the violinist and formed a silent "shh" with her lips.

I stood in front of the violinist as if I were enjoying the

music, but what I was really doing was trying to figure out why Angela was there. *Why didn't she arrest the guy? Was she waiting for the kid's contacts to arrive?* I didn't want to mess up what she was doing, but what I saw didn't make sense. I pulled some bills out of my pocket, and as I leaned over to place them in the empty violin case sitting opened in front of the young man, I saw Angela's hands were behind her back. She must have figured out what I was doing because she turned ever so slightly to her left to show me the rope around her wrists. I dropped the bills in the box and turned to leave. Instead, I pulled my pistol and turned back to the violinist.

He dropped his violin and ran.

I aimed at him with my gun and considered where to put the bullet. He was only seventeen, and I didn't want to kill him.

"Don't shoot, Chris," Angela said.

I still had the gun aimed at the kid as he rounded the corner and went out of sight.

"Chris, help me get this bomb off before they detonate it."

"What?" I put away my gun and walked to Angela.

"This," she said, nodding at the accordion. "It's packed with explosives."

I took the accordion off her shoulders and placed it gently on the floor.

"Get this rope off me. We need to get out of here."

When the rope was removed, she rubbed her wrists. "Thanks. Do you have a phone?"

"Here." I handed her my cell phone.

She tapped in some numbers and waited. "Angela here. I'm in sector B14 with explosives in an accordion. Suspect got away, and he may have the detonators." She listened. "Okay, I understand. I'm leaving now." She hung up and handed the phone back to me. "Let's go. They're sending the bomb squad, and they want us to leave the area."

She was six feet ahead of me when she turned around to face me. "I guess you don't understand the urgency here."

"You mean to get away from the bomb?" I walked slowly toward her.

"No. You must not have seen the news—the president is here."

When I reached her, we both walked a little faster away from the bomb back toward where I'd entered the passageway.

"The president of the United States is here, in Houston?"

"He's here in this tunnel—now." She said, enunciating each word carefully.

I looked back to where we had left the accordion. "All this time I thought they were trying to topple the buildings around here."

Angela grabbed my hand and pulled me along. "We've got to hurry. I'm sure they'd love to knock down every building in town, but with all the reinforced concrete here, that bomb wouldn't do it. They were after a human target; that bomb was intended for the president."

"At least we know where the explosives are and can keep the president away. Do you think there are more bombs around here?" I asked.

"Don't know. They usually have backups. I wouldn't be surprised if we learn there are several other suicide bombers here."

I was alongside her, and she dropped her grip on my hand. We continued walking rapidly side by side. Soon, we passed the point where I'd entered the tunnel with Tex and Liz. We kept walking, but I wanted to grab her and look her in the eye. She knew who the killers were. She talked about them as if she knew them well.

"Who are they?" I had to know.

"Al-Qaeda," she said without slowing down.

We reached a T in the passageway, and Angela immediately went left. She must have known where she was going. Then she stopped. I thought she'd changed her mind and we were going to backtrack and go the other way. Then I saw what she'd seen.

Liz was sprawled on the floor in front of Tex's wheelchair. The Galveston woman's son stood behind Tex with a pistol pointed at the back of his head. Another man with a gun stood nearby. Now it was too late to surprise them. We had been spotted and had nowhere to go.

I was surprisingly calm. I said a quick prayer and moved closer. Angela stood on my right and held out her hand to stop me from going any closer to Liz and Tex.

"Are you okay, Liz?" I asked.

She nodded, but I could tell by her voice she was frightened.

I glanced at Tex. "What happened?"

Tex spoke rapidly. "After we hit this dead end, we turned back toward the way you'd gone, and we saw this character. I tried to stop him and would have if his buddy here hadn't shown up."

We had one weapon up against two, but it was the pistol held a few inches from Tex's head that worried me most. *Tell me what to do, Lord.* I had to shoot the one nearest Tex first and make sure he didn't live long enough to pull the trigger. Then I would have to shoot the other man before he shot any of us. I couldn't believe God would put me in this position.

"Tex, don't stand up," I said as I pulled out my pistol and aimed it at him. The guy behind Tex laughed at what I said, and that gave me enough time to shoot first. Everything I'd learned at the pistol range came back to me as I pulled the trigger. I remembered the smirk on the killer's face when he shot Sarah, but I also remembered the look on this gunman's mother and my promise to find her son. Still, it had to be done.

I didn't look to see what happened to the seventeen-year-old. I did what I'd seen TV cops do. I hit the ground, rolled, and took a shot at the other guy, hitting him before he could get a round off.

Angela grabbed the guns of the two people I'd shot, and then she pulled Liz and Tex out of the way. The seventeen-year-old was alive. His right hand was bleeding. It was the first time I'd missed my target. Because of my promise to his mother, I'd aimed at his gun rather than his body and had hit his index finger instead. I was lucky the impact of the bullet hadn't caused him to pull the trigger and shoot Tex. I hadn't thought about that possibility until just then. The kid was alive and not seriously wounded, but he was probably too brainwashed to go back to being a normal teenager.

The other guy wasn't so lucky since I had to fire so quickly. Angela checked his pulse and shook her head.

I handed her my cell phone. "Get us some help here, please," I said.

She tapped in some numbers while I checked on Tex and Liz.

"Angela here. We've got two down in C3—one DOA. Civilians okay. Did you stop the president?"

There wasn't time for a response because of the explosion. It was probably the accordion; however, it was so loud I wondered if it was closer. *Were the exits still open? Would we be able to get out of here?*

I turned toward the laughter to see the seventeen-year-old holding an iPhone in his bloody hand.

"The detonator!" I ran to him and jerked it out of his hands, which seemed a little foolish since the bomb had already gone off.

"The phone's from Albuquerque," Tex said.

"We should have searched him," Angela said. "I know better. There was too much going on." She pushed the kid up against the wall and searched him.

"Let me borrow one of your costumes, Tex."

He reached around to his backpack and pulled out a shirt. I used part of it to bandage the violinist and the other part to tie his hands behind him.

"We better get out of here," I said. "We don't know whether there are more bombs or not."

The young man laughed again, this time a long, mad howl. "You'll never get away. We'll keep coming until all infidels are dead."

Angela helped Liz while I shepherded the kid. Tex was moving ahead of us all. He found the exit and waited for us to catch up, then he took the elevator, while the rest of us went up the steps. As soon as we walked out of the building, we were surrounded by a mob of police and news cameras.

CHAPTER TWELVE

Angela showed the police officers her badge, and two of them took the young violinist from her and handcuffed him. All the while, I watched as dozens of uniformed officers swarmed into the tunnel passageway we had just left.

I grabbed one of the police officers standing near the door to the elevator. "Watch for our friend coming up on the elevator. He's in a wheelchair."

The police officer nodded and opened the door to go in, but before he went into the building, I saw Tex rolling toward us.

Liz and I stood next to Tex as Angela talked to some guy in a black suit. The large video cameras aimed at her followed as she walked toward us. Liz smoothed her hair, and Tex sat up straighter. The news people were restrained by a barricade and were far enough away that they couldn't possibly hear what we were saying.

Angela spoke softly. "The president is okay. Three more bombs were found in the tunnel and disarmed. They've arrested about a dozen Islamic extremists." She paused and looked at each of us individually. "Thanks to you three, there's no longer a threat here."

I felt a relief I hadn't experienced since Sarah's death. We had finally done what we set out to do. I looked at Angela, not sure what to say.

She grinned. "Come on, someone wants to thank you personally."

We followed her to the street, where I saw a caravan of

black SUVs lined up at the curb surrounded by uniformed police.

A man dressed in a business suit led us to the vehicle in the middle. "Get in, he said."

I looked at Tex. "My friend prefers to wait here."

The man who had told us to get in opened the door and leaned into the vehicle. We couldn't hear what he said. Shortly afterward, he moved back out of the way, and the president of the United States stepped out of the SUV and stood smiling at the four of us.

"Angela, good to see you again. I should have known you'd be involved in this."

"I do what it takes, Mr. President," Angela said in a lilting English accent Chris had only heard when she'd gotten upset once. "But it wasn't me this time. My three friends here are the ones to thank." She held out an arm toward Liz, Tex, and me as she bowed ever so slightly.

"This is Chris McCowan. When his fiancée was murdered during a robbery, he went after the killers and wouldn't stop until we caught them today."

The president shook my hand. I thought how different he looked in person. He looked me in the eye as if I were the only person on earth.

"Thank you, Chris. We need more citizens like you."

I wished Sarah could have been there to share that moment with me. Then I thought about Angela. The president as much as said she'd saved his life before. *How could I have doubted her?*

"Thank you, sir," I said as I shook his hand. That was all I could think of to say.

Angela turned next to Tex. "This is Percy Thompson. We call him Tex. He helped Chris with the shadier sides of the search, but he's been clean for a long time."

Tex had never once been at a loss for words, but he

was silent. All of a sudden, he sat up straight and saluted, with the tip of his fingers touching the brim of his cowboy hat. Then, as if he remembered he wasn't in uniform, he removed his hat and held it reverently against his chest, looking at the president with admiration.

The president saluted him back. "Thank you, Tex."

I saw tears forming in Tex's eyes, and I knew why. Before his accident, he'd wanted to fight for his country, and now he had.

Liz stood at attention as the president approached her, but as soon as he turned his attention to her, she had her arms around him. A Secret Service–looking woman and man moved in, but Angela signaled them not to stop Liz.

"It's okay. This is Liz Siedo, Mr. President. She's our…uh…spiritual leader."

"Wonderful," he said, his voice subdued as he spoke. "She's a good hugger, too."

She released him and then beamed as she hooked arms with him. "Thank you, sir. Listen, I want to tell you an idea I have about how to solve this illegal immigration problem."

The president laughed as Angela coaxed Liz away from him.

"Maybe some other time. The president has a tight schedule today," Angela said.

"Yes," he said, "I'd love to hear what you have to say, Liz. I'll call you when I get back to Washington. And thanks to all of you for what you did for the country today." The president waved and climbed back into his SUV.

In a matter a seconds, the convoy was gone, and the four of us stood alone surrounded by news people, who'd inched in closer now that the Secret Service was gone and the barricades were removed. Two microphones popped in front of Angela simultaneously.

"I couldn't help hearing the president say you'd saved his life before? Who are you, and can you tell us about it?" The questions came from a woman with long, blond hair that was so stiff it didn't move at all as she walked.

Angela shook her head and smiled. "Oh, that was nothing. He was exaggerating some. Besides, here are the real heroes." She pointed to us. "These three are the ones who saved the president's life today. Talk to them."

As the news people moved in closer, I looked to Angela for guidance. I couldn't find her anywhere.

The reporters asked us questions, and we told them everything that had happened since Sarah's death. In a way, it was closure for me. I knew we hadn't found all the killers, but we had stopped an assassination, gotten a few bad guys off the streets, and identified the enemy for those who could do a better job of finding the rest. I was ready to get back to teaching. I just wished I'd had a chance to say good-bye to Angela.

***

It didn't feel the same, but Liz, Tex, and I went to the Austin History Center for our weekly meeting three days after the big adventure in Houston. Instead of the homemade chocolate chip cookies Liz usually brought to the meetings, she had a peach cobbler, along with bowls and spoons. It was the best cobbler I'd ever put in my mouth.

This would be our last meeting. Our part of the search was over, but we had promised Homeland Security we'd make notes about our Galveston trip and send them our research. Tex tapped his computer keys as we talked. When we reviewed what had happened at the warehouse, I used my computer to show them the cell phone photos I'd taken before police showed up and arrested us.

"Wait a minute!" Liz hollered. "What's that?" She pointed at a colorful image at the right corner of the photo on screen.

I couldn't make it out, but it was out of place with the rest of the objects on the table.

"Just a minute. I learned a trick about enlarging photos without losing quality." I hit a few keys, and we all watched as the object got bigger.

"Hey," Tex said, "I know what it is. That's part of the DVD cover for *Field of Dreams*. I have that movie at home. Remember the one about how some corn farmer in Iowa builds a baseball field, and all the great players from the past somehow come there to play baseball?"

"Oh yeah," I said, "I guess it doesn't mean anything—they probably just had it for entertainment."

Liz glanced at her watch for the tenth time. "Hey, y'all, wait a minute. I gotta check on something." She left the room.

Tex looked at me. "I wonder what's she's going to get now."

I shrugged. "Some ice cream for the cobbler would be nice."

Tex laughed, then took a big bite of browned pie crust dripping with peach syrup.

I went through the rest of the photos with Tex.

"I don't see anything special here. Guess we should send the whole batch to the feds and let them figure out if they mean anything. I'll give them the blow-up of the DVD case, too."

Liz returned with a man and a woman in tow.

When they were in the room, she moved to the side, exposing a couple in their sixties standing side by side holding hands. The man had a John Deere cap pulled down tightly on his head, with long, graying hair sticking out below the cap. The woman wore a white shirt and brown slacks under a tan coat. Her hair was faded blond, and it looked as if she'd combed it, but hadn't done much more than that. I could smell cigarette smoke across the room and knew it surrounded them both.

The woman's lips quivered as she released the man's hand. She gazed at Tex through tear-filled eyes, and I knew at once she had to be Tex's mother.

"Hello, Son," the man said as he pulled his cap off.

"Momma? Daddy?" Tex's voice cracked as he called out to them with open arms.

They knelt, one on each side of their son, and he placed his arms around them. Liz and I slipped out the door.

"How did you find them?" I asked.

"What do you mean?" Liz looked around the hallway as if expecting someone else.

I looked around, too, not knowing why. "I've been searching for Tex's parents for months and never found them. How'd you do it?"

"Well, Mr. Smarty Pants, I've been looking for them a lot longer than you have. As it turned out, they found us." She grinned as she said it.

"What do you mean?" I asked.

Liz rubbed my shoulder. "Simple. They heard about us in the news and called the library. I set up the surprise meeting because I wasn't sure Tex would go along with it otherwise."

"Good idea. He'd told me not to try to find them."

"Yeah, but did you see the way he looked?"

"I did. I bet he'll thank you later."

"Hey, where'd y'all go?" Tex hollered while holding the conference room door open. "Y'all come meet my folks."

Liz looked around once more.

"Who else are you expecting?" I asked. There was no

telling what else she'd done.

"Don't you worry about it. Let's go meet the Thompsons."

When we got to the O'Henry Room, she pushed me ahead, and I looked around to see her searching the hallway again before coming in.

"Momma, Daddy, this is Liz and Chris. Liz is my boss here at the library, and Chris is my professor at the college."

I shook hands with Mr. Thompson. "Nice to meet you. Tex is more than a student; he's my friend." Before I could greet Tex's mother, Liz had her in a full-body hug.

"Guess what?" Tex said. "They've been looking for me and want me to forgive them. Can you believe it?" Tex laughed.

Liz had an arm around both of Tex's parents. "I believe it." She turned to Tex's mother. "Mrs. Thompson, he's a good boy—a Christian boy, a son to be proud of." Liz moved over to Tex and gave him a kiss on the cheek.

After a period of awkward silence, Tex's father cleared his throat. "I guess we weren't strong enough to handle all you had to go through, Son. But we never once stopped loving you. I just want you to know that. And we're surely proud of the way you turned out. Imagine, my boy helping save the president of the United States."

His mother nodded, then grabbed her husband's arm for support. She looked into her husband's eyes as if urging him to continue speaking for them both. I thought he might say more, but he just shook his head and then wiped away a stray tear.

Tex helped them. "I understand, Dad. I should've let you know when I recovered. But I couldn't. I was too ashamed of the way I'd acted before. I didn't think you'd want to see me again. Then I lost track of where you were."

His mother finally spoke, her voice deep and full. "Of

course we wanted to see you. We prayed for you every day." She moved closer to him and had her arms around him.

"That's probably what saved my life," Tex said, and his mother stood, her face beaming.

Tex's father cleared his throat again. "We know about the charges in Galveston. We're going to stay with you here for as long as it takes. I've taken leave from my job, and we'll sell the house if you need money for a defense attorney."

His mother nodded in agreement.

Liz jumped off the floor in her excitement. "Wait, I haven't had a chance to tell Tex the good news, but the DA dropped all the charges in Galveston because of how your son helped protect the president in Houston." She turned to Tex. "You're a free man. You'll get the official papers in the mail soon. And there's more good news: Our benefactor says you can keep the van. He's transferring the title to your name. It'll be out of the shop soon."

Tex's mouth was open, but nothing came out. He took Liz's hand and shook his head in disbelief. Then he gazed at her and at me.

"But, wait, there's more. Tex, you also have a full scholarship to get you all the way through college. It pays everything."

Tex was silent, but his eyes were wide open in disbelief.

"I hope you'll keep your job at the library, though," Liz said. "I kind of enjoy you being around here."

"I'll keep working here until you kick me out," Tex said.

"And, Chris, we searched around for a special gift for you, and I think you'll like it. All your college loans are paid off in full. You're financially free of debt."

I was surprised. I thought I'd be paying for my education for the next twenty years.

"Wonderful," I said. "What a relief. Thank you, Liz."

"I've got an announcement, too," I said. "My dad called from Virgin Gorda this morning where he and Mom are vacationing. He'd heard about our activities in Houston in the news, but he also had a call from the FBI—seems they want the three of us to help them with another project. Of course, he couldn't say what, but I agreed for the three of us. I hope that's okay."

"Of course," Liz said. "I've never had so much fun."

"I'm in," Tex said. "Thanks, Liz. Thanks, Chris. Now I'm going to leave you two alone. I want to take my parents to meet my wife and kids."

Tex's father looked at his wife. "Kids? You mean we're grandparents?"

"Yes, sir," Tex said. "Two times over."

Tex and his parents left without waiting for a response from us, leaving Liz and me alone in the room.

Liz was beaming from all the happiness in the room. "They're meeting their grandkids for the first time. Have you met the children?"

I shook my head.

"Percy and Jane have two of the sweetest young'uns you'll ever know. Anna is four and Owen two. Percy is a wonderful father, and his wife is a hospital chaplain, you know."

We sat at the table. There wasn't much left to do, but I still had a feeling Liz was up to something by the way she kept checking her watch and looked around the hallway earlier. Whatever it was, it probably wasn't about Tex since she'd let him leave.

I glanced at her. "So, what are you going to do for fun now that we've finished this investigation?"

She leaned back in her chair. "You mean before the

next one begins? Oh, I'll stay busy. You wouldn't believe some of the things I get involved in." She laughed.

Actually, I would. Liz wasn't just nosy; she cared about people. She had a knack for spotting people in trouble and getting others to help. I'd seen some of what she was capable of, but Tex had told me many stories about her adventures over the years he'd worked with her. She checked her watch again, making me continuously wonder what was up.

I wrapped up the power cord and put it and the computer into the carrying case.

"Well," I said in the slow way some Texans speak, "I better get going, too."

"Just wait a minute." Liz sat up quickly. "I've been meaning to ask—are you okay with how this turned out?" Liz could make a question sound so sincere you believed what you had to say was the most important thing in the world to her. Every time she asked me a question, she looked directly into my eyes without wavering.

I thought about her question for a minute. *Was I happy? Satisfied?*

"I know we didn't get everyone responsible for Sarah's death. I never thought we would. Still, we caught some of them and stopped them from killing the president. I'm content to let the government handle it from here on out. Of course, if they ask for my help, I'll be glad to do what I can."

"I'm glad to hear you say that." It was Angela's voice.

I turned to see her peeking in the door.

"Angela!" Liz bounced out of chair, grabbed her, and pulled her into the room. "Good to see you again. Chris, aren't you glad to see Angela?"

I took that as a hint to give Angela a hug, too. So I did. "Sure I'm pleased she's here."

I knew now it was Angela who Liz had been watching

for. And I knew Liz had kept me there long enough to see Angela. I wasn't sure why, but I knew Liz had a reason for everything she did.

After the hugs, we sat at the table. I turned to Angela. "I'm curious about why the president knows you so well. Can you tell us, or is it an FBI secret?"

She laughed. "It's not much of a secret after the president blurted it out to you." She suddenly turned serious. "First, I'm not an FBI agent. You all thought I was, and I didn't correct you."

Liz looked surprised. "So, whom do you work for?"

"I work for MI5."

"Oh goodness," Liz said. "You're with the British Secret Intelligence Service?"

A lightbulb went off in my head. "Tim—you worked with Tim?"

"Yes, we were partners."

"Was that bomb in my apartment meant for him or me?"

"Him. Unbeknownst to us all, he'd been helping the terrorists. After he was killed, we learned he'd tried to end the relationship with them, and they killed him when he refused to help more. I'm sorry I had to tell you he couldn't have been the one who fired on you in Massachusetts. At the time, I truly didn't think it was him."

"That explains why the terrorists always seemed to know what we were doing. I thought it was you," I said.

"I'm sorry. Tim was the one."

"That also explains why you were so angry after his death."

"Yes, I'm sorry about that, too."

"And the president?" Liz asked.

"Ah, that. I was assigned to security a few years back when he was visiting England. Something happened, and he needed protection. I can't tell you what. It was never in the news. I happened to be the one on duty."

I had a new respect for Angela. Looking back at all that had happened, I wondered how I'd ever suspected her of trying to block our efforts. For just a second, I wondered if she was single. *But then what?* I was still in love with Sarah. No one would ever take Sarah's place. I remembered how she'd told me to be happy. *But how could I be happy without her?*

I looked up to see both Liz and Angela staring at me.

"Well?" Liz asked.

I shook my head to get the cobwebs out. "I'm sorry. What did you say?"

Angela laughed. "She invited us over for a Christmas dinner Friday night."

"Christmas? Wasn't that last week." I wasn't sure what I'd missed, but the conversation didn't make sense.

Angela stood as if ready to leave. "Yeah, but if I remember correctly, we were all busy Christmas. You and Tex were in the Galveston jail at that time, and everyone else was working to get you two out."

I thought about jail and how God was with me there. I turned to Liz, and I think she was remembering what I'd told her about it.

She just nodded her head before she spoke. "Chris had a wonderful Christmas, even though he was locked up." Liz focused on Angela. "Get him to tell you about it someday. Neither one of you has tasted my baked turkey and dressing, and I don't like to brag, but I've been told my pecan pie is better than what's made by most native Texans. Now, are you coming or not? We'll invite Tex and Jane, as well as the kids, and Tex's parents if they can come. We'll make it a party."

I looked at Angela and nodded. "I'll be there," we said

simultaneously.

Everyone laughed.

Angela walked toward the door, but stopped and turned back. "I want to hear about what happened to you in jail. Will you tell me Friday night?"

"Sure." It was nice knowing I would see her again in a few days. I still didn't know why it mattered, but it did.

I felt a strong need to talk to Sarah's parents and to Father Jesse. I owed him an apology. Better still, I felt it was time to return to my church. Sure it was Sarah's church first, and it would always remind me of her, but there was nothing wrong with having memories of the one I loved.

EPILOGUE

It was a year after the belated Christmas dinner Liz hosted, and I hadn't seen Angela again since then. At that dinner, I had taken Angela to one side and told her about the chaplain who had visited me in jail on Christmas and turned my life around. I'd only told Tex and Liz before that, and I was concerned Angela would think it was merely a dream brought on by the stress of the situation. But she acted as if she believed me. I remember her saying something about God working in mysterious ways.

The year went by so fast I was surprised when Liz called and invited me to the second-annual Christmas dinner. I said I'd be there. That's when she told me Angela was coming.

Liz, Tex, and I had been called on four times during the year to do some research for the government, but it wasn't nearly as exciting as it had been when we set out to find Sarah's killers. I missed the fieldwork, and I'm sure Tex and Liz did, too. I still worked out two to three times a week, and my leg hadn't hurt again since that night in the Galveston jail. I also practiced shooting my pistol at least once a month. Who knows, maybe we'd be called to the field again.

I was back in the classroom teaching a full load and working on a new textbook. With my educational loans paid off, life was sweet. Being debt free meant I could stay at Austin Community College, which I loved, and not be forced to go to a larger university for the money.

I called Mary Simpson in Rowe, Massachusetts from time to time to see how she was doing and to remind her how her photo helped find the killers.

In addition to the government research we did, Tex and I got together occasionally to visit and reminisce. I got to know his wife, Jane, and their kids, and it wasn't long before Anna and Owen were calling me "uncle." When I played with them, I wondered more than once if I would ever have children of my own. I thanked God for the time I'd had with Sarah, because no matter how short our life together had been, it was still the most wonderful experience I had ever had. She'd taught me to be happy and to trust God. She also taught me to accept what God presents to us no matter how difficult it is to do so. And, well, this one is hard to explain, but with her death, she taught me how to die.

Tex was now attending the University of Texas on the full scholarship Liz had found for him. He still worked at the library, but only because he loved it so much. The best news yet was that Liz had talked to the governor about what Tex had done to catch the terrorists, and she'd talked him into granting clemency to Tex. Not only was he off probation for his DUIs, but he was also pardoned. He had a clean slate. He was no longer an ex-con. He thanked me as well as Liz afterward, but I told him it wouldn't have been possible without what he'd done.

We could all be proud. What we ended up doing made a big dent in the fight against Islamic extremists. The photos we took in the Galveston warehouse turned out to be a major clue in rounding up more than a hundred more terrorists. Some researcher at Homeland Security suggested checking the farm in Iowa where *Field of Dreams* had been filmed. It was near there that they found a terrorist training camp, and after spying on them by satellite, the government moved in and arrested them all.

Even though I hadn't seen Angela, I'd talked to her a few times during the past year. She was usually in England. At other times, she couldn't tell me where she was. Our conversations became more personal over time, and I eventually learned she was unmarried and had gone to school in the United States. Her favorite food was Tex-Mex, and she loved cruises, beaches, pools, water-skiing, and anything else near the water. Her parents lived in York, England, but her mother was an American, so she had relatives in the United States, mostly in and around Atlanta.

And now I was about to see her again. She was coming to the Christmas dinner, and she'd asked me to pick her up at the airport. I was looking forward to seeing her more than I should have been.

After parking in the short-term lot at the Austin-Bergstrom International Airport, I went to the baggage area in time to take a call from her. My heart skipped a beat as I wondered whether she'd changed her mind about coming to Austin or if her work had forced her to be somewhere else. The call, and the possibility of not seeing her, made me realize how much I wanted to be with her.

"Chris?" Her voice was as lovely as ever. She used her English accent more ever since I mentioned I liked it.

"Yes?" I knew I sounded tentative, but I was afraid I was about to hear some bad news.

She was silent for a few seconds. "What's wrong?"

"Nothing." I tried to sound more cheerful. I didn't want her to know how disappointed I was. *After all, she had a job to do.*

"You sounded so different when you answered. Well, we're on the ground."

Here it comes. She's been grounded somewhere for the night—probably back East in the icy weather area or some secret base in the

Middle East. "So, where are you?"

"What do you mean? I'm in Austin. We just landed. Where are you?"

I took a deep breath and exhaled. "I'm here—in the baggage area waiting for you." I'm sure I sounded more cheerful this time.

"Good. I'll see you in a few minutes."

I watched her all the way down the escalator, and when she walked over to where I stood waiting, we hugged. I didn't know how it happened, but the hug turned into a kiss, not a peck-on-the-cheek kiss, but a long, passionate, and guiltless kiss—a kiss I'd never forget.

QUESTIONS FOR DISCUSSION

1. The book opens with Chris thanking God for bringing Sarah into his life. By the end of the first chapter Chris is cursing God and vowing revenge for her death. Have you ever experienced a tragedy in your life that made you doubt God's existence?

2. Why did Chris not want to attend Sarah's memorial service? If he loved her as much as he said, wouldn't he want to be there no matter what?

3. Sarah's brother, Andrew, blames Chris for his sister's death. Although her parents defend Chris, the accusation must have been painful for him. Why do you think Andrew reacted the way he did?

4. Why did Chris feel responsible for Sarah's death?

5. When Tex approaches Chris after class offering to help, Chris is reluctant to accept the offer. What changes his mind?

6. With all the problems Tex faces, how do you think he maintains his positive attitude about life?

7. When Father Jesse shows up at Chris' apartment, what is he carrying with him that makes Chis mad? Why would Chris be angry about this?

8. It seems to Chris that Sarah's parents get over the death of their daughter too quickly. Why? How does this affect Chris?

9. Chris is upset with Tex for inviting Liz to the Vengeance Squad meeting. How do they resolve their differences?

10. Liz is a loving person who hugs everyone she meets and wouldn't hurt a fly. How could a person like that help the Vengeance Squad?

11. The woman who breaks into Chris' apartment turns out to be a law enforcement official. When she is caught by the Vengeance Squad, how does she react?

12. Chris has some symptoms of a person with Obsessive-Compulsive Disorder. How does this affect the grieving process? How does it affect his detective work?

13. As the search continues, Chris becomes more and more concerned about what he has gotten himself into. What are some of the ways he reacts?

14. After visiting Mary in Rowe, Massachusetts, why is Chris concerned about her safety?

15. On several occasions, Chris wondered if he could trust Angela. What caused him to feel that way?

16. When Chris was arrested in Galveston, Texas with fake IDs, who did he blame? Why?

Author Interview

Q: When did you first know that you would be an author?

My earliest memory of writing is when my older sister, Barbara Cagle, decided we would publish a neighborhood magazine. We were living on Pete's Path in Austin, Texas at the time, so I had to be about twelve years old.

By publish, keep in mind the magazine was handwritten and each copy was handwritten as well. So there wasn't a wide distribution and the magazine only lasted for a summer. When school started we were too busy to continue it. But I remember getting to write and I remember the encouragement from my sister.

But, it wasn't until later that I had that feeling all writers must get that boils down to a need to create something. I started several novels, wrote short stories, had a newspaper column for a while, and was assigned writing projects at various jobs throughout my career in computing.

Q: Who are your favorite authors?

My all-time favorite author is James Michener. I love the way he researched and described a geographical area so that it came alive. My favorite authors of Christian fiction are Jan Karon, Dee Henderson, and Philip Gulley. I review books for several publishers and belong to a neighborhood book club so I read a variety of books by many authors.

Q: Share with us your journey to publication?

The idea for writing *Where Love Once Lived* came to me while driving a bookmobile back in the 1960's. I was a college student at the University of Texas assigned to drive for a feisty librarian who got us into trouble with the head librarian several times because of helping our patrons in ways unrelated to books.

The nudge to write the bookmobile story came again in 2004, and this time I said no because I knew it was too hard. The very next Sunday, my pastor, Dr. Jeanie Stanley, said this: "Trust the Lord God with your dreams and he will help you achieve them." Four years later I had a good start for what eventually became *Where Love Once Lived*.

Q: What advice do you have for aspiring authors?

I am often asked how one goes about writing a novel and getting it published. All I can tell them is about my own experience. However, I can add where I made mistakes so they can skip some of the trial and error I went through. For example, one thing I learned too late was that you should know the market before you start writing.

Another thing I tell people is to take classes. Not just for what you learn from instructors, but for what you learn from reading your classmates' work and what they say about yours.

AN EXCERPT FROM

WHERE LOVE ONCE LIVED

SIDNEY W. FROST

CHAPTER ONE

Karen felt loved on Tuesdays.

She was fifty-three and divorced with a college-aged daughter at home who'd probably flee the nest soon, leaving Karen to live alone. She'd missed her chance for happiness. Still, she wasn't sad. Teaching and her volunteer work as a lay minister, hospital chaplain, and member of her church choir fulfilled her. To be honest, she wanted more. She wanted the special kind of love she felt on Tuesdays.

She glanced at the clock on the wall as the familiar knock sounded. The third graders snapped to attention, turning their heads in unison toward the door. Today was the day. Every Tuesday about this time for the past six weeks, a fresh bouquet of flowers arrived. Karen opened the door and felt a rush of warmth when she realized today would be no exception.

Peeking around the blooms with his usual grin, his black curls poking out from under the well-worn blue cap that sat too far back on his head, the deliveryman thrust the vase toward her.

"Morning, Ms. Williams."

"Good morning, Sam. It must be Tuesday." She took the flowers, admiring this week's selection of red roses. Her friend, Cathy, warned her to be cautious because the flowers might be from a stalker, but Karen didn't think so.

"Yes, ma'am, 'tis."

Sam wasn't much for words, but his facial expressions said it all. He knew something she didn't know, and his eyes bragged about it.

"You can't tell me who's sending these, right?"

The scent of the roses overpowered the usual class-room odor. Without the flowers, her room smelled like a combination of peanut butter and floor cleaner.

"Nope." After he said it, he pursed his lips as if to hold in his secret.

Karen imagined the Tuesday delivery was a highlight for Sam because of the way he acted each week. She didn't want to disappoint him today.

"Don't know or can't say?"

"Can't say." He turned to leave, but suddenly spun around. "And don't know." His eyes sparkled as he backed out of the room, keeping his gaze on her all the while.

After Sam shut the door, she held the bouquet for the class to see. Let the children make their jokes so they could get back to the lesson. Nine year olds loved distractions, but they enjoyed this mystery most of all because it involved their teacher. The student teacher, Fran Rush, sitting at the back of the classroom, smiled and shook her head as if she knew what was coming next.

"Who are the flowers from, Ms. Williams?" Jose asked.

"Well, let's see." She placed the vase on her desk and pulled out the card, repeating the weekly ritual. As usual, all it said was, "To Karen, with love." She peeked over the card to watch Jose's response as she continued. "Oh, no. It's not signed."

"Again?" Haley asked, playing along.

Jose pumped his hand high in the air, his eyes opened wide. "I know! I know! It's from your secret a'mirer."

Karen couldn't guess who that might be or why the flowers came on Tuesdays, for that matter. Could it be Leon? He'd asked her out once, but she turned him down and never encouraged him. Besides, Leon wasn't the type to do something in secret. He'd be bragging about it to everyone in the church choir.

As she wondered about the mystery, Karen peered out the window at the florist's delivery van in the school parking lot in time to see it leaving. As it disappeared behind the administration building, another vehicle came into view, one that looked like a bus with no windows. On its side in large letters was Austin Public Library Bookmobile.

She'd once loved a bookmobile driver. Memories of that time with him poured in so rapidly she caught her breath. It'd been long ago, but her heart remembered. At first she thought of the love she'd felt back then, but the good memories didn't last long. She'd gone to the bookmobile as usual that last day, but nothing was to be the same again. She went to Brian with love and exciting news. She left alone. Not just without him, but alone in the world and apart from God.

This couldn't be the same bookmobile. Nevertheless, she had to see it. She had to walk into it and face her fears. She grabbed her jacket to shield her from the damp November day and rounded up her class.

"Get your coats on, kids. We're going to the library."

The children grumbled at the notion, but when they saw what kind of library it was, they stepped livelier. Karen walked inside the bookmobile after making sure Miss Rush had control of the children. She inhaled the familiar odor of used books. She traveled back thirty years with a single whiff. The librarian just inside the front door welcomed her with a smile. A man sat at a desk near the back of the vehicle. Karen pulled a book off the shelf and held it next to her chest, not caring what the title was. With her eyes closed, she could feel Brian standing next to her, loving her, and it was so real, she felt her eyes moisten.

Enough. That was too long ago. She dabbed her eyes and looked around. Fran was up front letting the children in a few at a time. "Fran, will you watch the children? I'm going to the room."

Fran nodded in a way that said she'd seen Karen's tears and was concerned. Explanations would be needed, but not now.

When Karen reached the back door, she gasped and froze. He wasn't supposed to be here.

"Brian?" she asked.

He looked more like a professor than the student she'd known in college. His blue eyes sparkled, and she recognized his smile at once. The neatly trimmed beard was new, but it didn't hide the strong jawline she'd once loved.

He jumped to his feet and moved toward her with his arms open. "Hello, Karen. I knew you'd come."

His movement frightened her, but there was nowhere to run. She blocked the embrace he was heading for by taking his hands in hers and pretending to want to shake hands.

"What are you doing here?" She was composed on the outside, but the rhythm of her heartbeat told her she was anything but calm. "I thought you were in California." She dropped his hands and pushed away, putting as much distance between them as possible in the cramped quarters of the mobile library.

"I was, but I moved to Austin about six months ago."

"Mister?" asked a piping voice.

"What's up, Haley?" Karen asked the student who was peeking up at Brian.

Haley pointed to the woman sitting near the front door. "She told me to ask the man where to find the biographies."

Brian moved to the shelves on his left and knelt eye to eye with Haley. "They're right here, young lady."

She loved the way he focused on her student, but knew she should get away now before she said something she'd regret. He'd hurt her in a way she couldn't easily forgive.

Then she saw the ring. On his right hand was the wide gold band with the Greek letters Alpha and Omega, the beginning and the end. She knew there was a date engraved inside that marked the start of their life together. She knew it was there because she had a matching ring in her jewelry box. A relic of the past she couldn't bear to toss when she'd married Steve.

"I've worn it ever since you gave it to me," he said as he stood and moved toward her.

Could he still read her mind, or had she focused on his hand a bit too long? She peered into his eyes, as blue as his shirt, and ignored what he said. "I see you have your old job back."

He laughed. "I tried, but the city doesn't have bookmobiles anymore. I had to buy this one myself."

His laugh. She remembered that, too, and it took her back to a pleasant time of her life. Their two-year relationship was with laughter. Even so, it ended with sadness so deep there was little laughter for Karen for years afterward.

"Why did you buy a bookmobile?"

He shrugged. "Looking for happiness, I guess. I'm not sure it was because of the job or because it was the time when you were in my life." He moved closer and gazed into her eyes as if waiting for a response.

She felt the heat of his body and smelled his familiar scent, both so strong she turned away. The last time she saw him was in a bookmobile long ago when they were students at the University of Texas. That was the day he broke up with her and left her alone. She didn't want to think about that day. She walked as far to the rear of the vehicle as possible, motioning him to follow.

When they were near the back door, she stood close to him so the children couldn't hear her voice. She felt her body shiver. "Why are you here? Why are you doing this?"

"Because of you," he said and smiled.

For years, she knew what she'd say if their paths ever crossed. She even rehearsed it from time to time for the first few years they were apart. Too many years had passed for that speech. All she wanted to do now was to find out what was going on and leave. A thought came to her.

"Did you send the flowers?"

"Yes," he said. "Did you like them?"

"Don't send any more." The secret admirer dream burst, or rather fizzled. "I still don't understand why you bought a bookmobile."

He beamed. "You should know."

An image leaped into her head. This time it wasn't one of the day he said goodbye. She remembered a time before that when they were alone in the bookmobile. It was a time when his lips were on hers as she leaned against a book-shelf. For a split second, it was as if they were still there, still in love, still touching.

"All I remember is your dumping me in a vehicle like this."

He grimaced then looked her eyes. "I'm sorry. I was thinking about a different time. I never wanted to break up with you."

She wanted to forgive him for everything and move in-to his arms where she once felt so safe and loved. Instead, she stared at him, waiting, listening. He'd never told her why he'd left her, and her pride had kept her from telling him her news. It was too late.

His eyes focused on hers, and his voice comforted her with his sincerity. "I knew you wouldn't want to see me again. That's why I bought this bookmobile. I wanted to make you curious enough to come in."

Sunlight streamed in through the door window, high-lighting new wrinkles around his eyes. She remembered his birthday. He was fifty-four, more handsome than when they'd first met so long ago.

"It worked. You got me to come in, but don't count on seeing me again. Goodbye."

She went out the door without looking back, finding it easy to resist the urge to forgive him.

***

Brian had planned this reunion for months after dreaming about it for years. He'd considered a multitude of possible reactions on Karen's part, but he hadn't expected her to walk away before he could tell her why he had broken up with her. If she would hear him out, she'd forgive him. After that, anything was possible. He had to stop her.

"Liz," he hollered toward the front of the bookmobile, "I'll be back."

He ran to catch up to Karen. "Please wait. Let me explain."

She was halfway to the school building when she stopped and turned toward him. "Why?" Her voice was stronger now, but her eyes were moist.

He hadn't counted on the tears. He'd hurt her enough for a lifetime and didn't want to see her in pain, but he felt he had to continue. "I know you're angry, but please let me tell you what happened."

She was silent. Could it be his long journey home would end like this? She had the power to extinguish the hope he'd carried for so long. He would've come back sooner if it hadn't been for his daughter. Was it too late?

"Okay, I'll listen. But just long enough for you to tell me why you walked out on me the way you did." She pulled back the left sleeve of her jacket and glanced at her watch.

This wasn't the way it was supposed to be. The reunion he'd dreamed of had them sitting together in front of a warm fireplace. He had his arm around her, and she looked at him lovingly, chin upraised slightly, ready and waiting for his kiss. Here they were standing in a parking lot outside an elementary school, and he was on the clock. He almost prayed for help before he remembered God had forsaken him. All he could do was hope honesty was enough.

"It happened when I went back to my parents' home for the holidays. That trip I took before we split up. I didn't want to go, but Mother begged me to. She wanted the whole family home for Christmas. I was so in love with you, all I could think about was our future together. I left here vowing by the next Christmas, we'd never be separated again."

"So, what happened?" Karen's voice was monotone and her face expressionless.

He'd never told anyone what he was about to tell her, not even his best friend. Phil probably guessed what happened, but he'd never brought it up.

"When I got to Redondo, a girl I knew in high school invited me out. It seemed okay at the time because it wasn't a date and she wasn't anyone special to me. It was like a reunion with a classmate, talking about old times."

Karen crossed her arms. He felt her tenseness and wanted to wrap his arms around her and comfort her.

"I still don't know how things went beyond that. Up until that time, I always thought of myself as an honest, moral person. If there's a God, I was tested and failed."

She raised both hands with palms down. "Look. You don't have to say anymore."

"Please. I need to tell you everything. I need your forgiveness."

When she dropped her arms, he continued. "I can't justify what happened next. I've often wondered why I did it. It was stupid, and I'll always regret it. Before I knew what happened she was pregnant, and she assumed I would marry her to give the baby a name. I never loved her, and she never loved me."

"You stayed married?"

"Yes. We raised our daughter together. Otherwise, we lived separate lives. I immersed myself in my work and she in her social life. As soon as Amy was grown, I filed for divorce."

"Where is your daughter now?" Karen asked.

"She lives in Redondo Beach, not far from where I grew up. Raising her kept me sane. We're very close." He heard children behind him and looked back to see Karen's class walking toward them with the other teacher. His time with Karen was ending. He'd told her the truth. Was it enough?

She sighed. Not a sigh of relief, but one associated with an onerous task.

"Thank you." Karen's voice softened. "I saw the pain in your face as you spoke, and I know it wasn't easy for you to tell me what happened." She paused and cleared her voice before continuing. "I'm just sorry you made your decision about marrying without discussing it with me at the time. I could've helped if you'd confided in me."

He loved the sound of her voice, but didn't understand her words. "What do you mean? I had to do the right thing. I had no choice."

"You had choices," she said. "You were my first love, the first person I trusted with my deepest feelings." Her head bent forward slightly as she swallowed, and Brian saw new tears forming. "And you broke my heart."

Her words hurt, but no more than the ones he'd said to himself over the years.

"But—"

"Wait." Her eyes pierced through the film of tears. "I listened to you. Now, you listen to me. I loved you then, and I knew you loved me. We had something special, and I, too, had begun to think about future Christmases together. Think how shocked I was when you broke it off without an explanation. Then later, when I learned you were married, I thought you must have been dating both of us at the same time, and I wasn't as important to you as I'd believed."

"I loved you. Only you." He moved toward her, wanting to take her in his arms and show his love. "Karen, I…."

She pushed him away. "You had a funny way of showing your love. Now, here you are, back in town with flowers and a bookmobile and your fancy words of remorse. I suppose you want to pick up where we left off."

She was mocking him, but he didn't care. "Yes."

"Alright then," she said with a strong voice. She pushed her open jacket away and placed her hands on her hips. "Where we left off was at the point where I didn't care for you at all. Nothing has changed." She turned toward the school.

He'd expected her to be mad about the way he'd broken up with her, but she was angrier than he thought she'd be, especially after so many years.

"Can't we back up to where you said you loved me?"

"Impossible." She shook her head. "Too much hap-pened after that." She joined the students when they reached the place where Brian and Karen stood, and she walked with them toward the school building.

"How about meeting after school?" he asked. "We need more time to talk."

She continued walking away. "There's no reason to talk more. And stop sending the flowers."

"Is he your secret a'mirer, Ms. Williams?" a student asked.

"Don't talk, Haley," Karen said.

"Think about the good times we had together," Brian said. The children giggled. He didn't care.

He stood in the parking lot until she disappeared into the classroom and the door closed behind her. When he turned to go back to the bookmobile, he saw Liz standing in the door, watching him.

Afterword

I hope you enjoyed this book and I hope you will also read *Where Love Once Lived*. They are different and there will be sequels to each. Liz and the bookmobile appear in both books.

You can keep up with the progress of the sequels here: http://sidneywfrost.com.

You may also want to climb aboard the Christian Bookmobile. See: http://christianbookmobile.blogspot.com/. This is where I talk about writing, review books, interview other Christian authors and occasionally talk about growing up in Austin, Texas.

I also respond to email queries and would love to hear from you: sidfrost@suddenlink.net